Vampire in Love

Enrique Vila-Matas

Vampire in Love

and other stories

Translated from the Spanish
by Margaret Jull Costa

A NEW DIRECTIONS BOOK

This edition is published by arrangement with Enrique Vila-Matas c/o MB Agencia
Literaria S.L.

This work has been published with a subsidy from the Ministry of Education, Culture
and Sport of Spain.

Manufactured in the United States of America
New Directions Books are printed on acid-free paper
First published in 2016 as New Directions Paperbook 1351

Library of Congress Cataloging-in-Publication Data
Names: Vila-Matas, Enrique, 1948– author. | Costa, Margaret Jull, translator.
Title: Vampire in love / Enrique Vila-Matas ; translated from the Spanish
by Margaret Jull Costa.
Description: New York : New Directions Books, [2016]
Identifiers: LCCN 2016027932 (print) | LCCN 2016033170 (ebook) |
ISBN 9780811223461 (alk. paper) | ISBN 9780811223478 ()
Classification: LCC PQ6672.I37 A2 2016 (print) | LCC PQ6672.I37 (ebook) |
DDC 863/.64—dc23
LC record available at https://lccn.loc.gov/2016027932

10 9 8 7 6 5 4 3 2 1

New Directions Books are published for James Laughlin
by New Directions Publishing Corporation
80 Eighth Avenue, New York 10011

For Paula de Parma

CONTENTS

A Permanent Home...1

Sea Swell 9

Torre del Mirador...21

I Never Go to the Movies 31

Rosa Schwarzer Comes Back to Life..............................35

In Search of the Electrifying Double Act 53

Death by *Saudade*... 69

The Hour of the Tired and Weary 83

They Say I Should Say Who I Am 89

Greetings from Dante.. 105

Identifying Marks..123

The Boy on the Swing 125

An Idle Soul 169

Invented Memories 183

The Vampire in Love 193

Modesty..209

Niño 217

I'm Not Going to Read Any More E-mails 241

Vok's Successors..245

A PERMANENT HOME

I never knew much about my mother. She was killed in our house in Barcelona, two days after I was born. The murder remained a mystery, until I thought I had solved it on my twentieth birthday, when my father, on his deathbed, demanded to see me and told me that, now the moment was fast approaching when he would be permanently silenced, he wanted to tell me something before that happened, something he felt it was important I should know.

"Eventually even words abandon us," I remember him saying, "and that's all there is to it really, but, first, you should know that your mother died because I arranged it."

I immediately imagined a hired killer and, once I'd recovered from the initial shock, I began to believe my father's confession. The image of a bloodstained axe was enough for me to feel as if the ground were swallowing me up, leaving behind, like so many pathetic doodles, all the scenes of joy and plenitude that had made me idealize my father and create the mythical figure of a man always up before dawn, still in his pyjamas, a shawl around his shoulders, a cigarette between his fingers, eyes fixed on the weather vane on some distant chimney, watching the day begin, and devoting himself with implacable regularity and monstrous perseverance to the solitary ritual of creating his own language through the writing of a book of memories or an inventory of nostalgias, which I always assumed would, when he died, become part of my tender, albeit terrifying, inheritance.

However, on my twentieth birthday, in Port de la Selva, any tender feelings that had previously attached to said inheritance vanished, and I felt only the terror, the infinite horror, of thinking that, along with that inventory, my father was bequeathing me the surprising tale of a murder, whose origins, according to him, could be found in early April 1945, a year before I was born, when, despite having already experienced two resounding matrimonial failures, he nevertheless felt he was still young and emotionally strong enough to embark on a third such adventure. He therefore wrote a letter to a young woman from the province of Ampurdán in Catalonia, whom he had met by chance in Figueras and who, he felt, had all the necessary qualities to make him happy, for not only was she a poor orphan—which made things easier for him, since he could offer her security and a not inconsiderable fortune—she was also beautiful, gentle and had the most sensual lower lip in the entire universe; above all, she was extraordinarily naive and docile, which is to say that she had a proper sense of woman as man's subordinate, a quality he particularly valued, given his two previous hellish conjugal experiences.

You have to bear in mind, for example, that my father's first wife, in a freak attack of rage, had bitten off part of his ear. He had been so very unhappy in his two earlier marriages that it should come as no surprise to anyone that, when he considered finding a third wife, he wanted someone who was both gentle and docile.

My mother possessed both those qualities, and he knew that all it would take to entrap her was a carefully drafted letter. And so it proved. So passionate and so skillfully written was his letter that, shortly afterward, my mother turned up in Barcelona, in the Barrio Gótico's labyrinth of narrow streets, where she knocked on the door of the old, soot-begrimed mansion owned by my father, who, it seems, either could not or chose not to disguise his emotion when he saw her standing there in the rain, clutching a small blue suitcase, which she put down on the carpet before asking, in a tremulous, humble orphan's voice, if she could come in.

"I could never forget that rain," my father said from his deathbed, "because when I saw her cross the threshold, it seemed to me that the savage rain was actually there in her hips, and I was filled by the most intensely erotic impulse I have ever felt."

That impulse seemed to know no bounds when she told him that she was an expert at dancing the *tirana*, a long-forgotten medieval Spanish dance. Beguiled by this slightly anachronistic hobby, my father ordered her to perform the dance immediately, and, eager to please him in every way possible, my mother danced until she dropped, ending up, exhausted, in the arms of a man who, without a moment's hesitation, affectionately ordered her to marry him at once.

That night, they slept together for the first time, and my father, afflicted by the sentimentality that accompanies certain infatuations, had a sense that, just as he had imagined, making love with her was like making love with a bird, for in bed she trilled and sang, and it seemed to him that no other voice could possibly match hers, and that even her bones, like her lower lip and her songs, were as delicate as those of a bird.

"And you were conceived that very night, beneath the murmuring Barcelona rain," my father said suddenly, his eyes very wide.

A long, slow sigh, always so troubling in a dying man, preceded a brusque demand for a glass of vodka. I refused to give it to him, but when he threatened not to continue his story, I was so afraid he might carry out his threat that I raced into the kitchen and, making sure Aunt Consuelo wasn't looking, filled two glasses with vodka. I realize now that I need not have taken these absurd precautions because, at that moment, Aunt Consuelo was entirely absorbed by her desire for a particular painting in the living room, a dark picture representing some angels flirting celestially as they climbed a ladder; she lived only for that painting, and her obsession doubtless distracted her from another: the constant anguish of knowing that her brother was dying, laid low by a gentle, but implacable illness. And he, at that moment, was entirely absorbed in feeding the illusion of his story.

Once he had slaked his thirst, my father went on to explain that they had honeymooned in two cities, Istanbul and Cairo, and that it was in Istanbul where he noticed the first anomaly in the behavior of his sweet, docile wife. For my part, I noticed the first anomaly in my father's story, in that he was confusing those two cities with Paris and London, but I preferred not to interrupt when I heard him explain that my mother's anomalous behavior wasn't exactly a defect, but more of a strange obsession. She collected bread rolls.

Right from the start, visiting Istanbul's bakeries became a kind of strange sport. They sampled various bread rolls, quite needlessly as it turned out, because they weren't destined to be eaten, but only to add to the weight of the large bag in which my mother kept her collection. My father protested and asked rather irritably why she was so enamored with bread.

"The troops have to eat something," she replied succinctly, smiling at him like someone humoring a madman.

"What do you mean, Diana? Is this some kind of joke?" my bewildered father asked.

"I think you're the one who must be joking by asking such absurd questions," she replied absentmindedly, adopting the gentle, dreamy look of the myopic.

According to my father, they spent a week in Istanbul and by the time they arrived in Cairo, my mother had about forty bread rolls in her bag. Since it was late at night, he knew he was safe from the bakeries of Cairo, and walked happily along, even offering to carry her bag. He did not know that those would be his last moments of conjugal bliss.

My father and mother dined on a boat anchored in the Nile and ended up dancing and sipping pink champagne by the light of the moon on the balcony of their hotel room. A few hours later, however, my father woke in the middle of the Cairo night and discovered, to his great surprise, that my mother was a sleepwalker and was standing on the sofa frenziedly dancing the *tirana*. He tried to remain calm and waited patiently until, utterly exhausted, she came back to bed and fell into the deepest of sleeps. Once asleep, however, she gave him still more reason to feel alarmed, for my mother began talking in her sleep and, turning to him, said something that sounded for all the world like a categorical, implacable command:

"Fall in!"

My father still hadn't recovered from the shock of that first command, when he heard her say:

"Right turn. Break ranks."

He didn't sleep for the rest of the night and began to suspect that, in her dreams, his wife was deceiving him with an entire regiment. The following morning, my father had to face reality, which, as far as he was concerned, meant accepting that in those last few hours, she had danced the *tirana* and behaved like a deranged general, whose sole concern seemed to be issuing orders and handing out bread rolls to the troops. He took consolation from the fact that, during the day, his wife reverted to her usual gentle, docile self. Not that this was much of a consolation, though, because, while on their remaining nights in Cairo there was no repeat of the sleep-dancing episode, the issuing of orders only increased in regularity and in vigor.

"And reveille," my father told me, "became a real torment, because every day, minutes before your mother woke, her snoring appeared to be imitating the unmistakable sound of a bugle at dawn."

Was my father delirious? No, on the contrary, he was perfectly aware of what he was saying, indeed, it was impressive to see how, at the very gates of death, he still retained his usual sense of humor. Was he making it up? Possibly, which is why I tried fixing him with an incredulous stare, but this didn't seem to put him off in the least. Grave-faced and impassive, he continued his story.

He described how, on waking, my mother would instantly become her usual gentle, docile self, except, occasionally, near a bakery, or when she was simply strolling down the street, she would shoot strange, melancholy glances at the soldiers standing guard behind barricades erected on the banks of the Nile (at the time, of course, Cairo was on a war footing). One morning, she even tried out a few dance steps in front of the soldiers.

More than once, my father was tempted to confront the problem directly and speak to her, saying, for example:

"You appear to have at the very least a dual personality. You're a sleepwalker and, quite apart from standing on sofas and dancing the *tirana*, you've turned the marital bed into a military parade ground."

He said nothing, however, because he feared that if he did broach the subject, it might work to his disadvantage and he would succeed only in revealing to her a hidden aspect of her character: a certain talent for giving orders. But one day, while they were out riding camels near the pyramids, my father made the mistake of telling her the plot of a short story he was planning to write:

"It's the story of a very well-matched, even exemplary couple. However, like all happy stories, this would be of no interest at all, if not for the fact that, at night, in her dreams, the woman turns into a soldier."

He had hardly finished speaking when my mother asked to be helped down from the camel and then, shooting him a defiant glance, ordered him to carry the bag full of Turkish and Egyptian bread rolls. My father was absolutely terrified, because he realized that, from that moment on, not only would he be condemned to carrying around that nightmarish collection of foreign baked goods, he would continue to receive order after order.

On their return to Barcelona, my mother was already issuing orders with such authority that he began to think of her as a general in the Foreign Legion, and the oddest thing of all was that, right from that very moment, she appeared to identify totally with that position, for she would go into a kind of trance and say that she felt she was lost in a universe adorned with heavy Algerian rugs, with strainers for making pastis and absinthe and hookahs for marijuana, and she was scanning the desert horizon from an oasis village in the luminous night.

When they arrived in Barcelona, back in my father's mansion in the Barrio Gótico, any friends who visited were astonished to see my mother smoking like a man, with a lit cigarette hanging from one corner of her mouth, and to see my father, his features hard and blunt as pebbles polished by the waves, half-blinded as if by the desert sun, and transformed into an old legionnaire flicking through ancient colonial newspapers.

At this point in the story, the only thing I understood completely was that—quite astonishingly for someone on the verge of dying—my father, true to his constant need to tell tales, was continuing ceaselessly to invent. Not even the proximity of death could take from him his taste for making up stories. And I had the impression that he wanted to bequeath to me the house of fiction and the pleasure of taking up permanent residence there. And that is why, springing onto the running-board of his carriage of words, I said:

"You are clearly confusing me with someone else. I am not your son. And as for Aunt Consuelo, she is merely a character I invented."

Before responding, he looked at me with a degree of unease. Then, deeply moved, he squeezed my hand and gave me a broad smile, that of someone who knows his message has reached safe harbor. Along with the inventory of nostalgias, he had just bequeathed to me the house of eternal shadows.

My father, who had once believed in many, many things only to end up distrusting all of them, was leaving me with a unique, definitive faith: that of believing in a fiction that one knows to be fiction, aware that this is all that exists, and that the exquisite truth consists in knowing that it is a fiction and that, nevertheless, one should believe in it.

SEA SWELL

I had a friend once. Indeed, at the time, I only had one friend. His name was Andrés and he lived in Paris, and, much to his delight, I traveled to that city to see him. The very evening of my arrival, he introduced me to Marguerite Duras, who was a friend of his. Unfortunately, that evening, I had taken two or three amphetamines. This was my regular daily dose, for I was convinced they would help me to imagine stories and become a novelist. I don't know why I was so convinced that this was true, since I had never written a word in my life and the amphetamines were largely to blame for this. They were also to blame for me losing all my money in secret gambling dens in Barcelona.

I was completely bankrupt when I traveled to Paris, and my friend lent me some money and introduced me to Marguerite Duras. Andrés was one of those people who believes that the company of brilliant writers helps to improve one's own writing.

"One of my attic apartments has just become vacant," Marguerite Duras said as soon as we met.

If I hadn't taken those wretched pills, I would have responded at once and said that I would very much like to rent it. However, the amphetamines always had a bad effect on me. I would fix people with mad, staring eyes, as bright as fog lamps, and there seemed no point in giving expression to any of my thoughts because I had already thought them. On top of that, they made me lose my appetite and, needless to say, any desire to write.

We were standing opposite the Café de Flore. Hearing me babbling a few syllables that stubbornly refused to cohere into words, my friend Andrés made a series of friendly gestures in my direction and came to my aid in his curious, heavily-accented French, making clear that I would love to rent that attic apartment situated in the highly desirable location of Montparnasse. And so it was that, without my having uttered a single word, Marguerite expressed her willingness to become my landlady. The rent was very reasonable and additionally she invited us to dine at her house the following evening. In fact, the rent was purely symbolic. Marguerite liked to help young writers in need of accommodation.

I went to the supper with Andrés, and with two or three amphetamines inside me. This was an act of sheer youthful recklessness, since behind that invitation lay Marguerite's desire to get to know me a little and find out if I would make a suitable tenant. Unfortunately, I only realized this when it was too late. Andrés told me when we were already standing outside her house. I panicked and roundly cursed the amphetamines. But, as I said, by then, it was too late.

The person who opened the door was Sonia Orwell, who had also been invited to supper. We went into the kitchen and said hello to Marguerite, who was embroiled in an unlikely struggle with some baby squid being cooked in their own ink, which—although I never knew why—were leaping and dancing around in the frying pan. With a cigarette clamped in one corner of her mouth, Marguerite seemed entirely occupied with these rebellious squid. One of them leapt out onto the kitchen floor and, quick as you like, Marguerite bent down and immediately restored it to its proper place in the pan. In doing so, her cigarette fell in among the squid and was instantly fried to a crisp.

We went into the living room, leaving Marguerite to finish preparing supper. Sonia Orwell offered us a cup of coffee, and I wondered if it was the custom in Paris to begin suppers at the end. Sonia Orwell soon cleared up this mystery by explaining that she was feeling really exhausted and hoping the coffee might perk her up. In an attempt to be nice, I made a supreme effort and said:

"Thank you very much. I love coffee."

I actually disliked coffee intensely, but saying these words cheered me up, even though I felt that I would find it as hard to drink coffee as to utter another word. Fortunately, Andrés again came to my aid, proving what a good friend he was. Knowing the deleterious effect amphetamines had on me, he began speaking for both of us. He did so by embarking on a discussion of the huge advances made by feminism in the modern world. (I merely nodded now and then.) Then he spoke about General de Gaulle and how fed up he was seeing him governing France. Then, suddenly, he began to talk about me. He explained that I had only been in Paris for one day and that he was the only person I knew there.

"The thing that has surprised him most about the city is seeing so many Japanese people," Andrés said, with a smile on his lips, indicating that while he considered me to be a friend, he also thought I was a complete hick.

Then he told Sonia Orwell about a strip club. He explained that, as soon as I had arrived in Paris, I had headed straight for the Quartier Pigalle, where I spent the little money I had staring at naked women and feeling bored.

"On the other hand," said Andrés, "a whore from Alsace told him that he was very handsome and complimented him on his sweater and, above all, on the color of his trousers."

I felt pretty embarrassed but, at the same time, unable to correct anything he had said, because I was incapable of speech.

"Speaking of whores," said Sonia Orwell, downing her second cup of coffee, "Marguerite suggests that we go to the Bois de Boulogne tonight. She wants to find out if it's true what they say in the newspapers."

"And what do they say?" asked Andrés.

"Oh, nothing much, just that some of the prostitutes there are dressed as if for their first communion."

Marguerite came into the room and said that we would soon be able to sit down to eat and that she just had to finish making the curry sauce. I thought this odd. Octopus doesn't need any sauce.

What was I thinking? It was squid not octopus I'd seen in the kitchen. I realized to what extent those wretched amphetamines were addling my brain. I glanced at Andrés, hoping he would continue to help me out and speak for me, but he clearly wasn't up to doing that just then. He rather resembled a coffee pot. A few words that appeared to be coming to a boil immediately behind his eyes were bubbling up toward his brain. Suddenly, his head began bobbing frantically up and down, as if it were about to explode, until, pointing at me, he said to Marguerite:

"Do you know, until he came to Paris, he had never seen a Japanese person?"

"Not even at the movies?" she asked.

I swallowed hard, recalled several movies about Hiroshima that I had seen, but was incapable of saying anything.

"But how is that possible?" she insisted. "Are there no Japanese people in Barcelona?"

I cursed the fact that Andrés occasionally forgot that I couldn't speak. And since he again failed to rescue me, I made a supreme effort and, attempting to be comical, I said:

"No, Franco has banned them."

Instead of accompanying these words with an ironic smile, my face became fixed in a harsh, horrific grimace. To conceal this, I tried to take a sip of coffee, but my hand was shaking so much that I nearly spilled it over Sonia Orwell's skirt. They all pretended not to have noticed, and I listened to them talking for a while. Then, Marguerite announced that she was going back to the kitchen to finish making the curry sauce and carried the coffee pot away with her. I understood this to mean that she would be adding coffee, not curry sauce, to the squid. So much for squid ink, I thought. God, I was in a state. I shot Andrés another pleading glance, a cry for help, but, instead, my face creased into a crazed scowl, which Marguerite saw as she left.

"We don't eat people here, you know," she said, coming back into the living room and this time bearing a tray containing a dish of rice with curry sauce, which was, apparently, to precede the squid cooked in their ink. I felt Sonia Orwell's eyes fixed on me, and had the distinct impression that she was beginning to view me as if I were a Martian.

"Help yourselves," said Marguerite.

When it was my turn, I piled my plate with rice.

"You're obviously hungry," said Andrés, knowing full well that I had no appetite at all. I thought this was because he wanted to draw attention to me and my piled-high plate. I forgave him, though, because it seemed to me that he was actually trying to draw me out and, like any good friend, was worried about what would happen if I didn't start behaving more normally—and soon. I knew that, deep down, he was acting out of the best possible motives.

I tasted the sauce and could barely keep from pulling a face. As for the rice, I knew, right from the start, that I wouldn't be able to eat it. When they had all cleared their plates (even soaking up the sauce with a great deal of bread), all eyes were turned on my plate, which remained scandalously intact. Luckily, this time, Andrés rode to my rescue. He said that only half an hour before, I had succumbed to the charms of some Tunisian cakes.

"You're making all kinds of discoveries," said Marguerite. "Eating Tunisian cakes, seeing Japanese people for the first time."

"Yes, that's true," I replied laconically.

I assumed I had lost any chance I might have of renting that attic apartment. I couldn't have been less charming. However, just then, someone rang the doorbell. Sonia Orwell suggested it might be Louis Jacquot, an actor who wanted to adapt one of Marguerite's books for the stage. He was, I learned, a poor wretch who had played so many different roles that he no longer knew who he was. We heard Marguerite talking to someone in the hall, and when she returned to the living room, she confirmed that it had indeed been the actor.

"He's gone now," she said.

"That was quick. What did he want?" asked Andrés.

"Oh, nothing. The usual thing," Sonia Orwell said. "He wanted to know who he is."

There was a brief silence, then Marguerite poured herself a glass of wine and declared:

"Poor man."

Andrés took charge of the bottle of wine and drank four glasses one after the other, almost without pausing for breath. Marguerite was obliged to open another bottle of Beaujolais.

"So you're from Barcelona?" Marguerite asked, as if giving me one last chance to say something.

Then, as if the question had been addressed to him, Andrés stepped in and said:

"Yes, he's from Barcelona, whereas I, on the other hand, come from Atlantis."

At first, one might have guessed this was the result of those four glasses of wine, but he hadn't really drunk that much. Knowing Andrés as I did, it was more likely that he had finally decided to behave as the most heroic of friends should behave in the most difficult of circumstances. It could be that he had chosen to adopt a diversionary tactic, which involved behaving like a mad eccentric in order to focus attention on himself and thus divert those dangerously perplexed and probing looks away from me. If so, it must be said that Andrés was a very good friend indeed.

"So you're from Atlantis, are you?" asked Sonia Orwell, with a smile on her lips.

"I am," responded Andrés succinctly, and tears welled up in his eyes. When we saw this, we all froze. A heavy silence fell. For a while, as we ate the main course, we listened to him talking about that lost continent. Gesturing dramatically, he summoned up certain marine images, which, according to him, were ancient memories from when he used to live in his real homeland. I had never heard anyone describe with such precision the unknown world of the sea bed. He spoke of paths carved out of the rocks, of the giant skeletons of fish, of shells and stones as pink as mother-of-pearl. He talked and talked, oblivious to the food on his plate, oblivious to the evening and to us. At one point, Marguerite suggested that he had perhaps drunk too much.

"I read somewhere," he said, "that when you've drunk a little, reality grows simpler, you can leap over the spaces in between things, everything seems to fall into place and you can say: yes, that's it. Well, that is what has happened to me tonight. You might think me mad or that I'm making it all up, but you're wrong. For me, tonight, everything has suddenly fallen into place. Ever since I was a child, I've always had a sense that, in another life, I used to live in Atlantis. Now, at last, I feel absolutely sure I was right."

And with that, Andrés finished off the second bottle of Beaujolais.

"Everything you've told us—and you told it very well indeed—is curious in the extreme," Marguerite said, "but it's very hard not to think that you've either drunk too much or are simply having us on."

Andrés did not bat an eyelid.

"And would you believe me," he continued, "if I were to speak to you of a sea that was always so calm that its waves barely rippled when they touched the foot of the cliffs? I remember, too, flocks of sea birds resting on the bluest waters that have ever existed. I remember the profound happiness of all my compatriots, because we lived on the very margins of history or, rather, entered into it only very superficially. We conserved so much energy in our cities that the cosmos itself threatened to be transformed into pure energy. I remember vividly the pieces of white tinplate with the top painted in red lacquer that we used to catch the sumaje fish, our only enemies."

He did not appear to be inebriated. True, he had drunk quite a lot, but he spoke with utter serenity and with a nostalgia that appeared genuine.

Perhaps trying to change the subject, Sonia Orwell pointed at me, still locked in my rigorous silence, and said:

"Your friend is so shy. Not only has he barely uttered a word all evening, he hasn't even dared to open his mouth to eat."

"My friend," said Andrés furiously, "is not in the least bit shy."

His sudden fury seemed to indicate that he wanted to keep their attention from falling on me. However, what he said next didn't exactly confirm that impression.

"My friend," he added, "has taken a few amphetamines and is constantly thinking about his novel."

I was horrified. He had just produced out of nowhere a novel that did not exist and about which I was probably going to be obliged to talk. This proved unnecessary, however, because Andrés went on to explain that I was writing "the memoirs" of a ventriloquist.

"Unfortunately," he added, "this very evening, he lost the manuscript. He left it in a taxi. The memoirs could be read as a novel, although the plot isn't in any way conventional; it is a fractured, uncertain thing and, unlike nineteenth-century plots, is in no way tyrannical, making no attempt to explain the world, far less embrace a whole life, but only a few episodes in a life."

"And what kind of person was this ventriloquist?" asked Sonia Orwell.

"I don't know," Andrés went on, "the kind of man who is always considering leaving everything behind, saying goodbye to Europe and following in Rimbaud's footsteps. I think, in the end, he did leave Europe, but the real cause of his departure does not appear in the memoirs."

"Why not?"

"Before he fled, he committed a murder, and he could hardly confess to that. In the Lisbon night, having bade an unexpected and final farewell to the stage and to his public, he went in search of the barber who had stolen from him the woman he loved, and in a deserted alleyway in the port, he stabbed him through the heart with the sharpened point of a sun umbrella from Java. He could not, of course, write about that in his memoirs and so he fled Europe. In his memoirs, though, what is repugnant and cowardly is disguised as something beautiful, cultivated and literary."

I was lucky in that, once Andrés had invented this story, he promptly forgot all about me and plunged back into his eager search for his origins. He spoke about certain still, hot summer days in his childhood, when the torrid heat weighed on the waters of the river, and it was easy to fall into a sleep so deep it resembled death and thus to retrieve that most distant of past lives on Atlantis.

"Even as a child, I had a sense that I came from there," he went on. "One day, I fell into the Manzanares river. I was a clumsy boy and didn't know how to swim, and, to be honest, I've never learned. I went right under, and then I noticed I was being transported to remote places that suddenly seemed very familiar, as if I'd been there before. It took three or four minutes for me to resurface, time enough to see, at the bottom of the Manzanares, the old palaces of my true homeland. I remembered them as soon as I saw them. The light had a silvery tinge to it. That was where my real life went on: the streets, houses, stones, the footsteps of my true compatriots. And there I was, too, telling stories to rapt and loyal audiences. I was a storyteller recounting the tales of people who had migrated from their bodies in order once more to inhabit their ancient land."

Someone commented that it was getting late. We were certainly surprised by what Andrés had said, but also somewhat weary and weighed down, although I was still grateful to my friend for coming to my rescue like that. That's what friends are for, I thought, pleased with his efforts on my behalf. I preferred to think that he had acted selflessly, rather than assume that he was simply drunk or mad.

"I would suggest," said Marguerite kindly, "that we postpone this conversation until tomorrow. It really is very late, and I'm beginning to feel sleepy. I wanted to go to the Bois de Boulogne, but I'm too tired now."

It really was very late, but Andrés seemed not to notice. He started talking about underwater currents stronger than life itself, currents that dragged one inexorably back to the lost continent.

"Perhaps the day will come," he said, "when I won't return.... My old suit is already very worn, I need to change it, I don't feel comfortable in it anymore. I am, I believe, in the same state as a snake just before it's about to shed its skin: the daylight becomes bothersome and then, like any good snake, it withdraws to its lair."

He paused so briefly that we didn't have time to interrupt. He went on to describe the fires that burned in every hearth in his homeland.

"The flames," he said, "used to rise straight up and gave off no smoke at all. They were fed by dry juniper branches that exuded an acrid odor. On every mantelpiece in Atlantis there were always shield-like candelabras, whose candles gave out a powerful blue light, like the deep, deep blue of our seas."

Someone said again that it was getting late.

Andrés agreed to put his coat on over that old suit, but first polished off whatever alcohol was left in the house. I put a friendly arm around his shoulder.

"Come on," I said, leading him gently to the front door.

"The attic is yours," Marguerite said, much to my surprise. "I'll show you around tomorrow. There's only a mattress, so you may have to buy some more furniture. Yes, I think there's just a mattress and a poster. A poster of Venice showing a very fine reproduction of a crystal chandelier. That's what the concierge told me anyway. You'll see."

I said goodbye, feeling very pleased at this unexpectedly happy ending. Then Andrés and I went out into the street. All the cafés in Paris were closed and, beneath the starry sky, they resembled silent mausoleums on the moon. It would be a difficult night to forget, I thought. And so it has proved to be. That night, walking home with Andrés, he told me that we would never see each other again, and he kept remembering with irresistible nostalgia a valley of streams and mauve waterfalls. He told me that he wanted, without further delay, to disappear by his own hand.

I didn't quite understand what he meant by this, but I assumed that "by his own hand" must be some reference to suicide. I thought that perhaps he was talking about a disappearance that belonged not so much to the realm of necessity, but to that of freedom. I was still pondering this when Andrés repeated those same words—"by his own hand"—and, in one bound, leapt into the icy waters of the Seine, vanishing from sight. My first thought was that he really was taking things too far; then I realized that it was up to me to save him, because there was no one else around to help. I took off my overcoat and, without hesitation, jumped into the Seine and soon managed to locate him beneath the waters. He was in a near-ecstatic—I would almost say blissful—state, as if he were allowing himself to be carried by those underwater currents back to his original homeland.

I grabbed him by one arm, but he struggled violently, as if I had interrupted his journey. I had no option but to punch him hard and render him unconscious. Then came the hardest part, because I have never done anything requiring such enormous physical effort. I dragged his body up onto the quay, but there was still no one else around. I covered him with my overcoat and waited for him to regain consciousness. When he did, he looked at me in bewilderment, felt his chin, and asked what we were doing there, soaked to the skin.

"Can't you remember anything?" I said.

"To be honest, no …"

Feeling confused and exhausted, I thought for a moment. I was afraid I might have caught pneumonia. Deep down, I was very angry. The water had wiped my head clean of the effects of those amphetamines.

The water had wiped my head clean of the effects of those amphetamines.

"Do you really not remember?"

"No, I told you, no."

"You mean, you can't even remember where we've come from?"

I immediately regretted asking this question, fearing that he might say: "I don't know about you, but I'm from Atlantis." But he really didn't seem to remember anything. I was glad I hadn't mentioned Marguerite Duras, a name he might have associated with the lost continent.

"Let's go home," I said.

Again I regretted my words, fearing that the storyteller might recall his humble home back in Atlantis. But no, he remained in a state of utter bewilderment. The problem was that I couldn't utter a word, because anything I said might trigger a memory. Alas, I was so upset with him that anger overcame both prudence and silence. Why had he done all that? I asked him.

"All what?" he answered with his most beatific smile.

"What do you think?" I said very loudly, my eyes wild.

He lay there, half-confused and half-thoughtful, until suddenly he gave signs of having recovered his memory.

"Ah, yes," he said.

I feared the worst.

"Why *did* I do all that?" He was clearly thinking deeply. "Well, the truth is, it really doesn't matter. I would say that I had to do it, do you see?"

I can still remember the hard look in his eyes when, shortly afterward, he stood up, and walking slowly backwards, as if about to take part in the hundred-meter backstroke, he said:

"That's what friends are for."

And again he leapt into the river, this time taking my overcoat with him, as if he wanted to find out just how far our friendship would go.

TORRE DEL MIRADOR

One morning, I received a phone call from someone saying that he was close to having a nervous breakdown and that he needed to talk to me because he felt so alone since separating from his wife.

"Why are you telling *me* all this?" I said, a logical reaction for someone who has been woken up by a complete stranger.

"Let me explain," he responded. "My wife was making my life a misery by going on at me all the time about how ugly I was. She used to say she hated my face. One day, I got so fed up that I decided to rent the apartment I'm phoning from now and from which I can see my former home, the villa where my wife still lives, alone and abandoned."

I thought this must be some friend of mine playing a trick on me. The other man was still talking.

"I needed to talk to someone and I picked your name at random from the phone book. I'm alone here with my binoculars and the enormous mirror I've installed in my bedroom."

This was either a joke or the man was mad, I thought. I suggested that he stop playing games and go back to his wife.

"I can't, it's too late. She thinks I've disappeared and doesn't realize that I'm spying on her. Haven't you ever wondered what will happen after you die? In the early days, I watched the procession of visitors, family, and friends. My wife, of course, seemed anxious and, above all, confused. She couldn't understand what could possibly have happened to me, she couldn't understand why I had vanished in that mysterious fashion. Lately, though, now that everyone assumes I've disappeared for good, she seems ever more resigned to her fate, happier. It wouldn't surprise me if, any day now, she decided to remarry. But that isn't what bothers me."

Out of politeness—and a touch of curiosity (it no longer seemed to me that this was a joke or that he was a madman)—I asked if what was bothering him, as he had mentioned at the beginning, was loneliness.

"Exactly," he said. "Loneliness and monotony. I get more and more bored with each day that passes, especially when I have nothing to spy on. For example, when my wife goes shopping, there's nothing happening in the villa or in the garden. So what do I do? I sit here getting mortally bored."

"Go home, man," I said, hoping to appeal to his common sense. "Whatever made you think of doing such a thing?"

"It happened, and now I can't go home again because I've gone too far. For some days now, I've had a completely different face. Even if I did go back, I doubt that my wife would recognize me."

Things were getting interesting. I had a rather unimaginative first cousin, who was always on the look-out for ideas for his movies. Perhaps I could pass the story on to him.

"You say you have a different face?"

"Yes. My voice has changed too. I took an intensive voice-training course and learned to use different registers. I used to be a doctor. Now I'm no one."

"What sort of doctor?"

"I used to be a cosmetic surgeon. I just got back from Brazil where some very competent colleagues of mine completely transformed my face. I'm not as ugly as I was before. Sad to say, though, I'm no longer a surgeon, no longer married, and no longer have a future. All I have are a mirror and a pair of binoculars."

I didn't know what to say. I could see myself reflected in my own wardrobe mirror, and it occurred to me then to ask why he had put an enormous mirror in his bedroom.

"So that I can get used to my new face," he said.

I fell silent, thinking about what he had said. My silence alarmed him.

"I know you want to hang up," he continued. "Everyone does. They think I'm some practical joker or else mad and they hang up."

"No, really, I find your story very interesting. In fact, if anything new happens, don't hesitate to give me a call. Although I would ask that you only do so once a week at most and only when something truly significant has occurred. Otherwise, hold back. Unlike your unoccupied self, I have a lot of things to do."

"And may I know what those things are?"

"If you do have to phone me," I said, as if I hadn't heard his question, "do so in the afternoon. I work at night and sleep in the morning."

"Are you a baker or an actor or perhaps a fireman?"

I could see he had a sense of humor.

"No, I'm an interpreter of dreams," I said on the spur of the moment.

He then started telling me his latest dream (something about some very discreet creature that wore the mask of pride), but I cut him off as soon as I could. I wasn't thinking of including any dreams in my cousin's movie. I again reminded him that I was a busy man, and he finally got it: that if he wanted me to listen to him on other occasions, it would be best to say goodbye.

"Of course, of course," he said, and, after thanking me over and over and saying sorry, sorry, so very sorry, for bothering me, he said goodbye and hung up.

The following day, I was woken in the early hours by the phone ringing. Before I could even say hello, I heard his unmistakable voice:

"I've smashed the mirror and now I really am all alone."

Calling me at that hour seemed to me deliberately provocative, and it made me think that he had purposely smashed the mirror just to have something to tell me.

"I no longer exist," he declared. "All that's left are various fragments of glass that reflect me in a broken, uncertain fashion."

With my acknowledged talent for mimicry, I did a perfect imitation of my Aunt Consuelo, who also happened to be my moviemaker cousin's mother:

"I'm the cleaning lady, dear," I said. "The master's in Rome at the moment. He had to go there urgently and he'll be away for the next few months. Who should I say called?"

When he didn't reply, I asked again:

"Who should I say called?"

"Damn!" he yelled and then hung up.

I thought I had rid myself of a potential problem and had no regrets about disconnecting myself from the whole story until, a few days later, my cousin, Cool, came to see me (we called him Cool because that was his favorite adjective), and when I told him about the phone calls, he got really annoyed with me. He protested at me using his mother's voice to imitate a cleaning lady, but he complained, above all, about my losing touch with a man who, in his opinion, was living through something really remarkable, really cool, the beginning of a story he would have liked to know the ending to.

"It would have made a really cool movie," said my cousin, regretfully shaking his head.

After expressing my doubts that all stories necessarily have to have an ending, I pointed out to him that he could still use the beginning of the story as the starting point for a really interesting plot. I had forgotten that my cousin had no imagination. He paced aimlessly about the room, staring into space, pretending to be thinking. I felt so sorry for him that, finally, I suggested a possible continuation:

"How about if one day our character discovers that there's no correspondence between him and his mirror. I can see it now. The angular reflection of our man as he approaches the surface of the mirror: he raises one hand to his slender neck, and, to his horror, sees that there's no corresponding gesture in the mirror."

"You mean the mirror doesn't reflect the gesture of raising his hand to his neck?"

"Exactly."

"That's just nonsense."

I could have cheerfully strangled him. And then he had the nerve to accuse me of not being in touch with the character. I heard a string of wild insults which concluded thus:

"Party pooper!"

"All right, all right," I said, unable to bear his shouting. "If you really want to track him down, I don't think it will be too difficult."

An hour later, we were at the Medical Association, passing ourselves off as journalists. We arrived equipped with borrowed raincoats, spectacles, piercing looks, pens, and notebooks. We were told that the doctor who had disappeared was not a plastic surgeon, but an ophthalmologist. We both felt this didn't change matters much.

We were given an address, and we both agreed that if it were a villa, then we would almost certainly have found the right place. We hailed a taxi and, a few minutes later, we were driving through a residential area, where the taxi pulled up outside 27 Calle Tucumán. It was a villa. We smiled. We got out of the taxi, and peered through the railings at a deserted, bourgeois garden in which a single elm stood, dozing placidly. A sign read: Torre del Mirador. There was only one apartment block nearby, but that was some way off. A large tennis club separated the villa from the ophthalmologist's probable viewing point. His binoculars would have to be very powerful, I thought. Then a woman's voice behind us said:

"Have you come to see the villa?"

"Yes, we have," Cool blurted out and, for a moment, I had no idea what was going on. Then I noticed that the villa was for sale, as indicated on a board.

The woman was about thirty and very beautiful, although everything about her was slightly antiquated. Her hair was caught back on either side with combs; she wore a string of pearls, and an old brooch was pinned to the narrow lapels of an old-fashioned gray suit. She had such an extraordinarily mobile face that it was impossible to know for sure what it was really like. It was as if her face were constantly traveling back in time, and she were continually becoming various ladies from different ages. Slightly troubled by this, I concentrated on her voice, which was grave, weary, almost masculine in tone.

"Please, come in," she said. And as we walked into the garden, I had the uncomfortable feeling that I had become binocular fodder.

I took off my glasses and shot a furtive glance over beyond the tennis courts, toward the apartment block where the ophthalmologist might be spying on us.

We strolled around the garden and paused for some time by a pool whose waters reflected the solitary elm tree. My cousin seemed very comfortable in his role as potential buyer. He asked the selling price and, when he was told, he stared ostentatiously at the algae in the pond.

Then we went into the house. The living-room walls were dominated by five very brightly colored paintings depicting the various stages of construction of what appeared to be a Ritz Carlton Hotel in some African city. We were looking at these ghastly paintings, when the woman said:

"Are you there, Leo?"

We thought she was calling a dog and so were rather surprised when we realized that Leo was a person. A curtain was drawn aside, and a man appeared, smoking a Havana cigar.

"May I introduce my friend Leonardo."

I quickly realized that their relationship was a recent one and that they were in love. There was no mistaking the way they talked and looked at each other. The man was about forty years old, had strange, brusque manners, and seemed somewhat irritated by our presence there.

Knowing human voices as I do, I was quick to realize that his rather dull, unresonant voice (what one might describe as "gruff") could easily be fake. I wondered if he was perhaps the ophthalmologist with his new face. Troubled by this thought, I studied that face, which reminded me of a gray paperweight that had belonged to my grandfather. His hideous eyes appeared to be submerged in a dark green ditch. He had protruding ears—the only promontories in that devastating, devastated face—huge ears, which reminded me of the lampshades on two Chinese lanterns of which my poor grandmother had been particularly fond.

He stubbed out his cigar and, after eyeing us rather suspiciously, began reading the sports pages in his newspaper. We left him there while we were shown around the rest of the villa and, after half an hour, returned to find him still reading. My cousin and the woman were already on friendly terms and entered the living room together laughing. Leonardo, making no attempt to conceal a flicker of jealousy and unease, felt obliged to intervene.

"Look at this, Lola," he said, pointing at the newspaper. "Look, there's an article about Timbuktu. Do you think your husband might have written it? It's signed by someone called Spacspack, but that must be a pseudonym."

"No, I doubt very much that he wrote it," she said with a faint smile.

"Is your husband a journalist?" my cousin asked rather too familiarly.

"No, he's a doctor," she replied. "An ophthalmologist. We think he might be practicing in Timbuktu now, which is a place he said he always wanted to go. If you do buy the villa, you should know that I'm selling it with my husband's ghost included. He's soon going to be declared officially dead in absentia, but he could return any day from Timbuktu or wherever he's gone, and then you'd get a shock."

"We're immune to shocks," my cousin said, and I thought he was referring to Leonardo's hideous face.

"You can't imagine what my husband looked like. I don't like to speak ill of him because he may be dead, but he looked like a character out of a horror movie. He was even uglier than those paintings over there."

"Are they supposed to show a hotel in various stages of construction?" I asked.

"As a young man," she explained, "he wanted to be a missionary in Africa, but the Jesuits told him he wasn't suitable. Then he met me. When we married and moved here, he wanted to call the villa something like Mirador del Africa. When I wouldn't let him, he took his revenge on the Jesuits and me by painting those five horrible paintings of some imaginary hotel in Timbuktu."

"They're not that horrible," said Leonardo, and this only made me more suspicious.

"Not horrible?" she cried, and she seemed genuinely angry. "It's time you knew my tastes, Leonardo. Those paintings aren't quite as ugly as he was, and you aren't quite as ugly as them."

Leonardo thanked her for the compliment, but it was clear that he wasn't at all pleased. I took the opportunity to try and sound him out about his profession.

"By the way," I said, "your face looks familiar. Are you an architect?"

"No, I'm not an architect," he replied. "I'm just a neighbor. And what about you?" he said, indicating my cousin and me, while his ears seemed to stick out even more wildly. "Were you married in church?"

"What do you mean?" asked my cousin.

"I'm asking if you're married."

Now my cousin is a man of violent, rather primitive reactions, and so I felt obliged to intervene before he did; however, the woman beat me to it.

"They're cousins!" she said, laughing.

When I try to reconstruct her face through her smile, I still can't do it. It's not because I can't remember, but because her constantly time-traveling features revealed too many faces at once.

My clearest recollection of that moment is Leonardo's fierce look: one of utter distrust, which only increased my suspicions that, equipped with his new identity, he was trying to remake his marital life. If this were true, his wife appeared to be entirely unaware of it. And my cousin Cool even less so.

"Well, the villa is really very splendid and the algae in the pond, of course, is truly intriguing," he said. "I think we'll buy it, that is, we need to give the matter some thought of course—but yes, I think we'll buy it. I just hope," he said, making an utterly tasteless joke, "that we don't have to pay extra for your husband's ghost."

This final comment seemed to bother her. Cousin Cool was taking too many liberties.

"I hope so too," she said, heading for the hallway, signaling unequivocally that our visit was over.

We were just saying goodbye when the doorbell rang. Another

buyer, she said. But when she opened the door, a man of about thirty appeared and, after standing motionless on the threshold for a few seconds, he said very slowly, in a voice heavy with emotion:

"It's me, my love. I've come back."

He was tall, dark, and rather handsome. She appeared completely bewildered.

"It's me, my love. Don't you recognize me?"

On the visitor's face glinted the lenses and gold frames of glasses that sheltered delicate, restless eyes. His glossy, black hair was parted in the middle and combed backwards in a long curve behind his ears; there was a slight wave in it left by his elegant black hat.

"Don't you at least recognize my voice? I changed my face in order to please you."

She still didn't respond, and it occurred to me that perhaps, like me, this man had heard the story over the phone, but was intending to take advantage of the situation by selling to her, at a high price, the information he had about her vanished husband.

However, to judge by her reaction after her initial bewilderment, I could only assume that he really was her husband. How else explain the way she contentedly examined that pleasant face, then melted into the visitor's arms, in a long, emotional embrace.

"Why did you do that?" we heard her sobbing. "Why?"

"I had to," he replied, with an infinitely serious laugh.

We were clearly in the way.

"We were just leaving," said Cool.

They didn't even hear. I would have liked to stay because I was suddenly filled with an intense curiosity, but Cousin Cool was already out in the garden. I was just about to leave too, when I happened to turn and take one last look at the house. Leonardo was making his escape through a window giving out onto the garden.

I remember that as we began to walk down Calle Tucumán, Leonardo was already ahead of us, but since he was almost running, he had about a hundred yards on us, Cool didn't notice he was there, because he hadn't seen him jump out of the window, and I hadn't bothered to tell him.

"So the movie has a happy ending," Cousin Cool said, "but I don't think I'll use the story. By the way, do you think her husband suspected us at all?"

"Which husband are you referring to?"

"What do you mean 'which husband'?" he said looking at me, extremely puzzled. "The elegant fellow we left back there in the house."

Just then, I saw in the distance that Leonardo was passing an impeccably handsome young man of about twenty, who was walking energetically and determinedly up the hill. It seemed obvious to me that, in the street of life, one was on the way up and the other was plunging into the shadows.

"It won't be long," I told my cousin, "before that same elegant fellow will be jumping out of the window and landing in the garden."

When my cousin continued to stare at me in utter confusion, I had no option but to explain:

"And very soon too that young man heading toward us now will ring the bell of the Torre del Mirador."

I NEVER GO TO THE MOVIES

for José Luis Vigil

At 10 p.m., on the dot, he was standing at the front door of Rita Malú's house, and a very tall butler blocked his path. Pampanini said:

"I'm one of the guests."

"One of them?"

"Aren't there others?"

"Please, come in."

Pampanini walked down a corridor toward a small living room. As he was directed (in a manner of speaking, since the butler had disappeared by then) through a complex network of rooms, he began to realize that this was just the kind of place where you know that, at any moment, someone is going to give you a nasty surprise. And so it was. Suddenly, a door creaked open of its own accord to reveal Rita Malú, who was leaning against a bookcase, smoothing her long, perfect, ivory-colored gloves.

"I'm so glad I could come," he said, going over to the hostess.

"So am I," she said.

"But isn't this your house?"

"Let's go upstairs."

They went up a spiral staircase to the roof terrace. There were various groups of guests, as well as many small red party-lights, a piano, and a certain air of gaiety. The view was splendid, but Pampanini felt slightly dizzy. Ever since that first encounter with the butler, he had had a sense of impending doom. While two ladies were throwing cream cakes at each other, an American named Glen mistook him for a now-deceased movie director. After greeting him solemnly, and oblivious to the cream-cake battle being waged, the American congratulated Pampanini on the great beauty of his work, laying particular emphasis on the thrilling sequence in which a female slave bathed naked in the Tigris. Pampanini was about to protest, when an old lady berated him for the atheism evident in his early films.

"At least you converted to Catholicism later on," she said.

"You're obviously confusing me with someone else," said Pampanini.

Glen, the American, slowly lit a cigarette. The old lady went off to fetch a man with a notable double chin and a very prominent belly, a certain Rossi, whom she asked to play the piano. The man sighed, got up, tripped over Pampanini's foot as he passed and, sitting down at the piano, bowed his head, remaining motionless for some seconds. Then, slowly and very carefully, he placed his cigarette in an ash tray and again bowed his head. He stayed like this for a good while until, finally, looking up, he dedicated his performance to the distinguished movie director who was, that night, honoring them with his presence. Pampanini interrupted in order, once and for all, to clear up the confusion as to his identity.

"That man died some time ago," said Pampanini.

Everyone laughed, thinking he was being witty, and some even applauded. Then Pampanini asked Rita to clear up the whole mess.

"You can do that better than I," she said rather haughtily.

Pampanini went over to the piano and, leaning against it, said in a firm, calm voice:

"You're confusing me with a corpse. I'm a professional calligrapher and I work for the local council. My name is Alfredo Pampanini."

More laughter and applause.

"I wouldn't mind this whole unfortunate mistake," he went on, "if it weren't for the fact, ladies and gentlemen, that I never go to the movies. Indeed, I've never even been inside a cinema, not even when I was a child, when it was fashionable to spend Sundays in one of those dark places. My imagination was and still is too full for me to waste my time staring at a screen and waiting for a few fleeting shadows to appear."

It was true. As a child, Pampanini was always so engrossed in his own solitary games that his parents never found the right moment to take him to the movies. When he grew up, he still didn't feel the slightest curiosity. Whenever someone suggested going, he would find some more or less convincing excuse to avoid what, for him, would be sheer torture. He suspected that the cinema was the most deceiving of all the arts and the only one in which nothing was ever true.

"You can't fool us," said the old lady.

But Pampanini had moved on. In one corner of the terrace, Rita was introducing him to two young female friends of hers. They were both called Genoveva. "That can't be true," thought Pampanini. The prettier of the two girls tried to warn him of a threat hanging in the air.

"See those birds?" she said.

There were quite a large number of birds perched on a wire.

"What about them?" he asked.

Rita took his arm and led him over to the other side of the terrace. On the way, she asked if it was true that he didn't like the movies. Pampanini said:

"Yes, it's true, and do you know why? Because in the movies nothing is ever true."

While he was saying this, Pampanini kept looking back to where he had left the two Genovevas. He really liked the less pretty of the two, and was just thinking that he'd like to have a longer conversation with her when Glen, the American, bore furiously down on Rita and told her off for having so little alcohol at her party.

"Why do you want to drink so much?" Pampanini asked.

"To get myself drunk."

"Your *self?*"

"Sit down!" Glen said.

Glen brought Pampanini a chair, and Pampanini, who did not dare to refuse, sat down. He was still recovering from his surprise when, to his even greater surprise, he saw Glen deal Rita a spectacularly hard slap across the face. Since Pampanini had never seen such a thing before, he was astonished. It can't be true, he thought. Then Glen fled over the rooftops with Rossi in hot pursuit. Shortly afterward, while jumping from one roof to the next, Rossi missed his footing and slipped. As he fell, though, he managed to grab hold of a gutter, while his hat plunged into the abyss. Some of the guests laughed like maniacs. No, it can't be true, Pampanini thought. And he sat there, literally dumbstruck.

ROSA SCHWARZER COMES BACK TO LIFE

Right at the far end of this museum in Düsseldorf, in the last and most remote of the rooms devoted to Paul Klee, the highly efficient guard Rosa Schwarzer is seated on an austere chair, in the same uncomfortable corner that has, for years now, been her lot; she is yawning discreetly and, at the same time, feeling slightly alarmed, because, for some time now, along with the sound of rain falling in the museum garden, she has been hearing, issuing from *The Black Prince*, the seductive call of that dark prince, who, hoping to lure her into the canvas, keeps sending her the arrogant sound of beating tom-toms from his native land, the land of suicides.

I know that, in a desperate attempt to resist the prince's influence and his tempting proposal to abandon both her life and the museum, Rosa Schwarzer's eyes have taken refuge in the subtle pinks of *Monsieur Perlanschwein*, which is another of the paintings in the room she so zealously guards and where, were someone to burst boldly in right now, the intruder would find her—this highly efficient guard—stifling a yawn, springing to her feet to ask him, please, due to the very sensitive alarm, not to go too close to either Monsieur Pink or Señor Black.

As I said, Rosa Schwarzer is slightly on edge this morning.

Does what happened to her yesterday have some influence on all this? I would say that it does. Yesterday, Rosa Schwarzer turned fifty, and, since the museum is closed on Mondays, she thought she would have the whole morning to prepare her birthday lunch. However, everything went wrong from the start. To begin with, she woke feeling full of angst, flailing around like a puppet in the insipid, colorless void of her sad life. Then that void took on a pale gray color, just like the day itself.

What is the point of my life?

I know that Rosa Schwarzer said this as she lay half-awake yesterday and that she said the same thing today, but yesterday, unlike today, she woke surprised that she had spoken those words, then began simply preparing breakfast for her husband and her two sons, who had assured her that, even though it was a normal working day for them, they would make a special effort and get together at lunchtime in order to enjoy, as they always did, the roast suckling pig that no one cooked better than Mama Rosa, as they all call her.

That's what they call me, thinks Rosa Schwarzer, as she listens to the rain falling in the museum garden, as she feels herself being drawn toward the sound of beating tom-toms from that land of suicides.

I know that the second setback she experienced yesterday, after waking feeling like an angst-ridden puppet, was the unexpected desertion of her eldest son, Bernd, who, over breakfast, said that he wouldn't be able to come home for lunch, which prompted his father to make his excuses, too, and say he was terribly busy at work, and ask for his portion of roast suckling pig to be kept for later that evening.

Rosa Schwarzer silently bit her lip and told herself that none of this need delay breakfast, which was almost ready; however what would potentially be delayed was lunchtime, for other dangerous obstacles were blocking her path, clamoring for her attention: allowing her eyes to drift distractedly around the kitchen, she had noticed—along with the coffee, the cheese, the tea, the rye bread with cumin seeds, the jams and the cold meats—she saw the solitary heart of a colorless bottle of bleach, which, had that bottle been endowed with life, would doubtless have taken the form of a sad puppet lost in the insipid void of that equally sad kitchen.

She thought how easy it would be to die and that she should not

36

let this splendid opportunity pass her by. A few sips of bleach, and the daily grind of gray images, heartless husbands and the deadly dullness of her job at the museum would be erased in an instant. But just as she was about to pick up the bottle, it occurred to her to think about her wretch of a husband or, rather, her poor, wretched husband, and suddenly she discovered that there was something in the morning air, something about being alone in the sad kitchen, that stirred her blood in a not entirely disagreeable way. In fact, her husband, who was openly deceiving her on a daily basis with the next-door neighbor (the wretch thought she didn't know), was deserving of compassion and needed guidance, and this was one good reason—simple but important—to go on living, to go on preparing breakfast, to keep trying to help her husband regain his happiness and become once more the delightful man she had met in the Hofgarten one marvelous Sunday morning thirty years ago, a morning that did not deserve to be erased by a bottle of bleach.

Before carrying the breakfast into the dining room, in order to celebrate having missed this excellent opportunity to take her own life, Rosa Schwarzer drank a cup of very strong coffee that prompted her to take another look at the landscape of the kitchen, this time ignoring the bleach's obsessive presence—that is, she saw the coffee, the cheese, the tea, the rye bread with cumin seeds, the jams and the cold meats, but either did not or chose not to see the wretched bottle of bleach.

The coffee brought her almost savagely awake, and, for a moment, as if it were a brief foretaste of what she would experience at the museum today, she saw in her mind the remote landscapes of that dark foreign prince's country. The coffee left her buzzing with energy, so much so that she entered the dining room at an excessively brisk and lively pace and almost emptied the contents of the breakfast tray onto the innocent head of her younger son, poor Hans, who, unbeknown to him, was fatally ill.

My poor, dear Hans, she thought as she opened the window, and the cold morning air suddenly filled the whole room. Rosa Schwarzer sat thinking about her son's awful fate, and it occurred to her then to hurl herself into the void, or, rather, into the neighbor's courtyard, to take advantage of that second opportunity, as easy as it was perfect, to take her own life and achieve freedom by detaching herself from everything and everyone, to leave, at last, this tragic, grotesque world. Then she realized that her son needed her even more than her husband did, and that this really was a reason to go on living. And to assure herself that she would remain alive, perfectly alive, Rosa Schwarzer cut herself a slice of cheese.

When the three men of the household left for work, she began getting dressed, and she did this so very slowly that she took far longer than usual. She carefully counted the gray hairs that had appeared overnight and considered buying a wig, until she remembered the strange individual she had known as a child, a man who, in a mood of tragic despair, had brutally plucked out the hairs from his wig. She didn't want something similar to happen to her. She thought: I wonder what became of that man? And another thing: where do wigs go when they die?

She continued asking herself such questions and deliberately putting off going out to buy the suckling pig, until, finally, when it was already quite late, she went out into the street. The air and the colors of midday unfurled themselves before her, fresh, invigorating, and new, while she sought to fill her housewifely duties with the loving passion that, though unconfessed, burns in the hearts of so many housewives as soon as they discover the secret sweetness and the furious fanaticism that can be brought to bear on the most ordinary of daily tasks, on the humblest of domestic chores; because deep down—thought Rosa Schwarzer—there is nothing to compare with the inner satisfaction of serving up a steaming hot dish of food with admirable punctuality, bang on the dot at lunch time.

That was what Rosa Schwarzer was thinking yesterday morning, but, at the same time, and in violent conflict with her innermost convictions, she told herself that the roast suckling pig could wait, in fact, there was no way it would be ready in time for lunch, and so she told herself to go slow and began walking at a more leisurely pace, on a low flame. And simmering over that low flame, her blood rose to her cheeks when she decided to prepare a simple potato salad (after all, that would be enough for her and Hans), and then she thought, no, she wouldn't prepare anything, and that, besides, Hans' unhappy fate was too awful for her to be planning optimistic salads, and life was definitely far worse than any stupid potato, and that she would kill herself, yes, without further delay, she would kill herself. After all, there, before her, lay the wretched tarmac road shining in the sun, offering her the opportunity to throw herself under the wheels of a car and be done, once and for all, with the tiresome business of the roast suckling pig, her unfaithful husband, the potato salad, the silverware and the tablecloth, the infinite tedium of mornings at the museum, the cabbage and the lettuce, her youngest son on the verge of death, the steaming hot dish of food served up with admirable punctuality, bang on the dot at lunchtime …

She was already on the lookout for the car that would cut short her life when she suddenly realized that, in the early hours of that morning, of that strange, cold morning, something had broken very deep inside her; because, when she thought about it, it was really very odd that, after years and years of never thinking about life or things in general, in the last few hours, she had done nothing but that. And she thought that it was actually very stimulating to see how her fragile life force had grown so very gloomy and dark, but, at the same time, become so dangerously attractive. In other words, on entering the kingdom of darkness and despair, her life had finally and paradoxically become rather animated. It was rather like going to one of those movies that begin with a black-and-white still photograph in which, by sheer persistence, you gradually see more and more, until the image begins to take on color, setting in motion a subtle plot. In just the same way her own life was becoming more colorful, not much, only very subtly, but it was better than nothing. So why end up horribly disfigured beneath the wheels of a car when the truth was that she was fascinated to know what changes the next few hours would bring—subtle changes, of course, but changes nonetheless?

All of this seemed to her more than enough reason to let this opportunity to commit suicide pass her by. To celebrate her decision to remain alive, she went into a local bar and ordered a tea, doing so with the satisfaction of one who has finally dared to make a long-postponed decision, because it had been years—ever since she got married or possibly long before that—since she had gone into a bar on her own. That is why, when she leaned on the counter and ordered a tea, she felt she was experiencing a few moments of intense freedom. She felt very pleased, almost happy, but when they brought her the tea, and just when she was beginning to see life through rose-tinted glasses—to which the pink upholstery partly contributed—she noticed a man, probably drunk, who was staggering about in the strangest way just a few yards from her. For some reason, he reminded her of the man with the wig whom she had known as a child. Even though it had stopped raining some hours before, the man in the café still had on the hood of his old, dark raincoat. So early in the day and so drunk, thought Rosa Schwarzer. And shortly afterward, with a certain feeling of dread, she saw him coming over to her. Then she recognized him and calmed down. He was a local man whom she had often seen before and of whom it was said that he was permanently drunk and could frequently be found weeping in the corners of various bars.

"Good evening," the man said, with exquisite, surprising friendliness. He was about thirty, rather good-looking and seemed very sad.

"You mean 'Good morning,'" she answered.

"Don't you know that only night and darkness exist? There is only one story that happens in daylight. Haven't you heard about the man who leaves a bar down by the port in the early hours of the morning?"

"Hey, Hans, don't bother the lady," said the waiter. Rosa Schwarzer was somewhat taken aback to learn that the man bore the same name as her doomed younger son.

"He's not bothering me at all," said Rosa Schwarzer, touched by the name of that extremely polite drunk, who also spoke with a certain verve, one might say lucidity. You would hardly know he had been drinking.

"That man," he went on, "has a bottle of whisky in his pocket and glides along the pavement as lightly as a boat leaving port. Soon he runs head-on into a storm ..."

"Ah, now I understand," she broke in, "now I understand why you're wearing a hood."

The man pretended not to have heard her and continued his peculiar story:

"Soon he runs head-on into a storm and, rolling from side to side, frantically tries to get back to port. But he's never going to reach any port. So he goes into another bar."

"And why does he drink so much?" she asked.

After giving the matter seemingly endless thought, after thinking long and hard about it, the man replied:

"Because reality is too unpleasant."

Rosa Schwarzer laughed shyly.

"How very amusing!" she said. "But isn't unreality equally unpleasant, my friend?"

The man got annoyed then and lost his manners. He began explaining that he was an inveterate night owl and hadn't yet been to bed and what he most enjoyed (and here he lowered his voice slightly to emphasize what he deemed to be a witticism) was to broadcast his relaxed and sinful style of life among the lost souls of the International Union of Onioneers, whose members were all long-suffering, tearful housewives. Rosa Schwarzer, who was in no mood for jokes and who, moreover, had noticed that he was the only tearful person present, decided not to be cowed and gave him a withering look.

"Who do you take me for?" she said.

And she's saying it again now. Who do you take me for? But now the question is addressed to the black prince, who insists on sending out, above the murmur of the rain, the sound of beating tom-toms from his distant land, the land of suicides.

"Who do you take me for?" Rosa Schwarzer said to the impertinent night owl.

"Are you sure he's not bothering you, Madam?" the waiter asked again.

"Certainly not!" she retorted, for the last thing she wanted was for this technicolor sequence in her newly animated life to cease.

"My apologies, my sincere apologies," the night owl blurted out, all politeness now and still rather cowed by that withering look from a Rosa Schwarzer who now felt capable of anything, for she was convinced that no one—certainly not that poor night owl—could possibly have had a more intense or dangerous morning than she. Always on the brink of death and always, at the very last moment, drawing back from the abyss. She had already thrown away three opportunities that morning, three clear, categorical chances to kill herself. This made her feel so safe and so full of self-confidence that she even dared to invite the hooded stranger to join her in a stroll around the shops.

"Won't you join me? I'm going to make a potato salad and need to buy a few ingredients."

"Yes, why not?" he said at once. She was deeply moved to see how unreservedly this stranger valued her company, and she so trusted him that she even confessed she had been on the verge of committing suicide three times in the last few hours. It took her a long time to tell him this, because she didn't want to gloss over what seemed to her the most significant details.

"In short," Rosa Schwarzer concluded after half an hour, "this morning everything seems new, none of what is happening has ever happened to me before."

The man was half-asleep.

"Hey, wake up! We agreed that we'd go out and buy some…"—she didn't dare to mention the word "potatoes" again. "Come on, wake up, please. You're obviously not as much of a night owl as you claim."

The man brightened, went off to the toilet, and came back seeming like a new man.

"It's incredible," he said shortly afterward, when they went out into the street and the trust between them was now mutual, so much so that they were already on first name terms. "It's just incredible, Rosa…. Now I want you to do me a favor. I was thinking it over while you kept talking and talking and I almost fell asleep—and the only reason I didn't fall asleep was because I was trying to follow the mysterious thread of your thoughts—anyway, I've thought it all through now and I want you to do me a favor, Rosa. The next time you feel like killing yourself, don't resort to bleach or your neighbor's courtyard or the wheels of a car. Those are very unaesthetic deaths."

"And what makes you think there will be a next time?" she asked, somewhat surprised.

By way of an answer, the man handed her a miniature bottle of whisky and told her that it contained a cyanide capsule and that she should keep it. She preferred to think this was just another of the night owl's jokes and put the bottle in her coat pocket.

"If necessary," he said, "all you have to do is take the top off the bottle and drink the poison down in one, it's that simple."

"Now you know perfectly well that what you're giving me is whisky, not poison," she said fondly, and smiling.

"No, really, it's cyanide. The bottle is simply intended to throw people off the scent, you see," he said, slowly putting down the hood of his raincoat with a gesture she interpreted as a sign that he was recovering after his night of drinking, that he was returning to reality, however unpleasant that might seem to him.

At two o'clock, they were still walking around, not having stopped at any shops or—despite his best efforts—any bars; they were now stumbling over the cobblestones of a part of town that was no longer hers and approaching the Hofgarten, far from her usual everyday landscapes and far, too, from any grocers or bars. The man seemed sunk in his own thoughts and tired as well, as if he were about to faint or fall asleep in some corner or other, but he was still half-paying attention as Rosa Schwarzer talked to him, telling him, at one point, that thirty years ago, she had met her poor, unhappy husband in the Hofgarten. And finally they sat down on a stone bench at the entrance to the park.

"Now," he said, "instead of guarding a room in a museum, you're guarding the whole of the Hofgarten. Not a bad swap, not bad at all. The whole of the Hofgarten …"

Rosa Schwarzer smiled, but said nothing, watching the clouds drifting across the ice-gray sky. My poor, dear Hans, she found herself thinking, and she didn't know if she was invoking the name of her son—whom she had just phoned to say that she was still at the hairdresser's and would be late for lunch and that he would have to make do with some cold chicken that was in the fridge—or whether she was thinking about this other Hans, her drowsy companion, poor, handsome Hans, so young and eager to please, the man with the hood and the cyanide capsule, who had led her far from her home turf, from her family, from her sorrow over her son's illness, from the tedium of her mornings at the museum, and, above all, from the unbearable monochrome that was apparent in every aspect of her bitter life.

"Anyway," she said, "you still haven't told me what you do, if, that is, you have a job, which I very much doubt."

"I can't work," he said in a rather affected tone, as if he were reciting a familiar speech. "I can only drink and weep."

"Haven't you ever worked?"

"Only occasionally, but I always ended up being destroyed, I mean dismissed. Now I live in abject poverty. There was a girl who used to help me, but she lost her job too. Lately, my father's been helping me out, but his factory has just gone on strike, so ... Now I have no one to help me."

"My father spent half his life on strike. He used to say it was his favorite part of the job."

They fell into a respectful silence, with her thinking about her father and him thinking about his, when, that is, he wasn't nodding off. It was wonderfully peaceful there, although the park itself was a very sad place because it seemed to be so utterly deserted. The ice-gray sky covering the park made it seem the coldest of landscapes. It was very cold and deserted.

"So we're both the children of strikers," he said rather glumly. And then his head drooped and he fell fast asleep on Rosa Schwarzer's shoulder.

She didn't dare to wake him, it seemed criminal to do so. Then she wondered what would happen if a relative or friend of hers should chance upon them. What would they think seeing her there with a stranger tenderly resting his head on her shoulder? Not that it mattered, largely because there was no one else there, for the park could not have been more silent and deserted, the same park where, thirty years before, she had also managed to wrench from life a few brief, but intense moments of great happiness. And precisely because she had experienced them, she knew that such moments lasted hardly any time at all, and so she very gently removed the amiable stranger's head from her shoulder and, leaving him there alone and asleep in the old, cold, deserted park, she began the slow, painful journey back to her part of town and her apartment.

On the way home, what was tearing her soul apart was her almost absolute certainty that she would never be able to express, however vaguely, and definitely not in actual words or even thoughts, those few moments of fleeting happiness. This certainty accompanied her on the return journey like a new, secret sorrow. And when, two hours later, she found herself back in familiar streets, another fear was added to all her other anxieties, because it occurred to her that her son Hans, who didn't work in the afternoon, might not have gone for his usual walk with his friends, but, given the special circumstances, would be waiting for her at home, for her to come back from the hairdresser's. In that case, things could turn very awkward, because he would see at once that she hadn't been to the hairdresser's and that she was concealing a great mystery or, even worse—a word that rhymed with mystery—a secret history. Fearful of being found out, she went into the local hairdresser's and, since she didn't have time to have her hair permed, she bought a hideous brown wig. She arrived home wearing the wig, but, fortunately, no one was there, only the bones of a sad cold chicken, the remains of her poor, dear Hans's lunch.

The indecisive Rosa Schwarzer's delight at finding herself alone quickly gave way to the completely opposite emotion, to profound depression at the awful emptiness of the apartment. She went over to the window. The sky was a grubby opaque white color, and, in her mind, a similar opaque whiteness began erasing the memory of what she had experienced with the night owl, whom she had abandoned in the park. In this state of tragic despair, she began furiously plucking out the hairs from her wig. Then she picked up a kitchen knife and considered committing hara-kiri, unceremoniously slicing open her belly, offering her entrails up to that whole unwitting race of long-suffering housewives whom the young night owl liked to scandalize before nodding off in the park of forgetting. She put the wig down on top of the fridge and sliced it in two with the knife, and such was the accumulated tension and effort involved in that gesture that she even sliced through the stale kitchen air. Exhausted, she fell to the floor. No, she wasn't going to kill herself now either. Her poor son, her beloved Hans, deserved a hot dinner that evening. She got up, threw what remained of the wig into the bin, gave a wild guffaw, and ate a slice of rye bread with cumin seeds.

However, later that afternoon, when her poor, dear Hans came home, he didn't even ask about the roast suckling pig or why she had spent so long at the hairdresser's, nor did he complain about having had to eat cold chicken for lunch, he didn't even look at her, and so didn't notice his mother's wild mane of wire-wool hair. He merely wished her a rather lukewarm happy birthday and asked her to sew a couple of buttons on his shirt. But he didn't look at her once. Rosa Schwarzer realized that her son wasn't interested in her at all.

Her eldest son Bernd's arrival home was even more discouraging, not because he remembered nothing about the roast suckling pig—in that respect he was the same as Hans—but because, having failed to remember that, he also failed to remember it was his mother's birthday—he had completely forgotten the whole business about the birthday lunch. All he did was fill the living room with cigarette smoke, turn on the television and lie down on the sofa. Rosa Schwarzer considered turning off the television, and telling her sons about the gesture made by the night owl, which, to her, had seemed to open up immense, unknown possibilities of love. But she knew she could never express the feeling of plenitude she had experienced only a short time before, and she knew, too, that even if she could, even if she were able to express what she had actually felt, her sons wouldn't listen or wouldn't believe her.

"What's for supper?" demanded her son Bernd from the sofa.

"Death," she said. "Death."

She said this so quietly, from the solitude of her kitchen, that they didn't hear, just as they didn't hear, at that same moment, a chicken having its throat slit. And the reason they didn't hear this was that the chicken was their own mother, who was imagining having her throat slit, which she did in order to distract herself and drive away a dangerous temptation that had just presented itself in the form of another opportunity to take her own life: turning on the gas and sticking her head in the oven. A horrible death, she told herself, meanwhile thinking that the worst thing of all, if she did decide to sacrifice her head—the wild mane of wire-wool hair included— was that her sons would take some time to realize it. They would sit in the living room arguing, as they did every day, over which bit of the sofa belonged to them. Imbeciles. Wretches. Only when it was all over would they find their mother's perfectly cooked head in place of the suckling pig. A horrible death, thought Rosa Schwarzer as she tried in vain to drive away that terrible temptation.

She was saved by her husband's usual violent irruption into the apartment. His unmistakable arrival—slamming the door and coughing the cough of an inveterate smoker—banished the horrendous temptation of the oven, because she was suddenly much more interested in picking up a jar of jam and hurling it at her unfaithful husband's face as revenge for his affair with the neighbor and, above all, for all those years of indifference and constant humiliation. It was worth setting aside the idea of the oven and briefly savoring her husband's look of horror and surprise when, for the first time in thirty years, he saw his wife rebel against the suffocating violence of his vast indifference. But, first, she told herself, before she threw the jar, she would turn out all the lights and terrify all three of them, not with the darkness, but by screaming out her own name in her hoarse, shrill, seagull's voice. And that is what she did, although, in the end, she didn't turn out the lights, but merely screamed:

"Rosaaaaa Schwaaaaarzer!"

Astonished, they turned down the volume of the TV and then they heard that name again, but this time pronounced like a rapid, syncopated echo, as if she were having an attack of the hiccups. When it was over, they heard her give a deep sigh of relief and contentment.

"Have you gone mad, Mama Rosa?" her husband asked, violently grabbing her arm. "Whatever's wrong?"

Another excellent chance to die, she thought. And I'm not going to let this one pass. I'll really wind him up, which is easy enough, and I'm sure he'll say that he's going to kill me and then I'll wind him up some more and make him kill me for real.

"A fine way to prepare supper," her husband said. "What on earth is wrong with you?"

She responded by hurling the jar of jam at him, but missed and instead hit the kitchen clock, which immediately stopped, and this pleased Rosa Schwarzer no end, because, she thought, at least in the kitchen, time had stopped, and, with a little luck, it would stop for good if, as she hoped, her husband decided to kill her. And her husband seemed about to do just that, because he had raised one hand and was threatening her, saying he was going to kill her. She had to make sure that this time those words did not, as they usually did, come to nothing. She could not let slip this perfect, matchless opportunity to die—the sixth in one day, who would have thought it?

From the doorway, her two sons were looking at her, half-appalled, half-astonished, almost reproachful. It was as if they couldn't forgive her for finally letting a little color into her slave's existence, as if unable to accept that, however timidly, she had finally been able to breathe again and come back to life.

"It's the museum's fault, I'm sure of it," Bernd said to his father.

Another jar of jam flew through the air and again missed its target. Shortly afterward, feeling weary and cast down by such a lack of understanding, Rosa Schwarzer surrendered. She sat down on a chair, where she remained for a while, sobbing quietly. Now and then, one of them would shout:

"Be quiet, Mama."

"I said 'Be quiet,' Mama Rosa."

She stayed there on the chair, as if she were sitting in the museum, until the television stopped broadcasting for the night. When it was time for everyone to go to bed, she did so listlessly, in the grip of a galloping insomnia, and spent the rest of the night imagining all kinds of stories, all of which took place in a cold, deserted park that transformed every visitor into a night owl. And after not having slept all night, she was heard to say when day was breaking:

"What is the point of my life?"

She said this as she lay half-awake this morning, just before she got up and prepared breakfast, during which she ate only a slice of ham as she apologized to her husband and sons for what had happened yesterday and explained that she had been feeling depressed at reaching the age she had reached, that was all, and asked them to forgive her.

Then, just as she had for years, she cycled to the museum, and now she is sitting on her usual boring chair, struggling to keep awake after that restless, sleepless night, yawning loudly as she tries not to be seduced by the call of the dark prince, who, in order to lure her into the canvas, keeps sending her the arrogant sound of beating tom-toms from his land, the land of suicides.

I know that, in a desperate attempt to fend off the prince, Rosa Schwarzer seeks refuge with her eyes in the tenuous pinks of *Monsieur Perlanschwein*, which is another of the paintings in the room that she so zealously guards and where, were someone to burst in boldly right now, the intruder would find her, this highly efficient guard, stifling a yawn and springing to her feet to ask him, please, due to the very sensitive alarm, do not get too close to either Monsieur Pink or Señor Black.

As I said, Rosa Schwarzer is feeling slightly on edge this morning. And so she should, because the tom-toms are calling to her ever more insistently, inviting her to leave both the museum and life, and so seductive is the black prince that, any moment, she might succumb to this new opportunity to take her own life. Seventh time lucky, thinks Rosa Schwarzer, and then she remembers that she still has the cyanide capsule in her coat pocket, and decides to try her luck. If it's only whisky, it might help wake her up, because she's almost dropping asleep; she has never tasted a drop of alcohol before and doesn't know how she'll react, but she'll take a chance. And if it isn't whisky, but cyanide, then she will travel to the other side of life, to that other distant, seductive world, where her lover, the prince of suicides, lives.

She swallows the poison down in one, and almost immediately the tom-toms wrap sensually, bestially around her, because such is the powerful impact of the liquid on her, that she feels as if she had dropped down dead. Dizzy with death, her head drops violently forward and, just as she is about to fall, she feels that she has entered the painting and is walking along a strange lead-gray corridor taking her to a garish esplanade on which stands an altar reached by various steps. The steps are carpeted in a green more intense than any she has ever seen before. Near the altar now and, in the shade of a gigantic palm tree, she discovers a statue depicting a man mortally wounded by a dagger he has plunged into his own heart. The heart of a suicide in love. It is the black prince, who, as he comes back to life, is beginning to celebrate the arrival of his love and, launching into a dance as wild as it is prolonged, he summons all the suicides of his kingdom to the vast esplanade, where, at the altar, the new arrival will be honored and greeted. From countless huts, alongside an ocean of crystalline waters, come his subjects in evening dress, and the ocean, as the prince explains to her, imitates the inimitable: the burning blue smoke of Africa.

Happiness kills, and what those suicides are imitating is not the inimitable, but the nonexistent, thinks Rosa Schwarzer, recalling, too, that unreality is also unpleasant. And despite the exultant beauty of the prince, the burning blue smoke and the dazzling land in which she finds herself, she is beginning to feel uncomfortable in this incomprehensible culture, in this distant, mysterious place where death is celebrated. As if he had read her thoughts, the prince—sad that she doesn't appreciate the bright stars which, in her honor, are shooting fireworks up into the cold, ancient sky— warns her that the only way she can reverse her journey is by inhaling the burning blue smoke of that land of suicides. It is a highly toxic smoke, and Rosa Schwarzer realizes at once that this would mean committing suicide again, but in reverse, a suicide that would make her fall not on the side of beauty, but on the opposite side, the side of life. And Rosa Schwarzer doesn't hesitate, she goes over to one of the columns of smoke and inhales as deeply as she can, and, in a matter of seconds, she is once again sitting on her chair in the museum, next to which, shattered into a thousand pieces, lies the intoxicating capsule.

No one witnessed her astonishing journey. And Rosa Schwarzer, the efficient museum guard, opens her eyes very wide, and, still feeling somewhat dizzy, she composes her features and sees that everything around her remains unchanged. Or, rather, *almost* everything, because she can no longer hear the loving, constant beat of the tom-toms from the land of suicides. The blacks of the prince and the pinks of the Monsieur are quite still now. Everything has been restored to its sad, perfect order. With a bitter feeling that is also one of relief, Rosa Schwarzer has a sense of entering once more into the monochrome of her life, and she feels fine, as if she had finally understood that, in the end, we do not know—as the poet put it—if in reality things aren't better like that: deliberately scarce. Perhaps they *are* better like that: real, ordinary, mediocre, and profoundly stupid. Besides, thinks Rosa Schwarzer, that other life was no life for me.

IN SEARCH OF THE ELECTRIFYING
DOUBLE ACT

> I know not all that may be com-
> ing, but be it what it will, I'll go
> to it laughing.
> — Stubb, in *Moby-Dick*

One April afternoon some years ago, when my name was still Mempo Lesmes and I was very young and a starving, unknown actor, I got lost in the labyrinthine outskirts of San Anfiero de Granzara, and I came across a large mansion surrounded by an overgrown garden—the Villa Nemo. I had no problem getting into the house. There was no lock, no knocker on the door, it was abandoned, abandoned, it seemed to me, in the fullest sense of the word, for I found signs that, as well as being abandoned by its owners, it was a house that had also somehow abandoned itself. I was fascinated by this idea and walked in the garden for a long time imagining the house abandoning itself to its own fate in the darkness of the night. In a state of great excitement, walking along one of the galleries open to the winds, I told myself that if one day I succeeded as an actor, the first thing I would do would be to buy that house and make of it my residence of choice.

Some years passed, and I became a successful movie actor. A minor (but very meaty) role in *The Trunk of Fools* shot me straight to stardom. People found the way I gnawed on a toothpick a revelation. My agent was thoughtful and astute enough to change my name to Brandy Mostaza, and from then on it was plain sailing. I was signed to star in *The Loves of Mustafa*, the comedy which, by opening to me all doors of popularity, wrought a spectacular overnight change in my life. Then, I achieved my greatest success with *The Many Moods of Young Brandy*, one of those television series that shone so brightly in the sixties and which now, like everything else I did, has been relegated to the most complete and humiliating oblivion.

What contributed to my irresistible rise was the extreme, comic thinness of my body (people laughed because when I walked, I looked like a leaf being blown along by the wind), but that same physical quirk was soon to tell tragically against me. I bought Villa Nemo, put the garden in order, and restored the house, I built a large swimming pool and I began throwing extravagant parties every Friday night. The labyrinthine outskirts of San Anfiero de Granzara filled with men and girls, who came and went like moths among the whisperings and the champagne and the stars. Every Friday, crates of oranges and lemons for the cocktails arrived from a fruiterer in San Anfiero, and every Saturday these same lemons and oranges left Villa Nemo by the back door in a pyramid of pulpless halves. I had lots of girlfriends, I danced boleros, I began many beguines, I sang songs to love. But misfortune was lurking in the most brightly lit corner of my festive garden, and, without realizing it, I began to let myself go, to abandon myself. As if there were some secret link between the house and obesity, I gradually began to put on weight, and when I realized what was happening, no diet could stop the irreversible process, the tragic transformation. And so I reached the last Friday of the seventies, all dressed up and without a girlfriend in sight, transformed into a Brandy Mostaza who was unrecognizable, a monstrous fatso who had lost his comic spark.

"For some time now, you haven't been able to see the wood for the fat," my agent warned me that day.

"What wood?" I asked, pretending that I didn't know what he was talking about.

"Oh, come on! Just tell me one thing: how long is it since anyone offered you a contract?"

Since I had earned a lot of money, the fact that people had stopped giving me contracts didn't particularly bother me. I was much more worried by the sudden, alarming absence of girlfriends and the steadily declining numbers of guests at my parties. I was incapable of seeing that everything, absolutely everything, was indissolubly linked.

"And tell me," said my agent, "why do you think no one offers you movies anymore, or, if they do, why they only want you for awful minor roles?"

"Well," I said, "I suppose it must have something to do with my putting on a few pounds."

"You suppose!"

Baron Mulder, who was quite blatantly eavesdropping on us, joined in the conversation.

"My friend Brandy's fatness," he said, toying with his monocle, "is a splendid monument to the flesh, to excess, and to human kindness."

You might think that he was saying all this because he was even fatter than I was, but I had an inkling, too, that, for some hidden reason which I couldn't quite pin down, he was trying to flatter me in order to gain my sympathy as a way of getting something out of me.

My suspicions were soon confirmed when, an hour later, I bumped into him again in the garden, and he started talking to me about his ancestors, the Mulders and the Roigers, revealing to me that both branches of the family had lived in Villa Nemo at one time and that they had suffered all kinds of misfortunes there. He was a bit drunk and very garrulous, and a shameless merchant of doom. From all that he told me (he even had the impertinence to ask if his ancestors' ghosts were quite happy haunting my house), I drew one clear conclusion: Villa Nemo had a baleful influence on all its owners. That was why I was surprised when, as he said goodbye to me that night, he asked how much I wanted for the house.

"My friend," he said, "I'll be honest with you. As a fat man, your future in show business looks pretty bleak. Let's not fool ourselves. The public preferred you thin. I know that before too long you'll be having money troubles and I'd like to help you out. Sell me Villa Nemo, submarine included, and then go off on a trip, a trip around the world."

I was just about to ask him about the submarine when his monocle fell out. I stooped to pick it up for him, but he ground it angrily into the earth. Then, he did a few eccentric tap-dance steps and fell flat on his face on the grass. Something strange happened to me then, for when I saw him fall onto the grass, I felt an enigmatic impulse rise up inside me, an unstoppable desire to turn a somersault in the air and perform a circus number with the baron at the end of this party, which, it must be said, had turned out to be positively soporific.

"Take my advice, as a friend," said the baron as he got to his feet, "and sell me your house."

Then he clapped me hard on the back and disappeared into the night. My agent was at my side and couldn't believe what he had seen.

"Brilliant, absolutely brilliant," he said. "Did you see the wit and elegance with which he crushed his monocle? Underneath, the baron is a high-voltage comedian. If you could go back to being as thin as you used to be—though alas, I fear you never will—you could be one of the most successful double acts the cinema has ever seen."

"You're not saying ..."

"Why not? I'm talking about those odd pairings of actors who were only able to give their best because—how can I put it?—because there was something odd in each of them that triggered the growth or emergence into the light of a hidden electricity lurking deep inside the other. An electrifying double act."

"I see," I said, coolly saying goodbye to two former lovers who had become fast friends, "do you mean like Laurel and Hardy?"

"Exactly, and Abbot and Costello, too. Your thinness and the baron's extravagant fatness could make you into a very successful double act. Unfortunately, the partner you need now would have to look very different from the baron. That is what I wanted to talk to you about."

He led me to a bench in one corner of the garden, near the swimming pool. And there, while I watched the painful parade of ex-girlfriends bidding me farewell with the most wounding and taunting of smiles, my agent showed me an album full of photographs of thin actors who might be able to save my career if I joined forces with them.

"Wouldn't a better solution be to ask the baron to slim down until he's reed-thin?" I said, joking, depressed by the parade of mocking girlfriends and by the fatigue brought on by the lateness of the hour.

"Well, it's your funeral," he said threateningly, saying goodbye with a look that told me he would take no further interest in my career.

But the following morning, apparently recovered and as if wanting to give me one last chance, he turned up again at Villa Nemo with his album of photos of thin actors.

"Look at this one," he would say, pointing to one.

"And look at that one," I would reply, taking it all as a joke. But the joke didn't last long. In the days that followed, I ended up doing tryouts with many of those thin actors, and they always ended in utter disaster. Seeing that there wasn't a single actor in the whole country with whom I could form an electrifying duo, we put advertisements in the papers. But that didn't work either. My agent then suggested that perhaps the actor I was looking for lived abroad and perhaps (and here began my downfall) he wasn't an actor at all, in which case, I would have to seek him in the street, or rather, in the streets of the world.

"You must exhaust every possibility," he said. And that reasoning carried me far off, it even took me to the streets of Hong Kong in pursuit of a thin man who turned out to be a complete nonstarter. Just when I was despairing of ever finding a partner and was already in deep financial trouble, my mother, may she rest in peace, came to my aid:

"In Calle Rendel," she said, "in the bookshop with the same name as the street, there's a skeletal assistant with a most unpleasant face and a name that would be more appropriate for someone working in a cake shop. He's called Juan Lionesa and he might just be the man you're looking for."

Some hours later, Juan Lionesa stood before me, his dark hair cut bowl-fashion, framing ruddy cheeks and an expression of mingled tedium and mystery. I had just asked him for a copy of *The Divine Comedy* and found myself studying him from head to toe. Instead of looking for the book, he did exactly the same, that is, he subjected me to a close visual inspection that verged on the embarrassing. Then he said:

"Didn't you used to be Brandy Mostaza?"

That "used to be" rather shook me.

"And you," I replied, "never used to be anyone, which is much worse."

"Oh, come on! You're not going to tell me my little observation offended you?"

I hate the word "observation" and I hated that pedantic, impertinent bookseller's ugly face. I gave him a rather angry look and silently, roundly cursed him, but he barely batted an eyelid. Suddenly, something extraordinary happened. When he did finally get around to looking for a copy of *The Divine Comedy*, he glanced over at a (rather empty) shelf and stood for a moment in profile to me. I saw then that in that position, Lionesa's features—his left profile—were curiously like mine in the days when I was thin and successful. His profile, reminiscent of a heron in heat, was enough to make the most serious-minded of mortals laugh. Unwittingly, Lionesa possessed the essence of the comic quality that I had lost, the secret of my former success, a real gold mine. My mother had been absolutely right.

"Listen," I said in a very confidential tone of voice, "I need to talk to you alone, outside the bookshop, do you understand? It's about a matter that might interest you. And since you obviously don't have a copy of *The Divine Comedy*, give me something else, something by Jules Verne, for example."

He arched his eyebrows, and the expression on his face changed radically, as if the reference to Jules Verne contained some transcendental message. And then, slowly and very respectfully, he said in a low voice:

"The cake will travel by balloon."

I could merely have assumed that he was mad or that he was simply making fun of me, but for some reason I had a sudden hunch that those words might be a form of password (and they were, but not the kind I imagined). At first, I thought that Lionesa had sensed in me a being who, in many respects, complemented him, and, because of that, he had invented a secret language just for the two of us, words that allowed us to understand each other, but prevented anyone else from understanding what we were talking about.

"The cake will travel by balloon," I said, thinking that by my reply I was doing no more than recognizing the strange electric current that seemed to unite us, thinking too that with those words I was acknowledging the secret language that had just sprung up between us.

"The cake will travel by balloon, and I'll be at Jacob's Bar at half past eight," he said. Shortly afterward, I left the bookshop with a copy of *Five Weeks in a Balloon* under my arm. I read the first few chapters while I was waiting at Jacob's Bar for Lionesa, who arrived punctually. He was wearing dark glasses and had his coat collar slightly turned up. He greeted me from a distance, with a lift of his eyebrows, but when he came over, he acted as if he didn't know me. He sat down on my left, at the bar, presenting me with his anodyne right profile. He ordered a beer and just when I was expecting him to ask me why I had brought him here, he acted as if he expected nothing from me at all, except the cake that was supposed to be traveling by balloon.

"OK," he said, still not looking at me, addressing me as "tú" and keeping his head absolutely still, "when I finish my beer, pass me the cake, and good luck, friend. Ah, one piece of advice. Next time, try to be a bit more clever and discreet, and make sure you get the password right."

So it *was* a password, but not the kind of password I had expected. I had stepped right into the eye of a hurricane, doubtless a plot, or some sort of espionage ring. I cursed myself for not having simply disappeared when I left the bookshop. I was angry with myself for not guessing that Lionesa was a conspirator awaiting some secret message about Jules Verne or about a balloon.

While he was slowly drinking his beer, which I would have to pay for, I was weighing up how best to extricate myself from this particular mess and I finally decided that I would simply say that, for reasons beyond anyone's control, the cake would be delayed for twenty-four hours. I told him this as boldly as you like, and no one has ever looked at me like that, with a look, first, of utter astonishment, immediately superseded by one of terror.

"There's no need to look at me like that, just because there won't be any cake until tomorrow," I said loudly, out of sheer nervousness.

That was how I talked when I found myself in difficulties. I would either go off on a tangent or race madly ahead. Lionesa, however, seemed unable to believe what was happening, while everyone else in the bar was under the impression that drink had just brought about the birth of a friendship between two complete strangers; one drunk even rewarded us with a smile and a burst of loud applause. It was obvious to me that the marked difference in our physical appearance made us an attractive pair. Lionesa was clearly not of the same opinion; indeed everything seemed to indicate that he saw in me someone who, for whatever reason, had just set him a deadly trap.

The strange electricity between us meant that suddenly, like someone throwing out the main ballast from a balloon, I lost all my nervousness and transferred it to him. I felt very calm then—I would go so far as to say that I have never felt more serene—and I decided that there was no reason to get alarmed, that the most practical thing would be to put the record straight and tell Lionesa the whole truth. I explained that I had gone to the bookshop because I was looking for a thin man to work with me in movies that were guaranteed to be a great success if only I could find the ideal partner.

"And that ideal partner is me, is that what you're trying to say?" he asked with so much aggression and distrust that I thought he might kill me.

60

"Yes, of course. Please, you must believe me. I have no interest in politics whatsoever. There's been a misunderstanding, that's all. I came into the bookshop because my mother told me that the man I was looking for worked there. I've been all the way to Hong Kong in search of someone who could help save my career. And now all I have is my house, Villa Nemo, because I've lost everything else trying to relaunch my career. I need you to join forces with me, to be my artistic partner. Otherwise, I'll have to sell Villa Nemo and I'll be out on the street. Help me, please."

"Take a good look at me," he said and in his coat pocket there appeared what might have been a gun. "I'm pointing a gun at you, so cut the crap, pay for the beers, and just walk out of here ahead of me, and no funny business."

It was like a nightmare. I paid for the beers, and we went out into the street. Lionesa hailed a taxi and, as he did so, we were walking so close to each other that our legs and overcoats became entangled and we both tripped and fell to the ground. I managed to trap Lionesa's tie beneath my great bulk, but he sprang up, slightly flustered, and again pointed his hidden gun at me. Everyone in the street started laughing and enjoying the spectacle, which confirmed me in my view that I had found my ideal partner and that, if only politics and that wretched gun didn't get in the way of our rise to stardom, we could be an electrifying double act.

When we got into the taxi, I realized how difficult it would be to escape once the taxi was moving, since I could barely get my body through the door and Lionesa himself had to heave me into the cramped interior. As we were driving through the city, past the area around Parque Rendel, I was filled by a feeling of profound melancholy. I looked sadly out of the window, wondering if I would ever again see those trees I had so often felt drawn to. And I wondered, too, if I should bid farewell to life. Even in the most desperate situations, I have never lost my sense of humor. I'm one of those people who believes that life is utterly laughable, that life itself is made up of pure laughter, and that, although we may have no idea what awaits us at the end, the best strategy is to go to it laughing, with a tragic lack of seriousness. Perhaps that was why I was able to look at Lionesa in a relaxed manner and say with a broad smile:

"May I know where you are planning to kill me?"

I saw the taxi driver trying not to laugh. It was clear—or so I thought—that from the very first, he had found us irresistibly funny; well, not everyone hails a taxi in a twosome, rolling around on the ground. To conceal how much he had enjoyed our circus act and how much we had made him laugh, or perhaps simply in order to participate in what must have seemed to him a great festival of humor, the taxi driver cleared his throat and said to Lionesa:

"Excuse me, it was the corner of Juárez and Verlás you wanted, wasn't it?"

"No, it was the corner of Verlás and Juárez," replied an angry Lionesa, who did not seem entirely himself. Lionesa's uncertainty, and the half-hearted laughter that had taken hold of me (I kept thinking I was about to die and found the idea highly amusing), encouraged me to move closer to him as soon as we stopped at a traffic light. I was, and still am, a great actor. I leaned forward in a strange manner, thrusting my chin forward and showing my teeth. I reckoned that Lionesa would not be prepared for that. My face, normally soft and bland, hardened into something resembling a stone mask, deathly white to start with, but deepening to a dark red that spread out from my cheekbones, and finally became black, as if I were about to choke. I thought Lionesa would be unable to bear it and would faint, but he didn't, he simply sat there, looking at me strangely.

"Such a pity, we would have made a mint," I said and headbutted him hard. I came down on top of him with my whole weight, stone mask included, and he lost consciousness. After some strenuous bodily maneuverings, I managed to get out of the taxi and take refuge among a crowd thronging an entrance to the metro. I glanced back and, seeing no one following me, I gave a sigh of relief. I got into a train on line 5, believing I was traveling toward freedom. Poor fool, I didn't know what still awaited me. That same night, minutes after talking to my agent, who didn't believe a single word I told him, the phone rang in Villa Nemo, and a criminal voice informed me that they had kidnapped my mother. If I went to the police to report the kidnapping, they would first kill my mother and then me. If I didn't pay them a million dollars in ransom money, I would never see my mother alive again. When I paid them and they set her free, little would change, except that my mother could be with me once more; but if I subsequently went to the police with the story, I would not be with my mother, since, as well as being a million dollars poorer, I would also be dead, and dead men don't live with their mothers.

I had no option but to sell Villa Nemo to Baron de Mulder. I told him that I needed the money in order to go on a long trip.

"I always knew that sooner or later you would get rid of Villa Nemo," he said. "It is a house intended for a large family like mine, not for a confirmed bachelor like yourself. You'd be better off traveling and having a purely functional apartment, where, instead of throwing parties for multitudes, you could have intimate suppers for two," and he winked lewdly. "Don't you agree, my friend?"

"I haven't thrown a party for ages," I said. "Not since I got back from Hong Kong."

With the money the baron gave me for the house, I paid off the ransom and they returned my mother to me, but she was a changed woman. Since I was now ruined, I had to go live with her, and she spent all day every day blaming me for the kidnapping.

"You got into bad company," she would say. "You can't fool me. You got yourself into some mess or other, and I was the one who had to pay. The proof is that you won't go to the police."

It was useless explaining to her that I suspected it was a band of thugs of the kind who enjoy killing for killing's sake. Going to the police would only provide them with the opportunity for a cruel reprisal. My mother didn't believe me, however much I declared my innocence. Then events conspired against me. My mother and I began receiving visits from members of the revived cult of British wizards, demanding information about unguents that would help them to fly and so forth. In the end, my mother lost all patience and disinherited me. Tormented by remorse, she began to age rapidly.

Although she no longer spent her days reproaching me, she wouldn't talk to me either, passing her time writing down in a red notebook the salient details of all the funerals that passed beneath her window. When she had noted down thirty-three interments with eighty or ninety different details, she herself died. She may well have died of grief for having so unjustly disinherited me, for she knew that she was leaving me destitute. It could be said that life wasn't exactly smiling on me, but, nevertheless, I remained true to my principles and I smiled back at life.

Moreover, I got a taste for the streets, and I became an interesting vagabond, simulating madness, which proved most profitable, because people took pity on me and gave me money. My madness consisted in walking all over the city carrying a pair of drumsticks and beating out on the pavement a rhythm as emphatic as it was meaningless. I leaned clumsily forward as I advanced along the street, drumming the hell out of the cement. My new life, including nights spent in the metro, became a source of great satisfaction to me. It was marvelous not having to read newspapers or receive visits from British wizards, to pass the Rendel bookshop occasionally as an anonymous tramp and give them the finger. It was wonderful being able to earn a living doing a version of street theater, a daily rendition of the most refined madness an obese actor could manage.

Since I read no newspapers and had only passing contact with other wretched tramps, it took a long time for me to find out that Villa Nemo had been destroyed by a fire in which the baron and all his family had perished. On the cold winter day when I learned this news, I thought to myself that the fire, which the police had written off as an accident, might well have been caused by the British wizards. It occurred to me that they might mistaken the baron for me. Unable to do anything more for him, I said a prayer in the company of another tramp, and, shortly afterward, dying of curiosity, I went to see Villa Nemo, where I savored the morbid pleasure of strolling around, bearded and ragged, among the ruins of what had once been my dazzling mansion. Only four walls remained standing and the house was very much like the house I had discovered one April evening years before, the house that had so fascinated me. The garden was beginning to grow wild again; there was no lock or knocker on the door. It had returned to being the same abandoned house I had seen that first time, a house so adept at self-abandonment.

I thought about Villa Nemo in the days that followed and an irresistible electric force urged me to return—to return and live there again. And last night, I came back to stay. Very excited, standing on one of the galleries open to the winds, gleefully looking out on the now totally wild garden, I decided to come live in the house, or rather, in what remained of the house. I told myself that, after all, not only was it an ideal dwelling for a vagabond like myself, it was also the most familiar, comfortable place I knew, and doubtless ideal for parties for one: intimate parties that would be held each night after my exhausting travails as a mad beater of pavements.

That is what I thought last night when I returned to live in what had once been my luxurious bedroom. And perhaps because I couldn't stop thinking about all that or perhaps because of the cold (which my one blanket could do nothing to disguise), I took a long time to go to sleep. Around midnight, I was again woken by the cold. I began considering making a fire out of what remained of a wardrobe that had partially survived the last blaze and which I knew very well, for it had once belonged to me. While I was weighing up that possibility—and as if the wardrobe had realized my intentions—the sound of creaking and moaning seemed to emerge from its depths. I thought it must be my imagination, but the creaking came again, and then the sound of chains, and finally, a heartrending cry.

"Who's there?" I said, lighting a match and still not entirely losing my calm.

No one answered. By the light of that slender match, the wardrobe seemed different from the one I had known. It looked like an upended submarine. It had an art-deco design, which I had never noticed before. I remembered the words of the baron when he had suggested I sell him Villa Nemo with the submarine included. And I remembered, too, when he had asked me if his ancestors' ghosts were quite happy haunting the house. The match burned out, and for a few seconds, as I stood there plunged into darkness, I felt a certain respect for the shadows, which I soon put paid to by lighting another match.

"Who's there?" I said again, trying to keep my voice firm and steady. I received no reply that time either, but just as I was preparing to go back to sleep, the creaking resumed. I realized that I must confront the situation whatever the consequences, and then, commending myself to all the saints in the world, I wrenched open the wardrobe door.

Nothing. There was nothing and no one inside. I went back to my bed, wrapped myself in my blanket, and tried to go to sleep. Once more I was considering turning the submarine into a good, blazing fire when the creaking recommenced, this time accompanied by an unmistakable lament.

"Don't burn me," I heard a voice saying. "If you do, I will offer no resistance, but I fear that, in the attempt, you will lose all your strength. I am a spirit."

"Who's there?" I asked again, feeling alarmed this time.

"It's your friend, Baron de Mulder. My ruin was forged in this very room, in this house I lost all my family, in this wardrobe I kept my finest clothes. This house is mine: let me have it."

I didn't dare light another match, afraid that he might think I was about to set fire to the wardrobe.

"I would never have recognized your voice, Baron," I said, trying to recover my presence of mind.

"If you could see me, you would appreciate the great physical change I have undergone. The fire transformed me into a pale, emaciated figure, who spends each night standing in this wardrobe. It's a pity you can't see me and have a good laugh. It's a pity you still belong to the land of the living and can't appreciate the truly comic nature of my slender, supernatural appearance."

I tried to explain that it didn't seem logical to me that, given he was a ghost and had the chance to visit all the most beautiful places on earth (for I presumed that distance now meant nothing to him), he should choose to return to the one place where he had suffered most.

"I know I'm foolish," he said, "but I enjoy it, just as I love being thin and miserable. Because, my dear friend, I have great natural reserves of laughter, and I laugh all the time, and, the more miserable I am, the more I laugh."

And he laughed. Had he not already been dead, he would have died laughing right then and there.

"You laugh in a terribly serious way," I said. "I don't know that you could really call it laughter as such. Listen to mine, for example."

I demonstrated to him how to laugh in a cheerful, carefree manner and, as I did so, I felt the gentle but powerful connection between his laughter and mine. There was a current of mutual sympathy between us, the stimulating solidarity of the wretched. And there was something very strange in both of us that triggered the growth or the emergence into light of a hidden electricity lurking deep inside each other.

I remarked on this, but he did not reply. I thought that perhaps it was because what I had said had made him anxious. What I had said was all very well, but the fact was we could never be a truly electrifying double act if I didn't take a fundamental step (which only I could take) that would place me, like the baron, outside my dirty, crumpled clothes, outside my beard and this room and this submarine, outside this life.

That is why I am now waiting for night to fall and for the baron to return to his wardrobe. I have everything ready, the strychnine with which I will take that last fundamental step and which will allow me at last to form an electrifying artistic duo, one that will soon have me going on tour, a triumphant tour of outer space.

DEATH BY SAUDADE

I was nine years old at the time and, as if I already didn't have enough to do, I had sought out a new occupation: I had allowed a sudden curiosity to grow inside me to know what went on beyond the walls of my house or my school: an unexpected curiosity about the unknown, that is, about the world of the street or, which came to the same thing, the world of the Paseo de San Luis, the street where my family lived.

In the afternoons, instead of going straight home from school, I began to linger for awhile at the top of the Paseo and to observe the comings and goings of the passersby. My parents didn't get home until eight o'clock, which meant that I could delay my return by almost an hour. It was an hour that I enjoyed more and more with each passing day, because something always happened, some tiny event, never anything extraordinary, but enough: a fat lady tripping up, for example; the wind from the bay carrying off what I imagined to be a most unhappy hat; a father slapping his son around the face; the much-talked-about sins of the box office clerk at the Cine Venus; the customers going in and out of the Bar Cadí.

The street began to steal a whole hour of my homework time, an hour that I recovered thanks to the simple method of cutting down the time I usually spent after supper reading great novels, until the day came when the charms of the Paseo de San Luis proved so alluring that they stole *all* my reading time. In other words, the Paseo replaced great novels.

One day, I didn't get home until ten o'clock—not a minute before or a minute after—just in time for supper. I had been kept out in the street by a great enigma. A woman was walking timidly and hesitantly up and down outside the Cine Venus. At first, I thought she must be waiting for her boyfriend or her husband, but when I went closer, I saw that, judging both by the clothes she was wearing and the way she went up to everyone who passed, she must be a vagrant. I was just about to give her what little money I had, when she walked straight past me without asking for anything. I thought perhaps she had taken me for what I was: a poor, penniless schoolboy. Shortly afterward, though, I saw her begging from Luz, our teacher's daughter, and noticed that when she did so, she whispered something into Luz's ear, something that frightened Luz, who immediately quickened her pace. I walked past again, and again the woman ignored me. Then a very smartly dressed man walked by, and the woman didn't ask him for anything either, but let him go. Shortly afterward, when another woman passed, she almost hurled herself upon her, her hand outstretched, and whispered some mysterious words in her ear, and that lady too, much embarrassed, also quickened her pace. Another man went by, and she allowed him to go on his way, too, saying nothing and asking nothing, simply letting him pass. But as soon as Josefina appeared—the one who works at the haberdasher's—she asked her for alms and whispered the mysterious words, and Josefina, too, quickened her pace.

It was clear that the vagrant only spoke to women. But what was she saying to them and why only to them? In the days that followed, this enigma kept me from my studies or from taking refuge in reading great novels. You might say that I was becoming someone who, after wandering the streets, also wandered around his own house.

"Why have you become so idle lately?" asked my mother, who had drummed the work ethic into me from an early age and was alarmed at this change.

"The enigma," I said and immediately closed the kitchen door.

The following day, the wind from the bay was blowing harder than usual, and nearly everyone had retreated to his or her house. Not me. I had learned to love the street and the elements, as much as my vagrant seemed to love them too. And suddenly, as if that shared love were capable of generating action, something unexpected happened, something truly surprising. A woman passed, and the vagrant approached her, whispering the terrible words, and the woman stopped as if pleasantly surprised and smiled. The vagrant then added a few more sentences, and, when she had finished, the woman gave her some money and blithely went on her way, as if absolutely nothing had happened.

There comes a moment in all our lives when we are given the chance to overcome our shyness for good. Realizing that this moment had arrived, I went over to the woman and asked what the vagrant had said to her.

"Oh, nothing," she said. "Just a little story."

And with that, as if blown along by the wind from the bay, she turned the corner and vanished from view.

The following day, I did not go to school, and at six in the evening, I walked past the door of the Cine Venus, dressed in some of my mother's clothes: a transparent black blouse, a blue skirt, red ankle boots, and a white hat with a very broad brim. I had painted lips, a beauty spot on my cheek and my eyes were very wide, as round as headlights. In case the disguise wasn't enough to get the woman to take the bait, I carried a handbag with a long chain over one shoulder and, in my left hand, a large bag of food—without jars or tins, so that it didn't weigh too much, but with bread rolls, ground coffee, two lamb chops, and a bag of almonds.

When I came alongside the woman, I smiled. She responded with a strident laugh, her eyes wide. Paradoxical though it may seem, her wild eyes were strangely magnetic. I had heard people talk about madness and realized that I was looking at it.

"We are all idlers," she whispered, holding out her right hand.

In that hand was an old coin, one that was no longer legal tender. And there was a rhythm to the vagrant's bare feet that was old, too. I stood frozen to the spot, and she went on:

"Isn't it true that we women have all the time in the world? So hear my story."

I felt a gust of wind strike my face and noticed that my legs were shaking. That same wind brought me the echo of the woman's strident laugh, and it seemed to me that her wild, magnetic, mirror-like eyes were trying to consume me. Then I dropped both bags on the pavement, wanting to hear nothing more, no more little stories.

I took off the ankle boots and, carrying them in one hand, fled as fast as I could; I fled in terror because I had suddenly understood that what I had just seen, with utter clarity, was the face of the evil ravaging the streets of the city and which my parents, in low, cautious voices, called the wind from the bay, the wind that drove so many mad.

When I got home, I quickly changed my clothes and, for the first time in days, happily ate my afternoon snack, and by seven o'clock, I was already doing my homework. I told myself that, from then on, I would go back to being very busy and, once I had done my homework and eaten supper, I would surrender myself with my old fervor to reading those great novels, which, on winter nights, used to keep me awake. But I still felt uneasy, because I knew that outside my bedroom window, in the Paseo de San Luis, the wind from the bay would keep on blowing, horrific, but alluring too.

At the time, I rarely complained about anything. Not like now, when I complain constantly. I sometimes think that I shouldn't. After all, I have nothing to complain about. I'm still young, I have or still have a certain facility for painting pictures that evoke scenes from my childhood, and I have a solid reputation as a painter, I have a pretty and intelligent wife, I can travel wherever I want to, I adore my two daughters. In short, it's very hard to find reasons to be unhappy. And yet I am. Here I am, walking through the Estufa Fria in Lisbon, feeling like a vagrant and ceaselessly filled with the temptation to leap into the void in this city so full of beautiful places where one could make that leap. Here, my eyes have grown as wild as those of the vagrant of my childhood, in this city in which I woke up today, crouched in a dark corner of my hotel room, weeping.

In this city so far from my own, I woke up crying for no reason, perhaps because of that painting I've been trying to paint for years, the one I often begin, but never manage to finish and that is intended to evoke the ancient rhythm of bare feet, the rhythm of the feet of that vagrant outside the Cine Venus, which, a week later, to my amazement, reappeared in the bare feet of Isabelita, the maid who used to pick up my friend Horacio Vega from school. I remember her as being immaculately uniformed, apart from her shoes, which she always carried in her hand, as if she had just emerged from an exhausting ball at a palace, as if she were trying to imitate my vagrant or perhaps me when I broke into a terrified run, clutching my ankle boots in one hand because of that wretched wind from the bay.

That is how I remember her, and I remember her very well, but I've never been able to paint her. She and the ancient rhythm of her bare feet always escape me, and perhaps that's why I'm here (because I can find no other explanation for my constant anxiety); I'm here tramping my sad, melancholy way around the Estufa Fria, feeling like a vagrant, and trying to drive off the temptation that so pitilessly assails me, the temptation to leap into the void.

I wander around like a vagrant and, from time to time, catch a glimpse of my fleeting silhouette reflected in the shop windows and I say to myself that life is not achievable while one is alive. Life simply doesn't live up to itself. There isn't the slightest chance of ever achieving a sense of plenitude. It's ridiculous being an adult, absurd that anyone should ever claim to be full of life. Everything is painful, why deny it? If I could at least hope that I would one day complete the painting that refuses to be painted, the painting in which Isabelita is frolicking around on the grass of the school soccer field, immaculately uniformed, allowing herself to be swept up by a rhythm that is as ancient as our fleeting silhouettes …

*

I really shouldn't deceive myself. In fact, I paint nothing. I paint nothing from life. Indeed, I don't paint at all. I've never really painted a single picture. Yes, I'm still young, I have a pretty and intelligent wife, I can travel wherever I want to, I adore my two daughters, but it is equally true that I have never really painted anything, not a single, solitary picture. Perhaps that's why I'm now walking sadly along Rua Garrett, feeling like a vagrant painting certain childhood memories (in my head without ever completing anything). I think that if Horacio Vega, my friend Horacio, who will be sitting in his office now, if he could see me, he would laugh out loud. Even when we were at school together, he used to warn me about my tendency never to finish anything.

"Not even comics," he used to say, "as far as I can see, you never finish anything you begin."

And he was quite right. Even when I attempted to respond to his words, I didn't actually finish my sentence. I was always slightly in awe of Horacio, because he was like a wise old child, often speaking as if he were a grown-up. One evening, as I was watching the moon coming up above the school playground, he said to me:

"You're in flight from a sense of plenitude."

I didn't understand a word of what he said, but that was nothing new. I didn't understand anything when he talked to me about his grandfather, Horacio, who had been an intrepid sea captain. When telling me stories about his grandfather, he would always use obscure and incredibly convoluted language. And since I didn't understand much of what he was saying, I would turn my thoughts to my own grandfather, who had been a mere tax inspector and a devotee of the preprandial aperitif, an ordinary, sensible fellow, not like Horacio's grandfather, who had risked his life in a thousand battles.

I almost never understood Horacio, but I always pretended that I did so that he wouldn't realize that the language he used went right over my head. I didn't want to lose him as a friend. That's why I was so upset when, one afternoon, as we were leaving school, in front of Isabelita and a few classmates, he began to criticize me for my flight from a sense of plenitude. The fact that he did this publicly made me think that I had been found out and that this was my punishment for pretending that I always understood his words.

I told myself that this was a personal matter between him and me, and that Isabelita's presence and the laughter of our classmates (all of whom seemed to agree) were superfluous. I decided to follow him to see if at any point he should be left alone (which was fairly unlikely, but there was nothing to lose by trying) and I could approach him to express my displeasure at his behavior. Unbeknown to him, I dogged his footsteps, following him and Isabelita to the top of the Paseo de San Luis, where he lived. And I was lucky, because she did leave him alone for a few minutes while she went into the dry cleaner's (which I now own); I crept up behind him as quietly as I could, then, with one mighty kick, overturned his heavy school satchel, and, without knowing what I was saying, I tried to intimidate him with these words:

"You're the one who's in flight from a sense of plenitude."

I raised my fists and, although I didn't rule out the possibility that the element of surprise would initially work in my favor, I was expecting that he would respond sooner or later with a slap or a punch or perhaps merely a disdainful, humiliating, indifferent look. Instead, I found myself before an entirely unknown Horacio, an Horacio who was suddenly sad and defeated and older than ever, his head bowed, as if my unthinking words had touched the deepest and most painful fiber of his being. This was a strange sensation because, seeing that man-child so profoundly wounded, I discovered that some words, however empty they may seem, are not innocuous; some words are often, without one realizing it, full of aggression. This idea seemed to be confirmed in the days that followed, during which Horacio, doubtless as a form of revenge, continued to torment me with all kinds of descriptions of his grandfather's adventures, with stories that took place in Malaya, China, and Polynesia. I believed that those stories contained a secret, aggressive message. Was he telling me perhaps that his grandfather had felt that sense of plenitude? But what was it about those words that seemed to affect him so deeply? His stories always had the same inexorable aim: to demand from me an immediate question, which I always refused to ask.

"The last few minutes of my grandfather's life," Horacio told me, "were the most intense of an already very intense life."

"And what happened in those last few minutes?" I was supposed to ask, but I didn't. I had already endured hearing about his grandfather's many battles. (It usually proved counter-productive not to ask, however, because he would simply return to the charge with yet another story.) Finally, I could stand it no longer, so one afternoon, I cornered him in the playground and said:

"All right, enough is enough. If you wanted to make me suffer, you've succeeded. Can you just get it over with once and for all and tell me how your grandfather died? I know his life by heart already, so tell me about those intense final moments."

"You really want me to tell you?" he asked, giving me an evil look, as if, in that playground oozing tedium, it were some kind of crime for me—yes, me, who never finished anything—to demand that he complete the picture, the life story of his beloved grandfather.

I held his gaze for as long as I could, until suddenly, in an unexpectedly emotional voice, he told me how his grandfather, at the end of his days, had fallen victim to a stroke and how, on one Sunday, while everyone was at mass, he had finally managed, with great difficulty, to place the barrel of a rifle in his mouth and shoot himself, using the big toe of his right foot to press the trigger.

This was the first time I had heard of such an impulse among men, an impulse called suicide, and I remember that I was very struck by the fact that it was a solitary impulse that happened far from other people's eyes and was performed in darkness and in silence.

And I remember that both of us, Horacio and I, stood there in silence that day, as if we were thinking about all those who, far from other people's eyes, had succumbed to that solitary impulse and experienced the only possible plenitude, the plenitude of suicide. And I remember, too, that the playground was as empty as a quadrangular eternity.

*

I am in a quadrangular space, made of gleaming, beautifully fashioned wood, as solid as a piece of antique furniture, with wooden benches along the walls and, on the walls, framed advertisements that speak of draper's shops, dry cleaners, and hairdressing salons. I notice that one advertisement is missing, doubtless torn from its frame by some delinquent. It's a disquieting feeling, because I know that, even if I wanted to, I could never read all of the attractive advertisements in this room that is now slowly beginning to rise up into the air. I'm in the Elevador de Santa Justa, and I know what awaits me when it reaches the top. I will find a huge balcony and a splendid view of the blue air wrapping around the city below, but only a partial view of the Baixa, because it is partly obscured by the metal fence built above the balustrade, high enough (fortunately for me) to stop any suicides who, as is customary in Lisbon, feel the temptation to leap into the void.

I think about all those people who, a while ago, I saw practicing *saudade* in the Campo das Cebolas. The whole city is full of solitary people brimming with a nostalgia for the past. Sitting on chairs that the town hall has placed on miradors and quaysides for that very purpose, the practitioners of *saudade* say nothing and stare out at the horizon. They seem to be waiting for something. Every day, with admirable perseverance, they sit on their chairs and wait, meanwhile evoking the past. They are suffering from melancholy, from a vague sadness. I think about them now as I tell myself how ridiculous it is for me to be wandering around here, feeling utterly desolate, when, among other things, I'm still young, I own a prosperous dry-cleaning business, I have a pretty and intelligent wife, I can travel wherever I please, I can attract any woman I might want to attract, I adore my two daughters, and I have an iron constitution. No, it seems entirely unreasonable that I should be here among the jacaranda trees of the Largo do Carmo, with childhood memories filling my mind and leaving behind an inexhaustible trail of a vague sadness.

I remember the day that I saw, parked outside the school, the vast convertible driven by a father I had always assumed did not exist.

I was dazzled by the red-leather seats gleaming in the sun. I was dazzled by everything about Horacio's father: his extraordinary height and build, his brown hat, his dark glasses, his pinstripe suit, his silk tie, his defiant moustache, and, above all, the fact that he existed. Horacio had always said that his father had disappeared into the underworld of the city of Beranda.

"He's reappeared, and that's what matters. He's come to wipe out a rival gang," Horacio told me succinctly.

I found it harder and harder to believe anything that Horacio told me, but I preferred to say nothing, just in case I was mistaken and would be made to look ridiculous and, worst of all, never allowed to ride in that huge car.

For two weeks, without fail, Horacio's father met his son at the school gates. Instead of Isabelita's bare feet, that enormous convertible would appear, its red-leather seats gleaming in the sunlight. I would gaze in astonishment at the spectacle afforded by Horacio's monumental father, complete with mafioso suit and silk tie.

Throughout the whole of the first week, his father walked with a firm, confident step. However, in the second week—from Monday onward—his father's footsteps became hesitant and almost fearful. On that Monday, we all spotted the presence of a stranger. A motorbike was discreetly parked some distance from the convertible, driven by a spy with very short blond hair and prominent blue eyes that never left the convertible. We soon took to pestering the spy and, on Tuesday, we even climbed into his sidecar. On Wednesday, predictably, he'd had enough.

"Don't push your luck," he said, raising his hand and speaking in a very fierce, threatening tone in what seemed to me to be a Beranda accent.

That same day, Horacio finally invited me to ride in his father's convertible. They drove me home. Seen from the back seat, the Paseo de San Luis took on another dimension; it appeared quite different. Horacio's father didn't utter a word during the whole journey, but now and then, he looked at me in the rearview mirror, then adjusted his hat. At the traffic light opposite the Cine Venus, he lit a cigarette and laughed to himself. I felt slightly frightened when we arrived at my house. He solemnly got out of the car and opened the rear door for me. With unexpected courtesy, he doffed his hat, bowed his head, and said:

"Goodbye, sir."

I assumed he was a worried man. The following day, attributing his behavior to the presence of the motorbike, I spread a rumor that a gang from Beranda was planning to kidnap Horacio, and that his father came to collect him from school every day in order to protect him.

"You shouldn't have spread such nonsense. Besides, Beranda doesn't exist," Horacio told me on Friday, and he seemed very different, as if something were going terribly wrong in his life, something that had robbed him entirely of his usual sense of humor.

That Friday was the last time I saw Horacio's father. The next school day—a cold January Monday in that odd-numbered year—there was no convertible at the school gates and no spy on a motorbike either. The whole Beranda scenario had vanished, and all that was left was Isabelita waiting on a corner, looking very serious, as if she had a bad cold, and with her shoes on. She came over to Horacio, whispered something in his ear, and unceremoniously led him away.

The following morning, in the midst of a torrential downpour, we entered school via the church door. We always had mass on Tuesday mornings, and it was announced from the pulpit that day that Horacio's father, who was also called Horacio, and who was only forty years old, no longer belonged to this world, but was finally at peace, having died.

"Goodbye, sir," I said, crossing myself.

I remember that it did not stop raining all day, and making the rounds at school were all kinds of versions of how he had died, each one more horrible than the last, and the only thing everyone agreed on was that Horacio's father had felt the temptation to leap into the void and had thrown himself off the very top of the Torre de San Luis.

The teacher of composition, a heartless, irascible man, told me the rest of the story. There wasn't a single teacher in the whole school who inspired me, but the most hateful and hopeless of them all was that irascible teacher of composition, who would lose his temper over the slightest thing and insult us with impassioned malice. My profound aversion for him led me to talk to him, convinced (quite rightly) that he was the ideal person to tell me the unvarnished truth that remained hidden from my classmates. He enjoyed being nasty and saw in me an unmissable opportunity. He never knew that I wasn't turning to him innocently, but guided by a hunch that I was on the verge of experiencing a very powerful emotion.

He told me that only two weeks before, Horacio's father had been released from the mental hospital. He had been allowed to drive the car he had bought in Caracas some years ago, but, at the same time, had been kept under close watch to make sure that he really was safe from the pernicious influence of the wind from the bay. The spy on the motorbike was, in fact, a doctor from the hospital, who was to give the final verdict. In light of what happened, what his verdict confirmed was that, true to a deep-seated family tradition, Horacio's father had exchanged the wind from the bay for suicide.

"It pains me deeply," the teacher of composition told me, "to recite the endless obituary of that family of suicides to which your friend Horacio belongs. Because although it's absolutely true, it seems so extraordinary that no one could possibly believe it wasn't invented. I could never write a convincing story based on the history of that family, because there are too many gunshots and too many leaps into the void, too much poison, too many people dying by their own hand."

It may have pained him deeply, but he nevertheless recited that endless obituary, reeling off a long litany of calamities: Uncle Alejandro, for example, one of Horacio's uncles on his father's side, had accidentally killed his best friend on a hunting trip, and this had plunged him into such a state of despair that, not knowing what to do with his life, he pretended to be ill and got himself admitted to a hospital where he stole a large dose of cyanide and killed himself.

Then there was one of Horacio's mother's sisters, Aunt Clara, who, before turning on the gas, left a letter for the judge, explaining that the direct cause of her suicide was her inability to control her fervent desire to live. And Aunt Clara's daughter, cousin Irene, had wanted to be a trapeze artist and ended up choosing the Torre de San Luis to perform, with consummate skill and daring, a triple somersault into the void, crash-landing shortly afterward on the cold, hard pavement near the top of the Paseo. Horacio's father's leap looked rather modest, even amateurish by comparison, although his was doubtless faster and more direct, perhaps because his most urgent desire was precisely that, to reach the ground.

More than thirty years have passed since the teacher of composition put me on to Horacio's terrible family history, and I can still feel the emotion of that day in my bones. Now, as I walk toward the Mirador de Santa Luzia—an ideal spot for a leap into the void—that experience seems to me to have been the closest thing to a personal revolution I've ever experienced, one which, although I didn't realize it at the time, changed my life. My friend Horacio rebelled against his suicidal fate and will now be sitting quietly at his desk; and if he could see me now, wandering around like a vagrant, he would laugh out loud and wonder what dark forces could have led me to make his family's tragic history my own, to become so suffused with melancholy and a vague sadness—for they say that *saudade* or nostalgia is a lighter form of sadness—as I evoke those days in which I discovered that life is not achievable while one is alive, that life simply doesn't live up to itself, and that the only possible plenitude lies in suicide.

But I won't leap into the void, friend Horacio. I will allow myself to be consumed by my feverish desire to recover my childhood memories, a nostalgia for the past which, as I approach the Mirador de Santa Luzia, I can sense is becoming more reconciled with the present, to the point where I no longer feel as if I were going back in time, but have almost eliminated time itself. I will sit down and wait. There will always be a chair for me in this city, and from that chair I will be able to sit and silently watch all the sunsets and practice *saudade*, with my eyes fixed on the horizon, waiting for the death that is already there in my eyes and for which I will wait, seriously and silently, for as long as necessary, facing the infinite blue of Lisbon and knowing that the vague sadness that comes from a rigorous period of waiting suits death very well.

THE HOUR OF THE TIRED AND WEARY

For Mercedes Monmany

It's six o'clock and already getting dark when I stop to observe the sudden irruption onto the Ramblas of passengers who have just got out at the Liceu metro station. It's a spectacle that never disappoints. For example, today, Maundy Thursday, from out of the multitude emerges a sinister-looking old man, who, despite his cadaverous appearance and despite carrying a heavy briefcase, is walking along with surprising agility. With astonishing speed, he overtakes a whole line of sleepy commuters, plants himself decisively before a poster advertising the Liceu Theater, and studiously reads the cast list for a Verdi opera, his face almost immediately assuming an expression of intense annoyance, as if he were profoundly disappointed by the choice of singers. There's something about this man, this walking cadaver, I say to myself, that troubles and intrigues me.

I decide to follow him. And I soon see that this will not be easy. Perhaps it's because I'm tired after a long, hard day at work, but the fact is that, although I'm only forty and he's twice my age, he's walking so quickly that when he turns off up Calle Boquería, I almost lose sight of him. I speed up and, for a few moments, I feel rather weak, as if I were about to collapse onto the pavement. Then I realize that I'm making a fuss about nothing, after all, I *am* still young, it's just that I frequently imagine myself to be on the verge of collapse because, to a greater or lesser degree, I'm always tired, tired of this dreary city, tired of the world and of human stupidity, tired of so much injustice. I sometimes try to overcome this state of mind and body and challenge myself; I set myself goals like this one, of pursuing a tireless old man, for absolutely no reason.

Suddenly, as if to give me breathing space, the man I'm pursuing stops outside a shop selling religious artifacts. I proceed calmly, keeping close to the wall, close to the shop windows, in no hurry now. I draw alongside him and see that he's peering inside, where a black man is buying a statuette of the Infant Jesus of Prague. I am just about to speak to the old man, when the black man bursts out onto the street, overjoyed with his purchase, and the old man turns and follows him.

The black man is clearly very happy, but, after only twenty paces, he suddenly slows down to the point where he is almost dragging his feet, as if buying the statuette had drained him of all energy, or as if it were suddenly that time of day when one inevitably feels weary. Behind him, the old man also slows his pace. And only now do I realize that the man I'm pursuing must have been following the black man for some time, although the latter appears to suspect nothing and would doubtless be most surprised were he to discover the spontaneous procession that has built up behind him.

All three of us—equally weary now, as if we had infected each other with tiredness—turn into Calle de Banys Nous at a very measured pace. The black man is an elegant, heavy-set individual, about fifty years old, with the appearance of a gentle, weary boxer. He clearly suspects nothing, because he stops suddenly to examine his new acquisition. He holds it above shoulder-height, as if he were placing it on an imaginary altar. Behind him, and so as not to overtake him, the old man stops abruptly, as do I. We form a curious Maundy Thursday procession. A few strange and seemingly interminable minutes tick by before the black man resumes his slow march, and, after a few more apparently eternal minutes, he ends up going into a bar, where he orders a beer and another and another. Occasionally, he laughs to himself and reveals horrible cannibal-like teeth. On the other side of the bar, the old man misses not a single second of this alcoholic ceremony, while I, at the old man's side, miss not a single second of his vile espionage. All three of us linger so long over every gesture that the barman loses patience with us and reveals himself to be totally allergic to any display of profound weariness, and, knowing full well that we have reached that crepuscular hour when even the shadows grow weary, he begins working like a maniac, meanwhile sending us terrible, hate-filled glances. If he could, that barman would happily shoot us. I put myself on a war footing and tell myself it's high time that the weary of this world formed a united front and finally put an end to so much injustice and stupidity.

While I'm thinking this, the old man starts scrabbling around in his briefcase. From the ticking sound, I imagine that he must have an alarm clock in there. Or—why not—a bomb. If it is a bomb, I can't see it. But what he takes out of the briefcase is something else entirely. Neither a clock nor a bomb. It's a red file with a big label on it that says "Report 1,763. Investigations into other people's lives. Stories not my own." Inside the file is a great wad of paper covered in notes in pencil and Biro. The old man hurriedly scribbles something down on a sheet of paper and, shortly afterward, closes the file, puts it back in his briefcase, stares up at the ceiling, and whistles a habanera. How very discreet, I say to myself, purely for the sake of saying something, but I can't actually work out what the old man is up to. I ponder the matter and end up wondering if he's an investigator, a pursuer of other people's lives, a kind of lazy detective, a storyteller.

Meanwhile, the black man pays for his drinks and, at his most urgent pace, heads for the door. By the time he reaches the street, the old man is paying for his coffee and I'm paying for mine, and I assume we'll be resuming our slow, stately march. But no. We reach the Baixada de Santa Eulalia, and the black man shows signs of having recovered his strength. Those beers have worked wonders, and the procession picks up speed. Anyone would think the black man had sprouted wings, because he goes streaking down the Baixada as if he had a world record to beat. The old man is clearly thrilled to be able to practice his favorite sport again. And I have no option but to follow them at a gallop. At that speed, you can't really enjoy the luxury of reflecting upon the time of day, which is the ever-mysterious twilight hour, vast, solemn, crepuscular, a motionless hour not marked on the sundial, as large as space itself, as light as a sigh, as swift as a glance: the hour of the tired and weary.

A hundred yards from the cathedral, I walk right into a wall, which deals me a knock-out blow; but what bothers me most is that the other two men, unaware of what has happened, continue their frenetic race. I reject both the help offered by various dishonest citizens and the perverse offer of last rites from a priest in a cassock, and, struggling angrily to my feet, I take up the pursuit again as best I can, leaving in my wake a pathetic trail of blood, the price of my madness, my foolish incursion into other people's lives, into stories not my own.

Near one of the side doors to the cathedral, I catch up with pursuer and pursued. I calm down, once again taking up my number-three position in that singular procession, although I'm not entirely calm because that collision with the wall has left me with a pain growing in intensity, and while I wouldn't say I see stars, I can see a globe of light, a chandelier lit by a thousand candles. Half-blinded by that light, I notice that the old man has stopped outside one of the side doors. He takes from his briefcase a vast key ring and goes into what must be the sacristy. Everything is happening very fast. And after slamming the door loudly behind him, he disappears from view without even an apologetic backward glance for having spoiled my fun. Without so much as a goodbye, a scornful or compassionate glance. Nothing. He's gone in a flash, leaving me to pursue the black man. I think that perhaps I've been quite wrong, and the old man wasn't pursuing anyone, perhaps he was merely carrying a bomb that will blow the cathedral to smithereens.

So what am I doing pursuing the black man? I watch him as he, too, goes into the cathedral and kneels down before the Holy Christ of Lepanto. That's quite enough for today, I tell myself. I feel extraordinarily tired. I think about my wife, my late wife, and recall the days when we used to arrange to meet in front of this same Christ figure. We, the weary, also have hearts, we, too, fall in love. I loved her very much. I remember a summer night and the two of us dancing on an open terrace, me holding her close to my weary body, thinking that I never wanted to be without the smell of her skin and her hair. And I remember that the band was playing "Stormy Weather." What a time that was. And then our meetings in front of this same Christ figure, and the promises we made never to part. We, the weary, are also very sentimental.

Almost instinctively—a relic from the past—I cross myself, I think of the Battle of Lepanto, I hear the roar of the cannon, I think of the bomb the old man was carrying and that I had better leave the cathedral now. I lean against a pillar. I decide to leave, to forget all about the black man; I turn and walk wearily out onto the cathedral square. I'm going in search of my own blood. I begin to retrace my steps. I walk toward the Ramblas, which I should never have left. I'm smoking a cigarette. After each puff, I walk through my own smoke and am where I was not, at the spot into which I exhaled that smoke. And suddenly, at my back, I hear heavy breathing and, shortly afterward, feel a sudden blow on the back of my neck. I spin around and see the black man giving me his best cannibal smile, and he asks me why I am following him. I'm astonished. I say that surely he's the one following me. He stops smiling and looks at me defiantly, angrily, but gives me a few seconds to provide him with a satisfactory answer. It's clear that if I don't come up with something quickly, he might well eat me alive.

Fortunately, I remember the old man's red file. I tell the black man that I am a pursuer of other people's lives, a kind of lazy detective, a storyteller. I tell him that I live outside myself. I explain that I really love being outside and keeping my eyes wide open. I tell him that I follow people in order to find things out about them, things that I then introduce into my stories. He places a huge, threatening hand on my shoulder and asks me the title of the story I'm working on now. I say the first thing that comes into my head: *A pair of dark eyes for sale*. Looking at me with profound suspicion, he tells me that he doesn't want to be a character in a story. He shows me his fist and assures me that it's bigger than Cassius Clay's. No, no, no, he says—I think—I don't want to appear in that story. I tell him I'm very tired, that I've decided not to include him in my story and I ask him, please, to let a poor weary man go his way. Surprisingly, all the anger drains from his face. The word "weary" appears to have worked a miracle. Once again, he becomes the gentle, weary boxer I saw in Calle de Banys Nous. He tells me his name is Romeo and asks if he can accompany me as far as the Ramblas. Giving a sigh of relief, I say, of course, and on the way, I will tell him the story of a weary, anarchist sacristan I was following today. We walk along, leaning on each other, feeling utterly exhausted. It's dark now, and in the distance a clock is striking seven. The black man is telling me that he would like to give me the statuette of the Infant Jesus of Prague, when, as we turn down Baixada de Santa Eulalia, we hear a loud explosion. Gas, says Romeo. More likely it's an old kamikaze, I tell him. He grows still gentler and more sentimental when I tell him that the cathedral has just been blown to smithereens.

THEY SAY I SHOULD SAY WHO I AM

They say I should say who I am. They say that in order to satisfy my personal vanity (of which I have none, but there we are) and also the inevitable curiosity that a reader might feel about the author of this possibly interesting (they say fundamental) testimony about the obscurest episode in the life of the great painter Panizo del Valle, I should say a few words about myself, my very modest, humble self, because I am just a poor devil who was born in Catalonia, in the delightful town of Tossa del Mar, where I am writing this now, meanwhile telling myself that I live in one of the best places in the world, and I say this not just because I was born here, because there are, in fact, other places I like more and to which I feel far more emotionally attached, Babákua for example.

In my young and my not so young days, I was a boatswain's mate, second class, regularly calling in at ports along the southeast coast of Africa—mainly those of Bikanir and Mozambique (my slippers bear the same name, a homage to those two fabulous countries)— and there are two things of which I am proud—(two like my slippers and those two countries). One is being an autodidact (whenever possible, I like to give the lie to that old stereotype according to which an old sea dog cannot also be a sensitive, educated man); the other gives me goose bumps and is that I piloted a whaler along the southern coast of the Babákua peninsula (so famous everywhere for the portraits of the Babákua natives painted by the great Panizo del Valle, but, at the same time, so scandalously unknown and un-visited, including by Panizo del Valle himself), a peninsula where, as it happens, I am a respected and much-loved man, and where I would like to be able to return one day and even be buried, with these simple words written above my grave: "He piloted a whaler along our coast."

As luck would have it, on a cold, moonless night on the high seas—a night of fine, persistent rain when we were still some miles from the southern coast of Babákua—the great painter Panizo del Valle, who was wearing a gray windbreaker almost identical to mine, happened to come and lean on the same stretch of ship's rail as I was, on that ship so proud of its past (none other than the *Bel Ami* with its historic keel), which was carrying us to that remote land where I am so respected and well-loved and where I had once piloted a fantastic whaler—ah, what times those were, when we traveled blithely, unaware that time was traveling with us.

That was the night of the fifth of January, 1917. We were wearing similar windbreakers and, in the dark of the pitch-black night, we were two rather symmetrical figures. However, we were going to Babákua for very different reasons. I was going there to pick up or pack up my things (as people usually say) and to make preparations for my return voyage, possibly my last, to my birthplace of Tossa del Mar. For his part, Panizo del Valle was traveling to Babákua, strictly incognito and on a voyage that was as solitary as it was emotional, for he was traveling to the land of his imagination, the remote peninsula to which he owed his vast fortune and that he had been indefatigably painting for more than twenty years (mainly portraits of its inhabitants, as if he were a new Gauguin), but which he had never once visited.

I remember that the two of us stood for a long time in silence, side by side, until, on the ever-deceptive horizon, the outline of the south coast of the peninsula began to appear in the form of a geo-metric figure, black and angular, silhouetted against the somber sky. Then, as if moved by some strange mechanism, the painter turned slowly toward me and stared fixedly at me. I immediately did the same thing, giving him a look as fixed and insolent as his seemed to be.

And there we remained for several seconds, which seemed to me interminable. We were accompanied by the plaintive song of the ship. All around us, everything, absolutely everything oozed sound: the hoists, the handrails, the rigging. It was as if a sorrowing soul had taken possession of that whole area, so like the end of the world. In order to maintain the initial intensity of my gaze, I remember that, during those interminable seconds, I began thinking of other things, especially the swaying movement of the lamp in the bulkhead of my cabin when it drew a perfect circle above my rocking chair. That image kept my gaze both aloof from and firmly focused on that very tense situation, which appeared to be an entirely gratuitous stand-off. For his part, Panizo del Valle also managed to keep his eyes fixed on mine; indeed, the only thing I regret now is not knowing what distant and possibly evocative images he was resorting to in order to match the intensity of my gaze.

Thus we stood for a few brief, but intense seconds, while I kept telling myself: "You have to think of other things to fend off those who dare to challenge you with their gaze." Thus we stood until the southern coast of Babákua began to take on its first purplish tones, and Panizo del Valle finally decided to speak. I don't know how he guessed I was Spanish—he had probably heard me speaking to the boatswain—but it was in Spanish that he spoke to me.

"You're not from Babákua," he said, smiling. These words were apparently uttered in a very friendly fashion, but the truth is that no words have ever troubled me more. Because he did not ask or suggest; no, he stated it as a fact. You're not from Babákua. Who was he to say that? Such gratuitous smugness troubled me. It angered me that he should consider himself an expert on the natives of Babákua, when I knew that he had never even bothered to set foot there. It angered me above all (we autodidacts, I agree, tend to be over-sensitive), because it hadn't even occurred to him that I might have recognized *him*, that I might have detected on that ship the presence of the great Panizo del Valle. He probably assumed I was a poor, old, ignorant sailor, one of those sea dogs who know nothing about the world of art. This bothered and angered me deeply.

"I've seen all your Babákuans," I said.

"I'm sorry?"

"It's not me you should say sorry to."

"No, I mean, I'm sorry, I don't know what you mean."

"I know them well."

"Who?"

"Those portraits of natives ... so *un*faithful."

He tried to remain composed, to pretend he still didn't know what I meant. He was pretending that he wasn't Panizo del Valle, but was humoring me as if I were a madman. He knew perfectly well what I meant. Besides, his unease betrayed him.

"Do you mean that the natives or the portraits are unfaithful?" he asked at last, with a horribly forced smile.

"No, your brush is."

He saw at once that there was no point in keeping up the pretence. He was no longer traveling incognito.

"Should I assume you know who I am?" he asked.

It seemed to me that I inspired in him, as doubtless most things did, a deep-seated distrust.

"Yes, you should." I answered.

"And what do you know about me?"

With that question he managed to anger me again. He was still refusing to see me as an educated man. Why shouldn't I know all about him and his work?

"Well, I know, for example, that you have never seen a real Babákuan."

"In my imagination I have," he joked feebly, doubtless taken aback somewhat and surprised to see that a poor devil like me should know so much about his life.

"And I also know," I said, "that if you had ever bothered to visit that diabolical place, you would know how very unfaithful all your paintings are. It makes me laugh to think of those critics who call you the last realist. How crass."

"Oh come now," he protested shyly. "Why so angry?"

"I'm angry," I replied, pointing at the mist—as sudden as it was opportune, that had just made its appearance and was growing denser by the minute, half concealing the southern coast of Babákua—"because I cannot understand how you could continue to portray the Babákuans in a way that has so little foundation in the truth."

"Who? Me? Well, that's the first I've heard of it," he said and laughed. His behavior ensured that I continued to feel very angry with him, so I went on the attack.

"I feel sorry for them," I said, "your ridiculous Babákuans, those portraits of pure, angelic, indigenous souls. Your paintings are a puree of errors. Because in Babákua, you're not going to find any stupid natives with a bone through their nose. You need to know that. They are people who love the truly diabolical. They *are* diabolical! They have nothing whatsoever to do with what you paint."

"Really," he protested, "are you serious? You seem to want to spoil my fun. Besides, I've never painted any natives with bones through their noses. I've painted them as civilized beings, sitting quietly in cafés in the evening, for example."

"But you've painted a people who don't exist! You've painted men and women I've never seen in Babákua, where everyone is worse than the devil himself. You've painted nice, quiet people, happy and friendly, utterly genuine, not twisted in the least, but adorably Christian, kind, and stupid. Nothing could be further from the truth."

He looked at me almost incredulously.

"What do you mean 'stupid?'" he asked.

I pretended not to have heard him. I didn't want to have to explain my choice of words.

"All I'm saying," I went on, "is that they are a people in whom the truly diabolical is constantly made manifest, perhaps more so than in any other corner of the planet and remember, we are at the very outer edge of the planet."

"The very outer edge of the planet," he repeated with a little smile, as if I had expressed myself incorrectly.

"Have I said something wrong, something incorrect, Mr Smile?"

"You say some very odd things," he answered.

"It must be the fault of this mist," I said, trying to confuse him with a completely irrelevant remark.

"Very odd," he repeated.

For a few seconds, we did not speak, as if our brief conversation had exhausted us. In the end, I broke the silence.

"I imagine you must be wondering what the devil I mean by the truly diabolical; am I right?"

"I wasn't wondering anything," came his irritating response.

"Of course, you prefer to look at the sea."

"No, it's not that either. With this mist, who wouldn't be looking at the sea …"

"So do you want to know what I mean by the truly diabolical?"

"Frankly, no, but if you insist.… All right, I'll ask you. So, my good man, what do you mean by the truly diabolical?"

He thought he was being so clever, but he succeeded only in making me loathe him even more. Him and his paintings. The great Panizo del Valle. The last realist.…

"All right, you asked for it," I said. "To begin with, I should just say that your famous portrait of a young Babákuan girl holding a rag doll is the constant butt of jokes in Babákua. Not a day goes by without someone there making an ironic comment about that crassly unfaithful portrait."

"I don't know why you describe it as unfaithful. I simply made a masterly copy of a photograph. I can't see the problem, my friend. I painted the girl in that photograph as faithfully as I could. That's all."

"Yes, but that is *precisely* the problem. At the risk of seeming pedantic, I should just say that for me, snapshots are a diabolical manifestation of the modern, and they always deceive."

"Oh, come now, who gave you that stupid idea?"

"It is *my* idea and not in the least stupid," I retorted furiously. "What is stupid is your painting of that horribly precious little girl holding a rag doll. She's only stupid in your portrait, though, because in reality her name is Yvne, and like all the other Babákuans, without exception, she is a highly intelligent and a highly diabolical creature, notable for her tendency to harbor feelings of resentment and malice, or, which comes to the same thing, envy. And envy, in case you don't know, is one of Babákua's national passions. And envy, in case you don't know, is one of the clearest manifestations of the truly diabolical."

"I'm so very sorry, sir, to have painted that little girl as sweet, serene, and entirely unenvious. Please be sure to give her my apologies. But is it such a very terrible thing not to have painted her as a creature consumed with envy?"

"Yes, it is," I said with feeling. "Especially in light of your perennial boast that you have always painted the reality of life in Babákua, and yet you are ignorant of the most elementary facts, for example, that *all* the women of Babákua are consumed with envy. As children they always want their best friend's rag doll. And when they grow up, they all want to be the husband of their best friend, I mean, they envy their best friend for having the husband she has."

He gave that smug little smile again, this time because I had got myself in rather a tangle. But I carried on regardless.

"And the men of Babákua," I said, "kill out of envy. They will commit murder in order to get the rag doll that looks least like theirs. The Babákuans are an envious, murderous race, and yet you had no idea."

He looked at me hard, as if trying to work out if I were mad or telling him the truth (and merely warning him of the horrors he would find in Babákua), or if I were simply a charlatan and a bore.

I preferred not to get involved in another staring match.

"Listen," I said, "you may think I'm just a poor, ignorant sailor, but I've seen a lot of paintings, a lot. And I must tell you that all I ask and demand of a painter is that he should have a direct relationship with what he captures on canvas, free from all possible error, a real relationship, even if that reality has no life or form beyond the painting itself. That's why your extravagant, irresponsible relationship with the reality of Babákua angers me so much. You have no sense of commitment to what you paint. You have painted Babákuans as if you were painting pictures for a prayer book. I find your frivolity despicable."

"I envy you your good humor," he said.

I tried to conceal my sense of failure.

"You seem determined not to understand me. I'm trying to make you see that you still have time to accept the reality of Babákua and involve yourself in it."

"That's enough now, my good man. What I do still have time to do is to leave you here alone with your ship's-rail nonsense."

I realized then that, although he was trying hard not to show it, a degree of unease had entered his mind. When he said he still had time to leave me there, he had unwittingly revealed a feeling that he couldn't stand much more of the truths I was telling him about his mendacious, unfaithful paintings.

This gave me wings. I returned to the charge. I said:

"You must feel very proud, for example, of that celebrated series of paintings about the priests of Babákua. All those famous paintings of priests preaching the truth, always with the ineffable Erif volcano in the background. Beautiful paintings, no doubt about it, but totally and utterly unfaithful, because they do not, for one moment, reflect the reality of Babákua. They are pure imagination. I'm sure you must be very proud of your work, but I just want to say one thing, and, forgive me, but I feel it is my duty to do so, I just want to say this: You should be mortally ashamed."

"You obviously have it in for me *and* my work," he said, trying to appear unaffected by my words. "Let's see now, what is so very wrong about my paintings of the priests of Babákua? Are my paintings of them so very bad?"

"Your paintings couldn't really be worse. There is nothing further from the reality of Babákua than your paintings of the priests. You should know that, in Babákua, everyone, the priests included, cultivate the art of the lie, and it's as clear as day that you don't know that. Lies, you see, are another of the most obvious manifestations of the truly diabolical. And in Babákua lies are everywhere. There are even monuments erected to The Lie. It's another of their national passions. And yet you, my good man," I said, returning the insult, "paint those crazy preachers as if they were preaching neither more nor less than The Truth with a capital T. You don't appear to realize that those preachers love lies. And do you know why? It's very simple. So as not to lose their congregations. They know that what their parishioners want are lies, and so they give them what they want: one lie after another. That's what's so pathetic, or, rather, so comical about the paintings in which you depict preachers who are all integrity and holiness."

"I don't believe it," he said, and it seemed to me that he was beginning to feel worried.

"More than that," I went on, "in Babákua, they're all slanderers too. They are all, without exception, constantly spreading false rumors about their neighbors. That's another thing that could not really be said to be there in your sublime paintings of evenings in cafés packed with serene Babákuans, incapable of speaking ill of anyone. It's just laughable all those Babákuans gazing out at the horizon. And they're so quiet. You apparently don't know that in the evenings, the cafés are packed with people all happily engaged in the great sport of slandering others. If you had painted the real Babákua, you would have had to entitle your paintings: *Venomous Evenings on the Peninsula of Evil.*

Panizo del Valle slowly bowed his head and appeared to be growing increasingly anxious.

"You'll see for yourself soon enough," I went on. "It won't be long before we arrive, and then you'll be able to test the veracity of everything I've been telling you. And you'll find out at once, because I wouldn't be the least bit surprised if they didn't start slandering you pitilessly the moment you set foot there. Even if they don't recognize you, it doesn't matter; they'll still happily start slandering you. That's what they're like. They're always waiting for new people so as to widen the scope of their slanderings. They just love their national sport. Slander, just in case you didn't know or hadn't guessed, is another of the clearest manifestations of the truly diabolical. Their enthusiasm for it knows no limits. And yet, you have always painted the Babákuans as pure, uncontaminated souls. You even titled one of your paintings *The Innocent Life of the Savage*. I had to laugh."

"Neither that painting nor that title are mine," he protested.

"But they could have been. Because that is the philosophy I see behind your most successful paintings. I'm referring to the ones depicting natives dancing on the beaches at dawn around a fire. The underlying philosophy of those paintings is obvious: *The Innocent Life of the Savage*."

I laughed to myself, feeling that victory was mine. I had only to look at Panizo del Valle's anxious face. Then I went on:

"And what you don't know—because you know nothing about Babákua—is that even when they dance, they are busy slandering, although, in this case, they communicate their slanders to the fire, which is a representation in miniature of the Erif volcano. That is why they dance so much. Since they love to slander and the fire is happy to hear them, they are tireless when it comes to dancing on the beaches in the mornings."

He was, I saw, feeling simultaneously weary, worried, and bewildered. He appeared to be troubled by what I was telling him, especially because he had begun to realize that I wasn't lying, but putting him in touch with the harsh reality he would encounter when we disembarked in Babákua, a reality so far removed from that depicted in his paintings.

"They are a diabolical race," I said again, looking him in the eye.

I sensed in him a desire to retreat, as if he could stand no more of my company. Seeing that he wanted to escape, I did all I could to keep him there.

"Not that it matters if they do slander you as soon as you set foot on the peninsula," I said, "because they haven't had a good word to say about you for years. Did anyone ever write to you from Babákua? I doubt it. I doubt very much you've had any contact with the locals at all."

"On one occasion, a Babákuan woman wrote to me and told me that she belonged to a very contented race, such as is hard to find anywhere on Earth."

"As I said, they love to lie."

"I really don't know what to think."

"They say you must be the biggest dope fiend in the world, which explains why you have never been able to paint Babákua as it really is."

He appeared then to be plunged in gloom.

"Forgive me for being so frank," I said, "but right from the start, I felt it was my duty to warn you about what you would find when you disembark in Babákua."

"Sir, it's been a pleasure," he said, attempting another escape. "I don't know if what you tell me is true, but I'm leaving anyway. I prefer to know nothing more."

He turned and set off toward his cabin. The mist appeared to be dissipating. Soon, the troubling silhouette of the southern coast of Babákua would reappear. Soon, we would be able to make out that geometric figure, angular and black, against the somber sky.

I decided to try my luck and keep him with me for a while longer.

"All Babákuans can read and speak backwards," I shouted.

He paused, then very slowly turned and began walking hesitantly toward me until he was again standing at the rail beside me.

"What did you say?" he asked.

There was a glimmer of hope in his eyes.

"If you had, just once," I said, "given one of your paintings a title written back to front, then you would have at least been faithful to the perverse spirit of the Babákuans."

He looked suddenly very happy. And I felt happy, too, having laid this magnificent trap that had successfully lured him back.

"For years now," he said, "I've known that they do sometimes like to read or speak backwards. That's why several of my paintings do have back-to-front titles. So, at least in that respect, I have not been entirely ignorant of the reality of Babákua."

He remained thoughtful for a few seconds. Then, visibly pleased with himself, he added:

"Do you really know my paintings?"

He was clearly filled with glee at the possibility that, up until then, I had been lying.

"Are not you," he added, "the liar, the slanderer, the truly diabolical and all that?"

He laughed, such was his sudden joy that his face took on an expression that was, at once, amused and utterly deranged. He had been so nervous and upset before, and that always takes its toll.

"I would rather not say," I said.

Of course I knew about those back-to-front titles. Any connoisseur of Panizo del Valle's paintings would: indeed, it's the first thing anyone mentions when his name crops up in conversation. He's the painter with the back-to-front titles, they say. I had only pretended not to know because that seemed to me the ideal way of keeping him there with me on the deck. I didn't like the prospect of being left without a sparring partner.

"Are not you," he said again, exultantly this time, "are not you the liar, the slanderer, the one consumed with envy? Ah, now I understand. Why didn't I see it before? Everything you've said stems from the envy you feel for my fame, for my success, for my extraordinary, deep-seated connection to reality."

He had suddenly regained all his confidence, which was amusing in its way, because not five minutes before he had seemed the saddest man in the world.

"So you don't know," he went on, beaming, "that some of my paintings, the most famous ones actually, have back-to-front titles? Well, that's upset your apple cart, my friend. Now who's back to front? You weren't expecting that, were you?"

I could have put paid to his fragile joy simply by asking why the portrait of the girl, Yvne, and her rag doll didn't have a back-to-front title, why it was simply called *Envy*. That would have been enough, but I said nothing. I preferred to be prudent, and merely repeated his last few words backwards.

"Taht gnitcepxe tnerew uoy," I said, and waited to see his response.

He looked rather bewildered, even pale, I would say. He was no fool. He immediately grasped that I had repeated his words backwards. After a brief, awkward silence—during which he kept his eyes fixed on me—he finally said:

"You're from Babákua."

This enraged me. He still considered himself an expert on the subject. He apparently thought *he* could decide on my nationality at will. Before, he had taken me for an ignorant old sea dog, now he saw me as a native with a bone through my nose. I couldn't help but blurt out:

"You must be mad. And to think people describe you as the last realist …"

"Sir," he said, trying for a second time to take his leave, "it's been a pleasure."

As he held out his hand to me—proof that he was still not sure whether to take his leave or not—I began describing more horrors, things I hadn't yet had time to explain to him about the terrible, infernal nature of the Babákuans. Panizo del Valle continued to eye me oddly, as if I were a madman. He was clearly still unable to judge whether I was telling him the truth or not. He seemed to be saying to himself over and over: I can't believe it, these people cannot possibly be so utterly evil.

I explained in great detail that the Babákuans were not only, as I'd already said, mendacious, envious and slanderous, they were also malicious, mean-spirited, petty tyrants, and ruthless poisoners of innocent souls.

"Those," I said, "are their seven most distinctive qualities, and they are also the seven essential manifestations of the truly diabolical. And there you are happily painting them as little angels."

"Sir, it has been a pleasure," he said again and turned to go. And this time he did seem determined to leave me alone on the deck.

Then I made my first mistake.

Up until then, I had confined myself to warning him about the sinister reality he was about to encounter in Babákua. Up until then, I had invented nothing, but confined myself to telling him what he would find when he disembarked. However, seeing him so determined to return to his cabin, I began to invent. I, too, turned traitor to the reality of Babákua, and all because I couldn't bear to be left alone, because I wanted to keep Panizo del Valle with me for a few more moments.

That was when I made my mistake.

"Have you seen these photographs?" I asked.

I showed him three horrific pictures that someone had given to my friend José, the boatswain, in Mozambique. They showed the catastrophic consequences of some recent tribal conflicts. However, I told Panizo del Valle that they had been taken a few days before in the cemetery of Stsitra Dab, better known as the Violet Graveyard of Tormented Realists. In Babákua.

"All those corpses, horribly tortured, vilely mutilated, have been left to dry in the sun, in accordance with an old Babákuan custom, before being taken to their final resting place, the foot of the Erif volcano. And photographs never lie," I said, reminding him of his own words.

I have to say that I regret having lied like that, but I didn't do so out of malice. I simply wanted to keep him there. I wanted Panizo to stay a while longer on the deck with me. I regret it now, of course. It leaves a bad taste in my mouth. But how was I to know that those Mozambican photographs would prove to be the final scrap of evidence forcing Panizo del Valle to accept the truth, the now unquestionable truth that he had been a terrible painter all his life?

The bad artist somehow always knows he is bad and has an uneasy conscience about it. All I did was to help Panizo del Valle confront that reality to help him understand that art is nothing if it is not *dangerous*.

"I'm going. Yes, I think I'll go," he said, and I read or thought I read in his face a look of profound unease, possibly his own uneasy conscience. "With whom have I had the pleasure or, rather, displeasure of speaking?"

The word "displeasure" displeased me, if you'll forgive the play on words. Then I made another, I think, very grave mistake. One misunderstanding often leads to another, and the same thing happened with my mistake.

I showed him my passport.

My two reassuringly Catalan surnames must have brought him some relief, only momentarily, but relief nonetheless.

His relief did not last long: only the time he spent looking fondly out at the horizon, where we could already see, quite clearly now, the southern coast of Babákua with the Erif volcano in the background. The mist had lifted—later on, it would suddenly return, indicating the strange out-of-kilter natural laws prevailing around the peninsula—and a few moments of calm followed. A unique, unforgettable moment, which turned out to be the last, because, shortly afterward, it suddenly occurred to Panizo del Valle to read my initial and surnames backwards and say them out loud.

"Satam Alive," he said.

I think probably the whole ship heard him say it. And his scream finally merged with the gloomy, plaintive song of the ship.

"Yes, it so nearly spells Satan Alive, doesn't it?" I said in a falsely innocent voice just to clarify matters.

To say he turned pale would be an understatement.

And so the drama reached its abrupt conclusion. Looking utterly distraught, Panizo del Valle finally set off to his cabin, where he remained until we reached Babákua. He didn't even say goodbye.

The mist had come down again, and the jungle was black and drenched when we reached the port of Fiu in Babákua. The dampness dripped from the rigging onto the taut awning sheltering the bridge. It was an icy morning, unusual at that time of year, although, to be frank, nothing about that climate was usual.

On that icy dawn, my second-to-last glimpse of Panizo was of his somber, blurred profile. He seemed to be running away from me, from himself, from his horribly unfaithful paintings, from everything. Then I saw him jump down onto the quay. He was wearing only a pair of baggy trousers—doubtless his pyjama pants—and a floral vest. Without any luggage. He had left it all on board.

That morning, as I watched that mad, pyjama-clad figure heading off into the inconstant mist, I thought to myself that I would probably never see him again. And so it proved. He plunged into the jungle, although not without first shooting me a farewell glance (some friends said it was more likely a glance of eternal loathing for being such a pest, but I really don't think so); it was a glance as resigned as it was unhinged.

And now I can only hope that this account of the events preceding the departure of the great Panizo del Valle in those furious pyjamas will shed some light on the mysterious circumstances surrounding his disappearance. I would only add that, in my modest opinion, no one dressed only in pyjamas is likely to survive the dangerous jungle of Babákua. And this leads me to think that, at the last moment, and in a gesture as admirable as it is touching, he had decided, for the very first time in his life, to take a risk and to plunge alone into reality.

As for me, as I think I said earlier, I am just a poor devil. *The* poor devil to be exact. I am weary of being who I am. I've spent far too many years playing cruel tricks on people. While I write this, it occurs to me that I, too, long to disappear. I've reviewed all the possible ways of committing suicide and, finding that each of those possible deaths has its drawbacks, I have decided to tickle myself to death. And then let me be buried in Babákua, along whose coast—as I think I've made clear—I once piloted a whaler, a really fine whaler.

GREETINGS FROM DANTE

The few friends and relatives who still had the courage to visit the house would always tell me—I assume, to ease my anxiety—that everything was fine. That unpresentable son called Tito, born, alas, from my womb, had not uttered a single word for ten years—exactly ten, from the day he was born—not a sound in his entire life. He was dumb, utterly dumb, but, they would tell me, there was no need to worry, he'll talk eventually; any day now, you'll see, he'll start talking and there'll be no stopping him.

A poet friend of mine, who has always been a lucid fellow, albeit sad—a poète maudit who tends to say very complicated things which I carefully note down so as to pore over them quietly later on—took to its logical extreme the theory that everything was perfectly all right and told me that I shouldn't be in the least worried, since, after all, just as death never speaks, so chance, too, has no access to the word—indeed it is in silence that chance finds its fullest expression, where it is, in short, most able to speak.

But not even those complex, beautiful words could help me. Nothing and no one could do anything for me, and that was the sad reality. My poor, unfortunate son was almost ten and had still said nothing, had still not pronounced a single word in his whole life. It wasn't that he was a deaf-mute or an idiot (for those, at least, would have been perfectly convincing explanations). The child could speak if he chose to. All the doctors I consulted agreed that there was no physical defect preventing him from doing so, that it was perhaps simply that he did not wish to embark upon the human adventure of the word, and that although this was obviously a serious matter—it would require visits to a psychiatrist—I should not be overly concerned, because one day, when I least expected it, the child might yet take the infallible and ineffable step to show that he was just like everyone else.

"I don't believe your son will be able to bear being like this all his life," Dr Valente would say; he was the first psychiatrist to examine Tito, and that was all he ever said.

"But you must have some idea what's wrong with the child."

"It would be much worse," he would say, deftly changing the subject, "if we were confronted by one of those cases in antiquity of children born covered in scales, or children with two heads, who spoke out of one mouth in one language and out of the other mouth in another."

"A trauma experienced at a very early age," said the pedantic Dr Sastre, the second psychiatrist I consulted, "a trauma that must have created a vision of something, which, to the child, may have seemed monstrous."

"Like what, doctor?"

"Your guess is as good as mine! We would only know if the child were to speak, but since he doesn't … It's a complete puzzle, a fish biting its own tail." He paused thoughtfully. "Perhaps that's what he saw, a fish biting its own tail, and the sight seemed to him utterly horrific. It wouldn't be the first case of a child who went fishing with his parents and discovered the horrible death by asphyxiation suffered by a fish out of water."

"But we've never taken him fishing."

"It's a unique case," said Dr Trecillo sorrowfully; he was a psychoanalyst, who had been recommended to us as a rather better-read class of practitioner. "It's a difficult case, a puzzle, a fish biting its own tail."

"Oh, no!"

"I'm afraid so, Señora. It's a diabolical circle, because if the boy were to speak and, by some slip, without realizing it, lead us to the source of his trauma, then, knowing exactly what that trauma was would be the very least of it, because the problem of his lack of speech—which is why we're here and what really matters to us—would be solved and, of course"—here his tone of voice grew still more arrogant—"the trauma would disappear as quickly as the demon that used to live in your part of town."

The mention of a demon seemed to me entirely gratuitous. Nevertheless, I asked him to explain, I asked what devil he was talking about.

"You live near Plaza de San Boal, don't you, near where Calle del Aire used to be?" he said.

"I live in Plaza de San Boal itself."

"Well, in Calle del Aire, in the sixteenth century, there lived a Portuguese student, an excellent guitarist. This young man lived at an inn on that street and he would shut himself up in his room to eat the food brought to him in a covered basket by a silent servant. One day, he left the door to his room open, and a maid who worked at the inn saw with horror what the Portuguese student, Domingos, was eating: he was dipping into a bowl of flies with a spoon. It turned out he was a demon, and off he flew."

After thanking him for this information about the history of my neighborhood, I reminded him that I was there to find out why my son, though able to speak, chose not to.

It irritated him enormously to be reminded of this.

"I thought I'd told you that already," he replied. "It's a new affliction about which our Science, still very much in its infancy, knows nothing. An affliction which we hope will prove transitory. It's very difficult to diagnose and most disconcerting for us.... A psychoanalyst is basically someone who listens, and if, as is the case with your son, the patient doesn't say a word, well, there's really not much we can do."

At the time, those words struck me as a crude excuse to cover up his complete and utter ignorance.

"Shifting sands," he added, when he saw my indignant look, "uncertain terrain."

So, the only certainty was that not a single word had ever once escaped Tito's lips. He gave the occasional shout, broke into spontaneous laughter (he was capable of laughter), emitted guttural, rather mocking sounds, but made few other noises.

"A shut mouth catches no flies," his ingenuous, long-suffering sister Inesita used to say; she's a year older and is as patient as a saint with him.

One evening, Inesita decided for some reason to alter the wording of that proverb and the poor girl said instead:

"Tito's mouth is full of flies."

The boy didn't think twice and dealt her a fearsome blow that left her utterly stunned. I just froze. That was not, unfortunately, the first time he had hit her, but it was much more violent than usual. It seemed to me—and I was quite right—to signal an escalation in the display of cruelty and the evident taste for Evil that had plunged his own father into such despair that he was left desolate and behind bars for the rest of his life, the poor wretch, cast down by his own cruel, silent son.

That day, I managed to stop myself hitting Tito; I didn't want to cause him any more harm. He might be suffering some profound hurt that was preventing him from speaking and I didn't want to deepen what I imagined to be an already deep wound—and so I merely asked brother and sister to make peace and then applied a large dose of mercurochrome to poor Inesita's eye. For a whole terrible week afterward, her face was all swollen—I kept her well away from any mirrors—and she had a high fever.

Every evening, I would corner Tito in the kitchen.

"Why do you treat your sister like that? Do you think what you did is right?! Why were you so cruel to your father?! Why do you continue to be cruel even though you know he's in prison? Why?! Why!" It was driving me mad. "Why don't you speak?"

Always that same infuriating silence in response. There were days when Tito would sit staring into space, making horrible clicking noises with his tongue, as if he were drinking a glass of wine, and then he seemed to have only the most superficial, ephemeral sensations. Other days he would spend biting his nails in that irritating way peculiar to him, not raising his finger to his mouth, but lowering his mouth, his hand turned away from him, his elbow lifted.

"Why don't you speak?"

One evening, as on so many others, I asked Tito that question while standing with my back to him, washing the dishes. Suddenly—and to think I had turned away quite calmly, not expecting any reply!—something made me look around, utterly horrified, as if someone had stuck a goad into me. Ringing in my right ear, drilling into my head, was an incredibly piercing note, like the shriek of a bat, only slightly louder: it was the kind of experience that makes you wonder if there's something wrong with your brain.

It seemed impossible that the noise could have come from outside me, it seemed more as if the sound were resonating inside my brain; and yet I sensed that it was the boy who had emitted that note. I held my breath, covered my ears, and looked at Tito. And when he saw I was observing him, he went back to staring into space again, clicking his tongue.

"Did you do that?" I asked him. "Did you make that noise?"

I said to myself that if that bat shriek had indeed come from him, I at last had some information about my son's mind, a terrifying piece of information, because the shriek had been entirely without emotion and, even more alarming, without the slightest hint of intelligence; it was the shriek of a stupid, utterly unfeeling bat.

Again I was troubled by the thought that my son was simply mentally retarded, and, again, in the days that followed, the doctors denied this.

When I was least expecting it, I heard that shriek a second time, and it shook me even more, making me think again that it must be some tragic inner cry of my own, and that I, affected by my son's pitiless silence and by the absence of his father, was going mad.

It happened the second time, as I said, at a time when I least expected it, when I was making an investigation, by now almost routine, into Tito's frenetic activities in the small but idyllic back yard of our house in Plaza de San Boal. In one corner, almost completely concealed by a bush, there was a kind of hut where we used to keep the gardening tools, and where the boy had created a small shelter, which, in appearance, was half play-room, half-cathedral. For there he kept his tin soldiers and a Bridge over the River Kwai he had inherited—an almost perfect miniature—as well as a kind of altar dedicated to a chicken that he adored. I suspected that Tito used to talk to that chicken. Often, as I crept up to the hut, I would see his lips move as he sat opposite that singular pet. I was almost sure the boy confided in it, for on more than one occasion, I witnessed the moment when, after making the same movements with his lips—possibly performing some act of thanksgiving—the boy would pick up the egg that the chicken left there each afternoon and suck it with great pleasure and enjoyment, first carefully piercing it with a pin. He performed this ceremony every day for a fairly long period of time, an enigmatic ritual that I occasionally watched, hidden behind the bush, glimpsing what details I could of that mysterious encounter with the rough, feathered creature on which, as far as I could see from my awkward viewing point, Tito showered every affection.

On that day, as I approached the hut and the bush and was just about to take up my ideal position for spying—always hoping to get some definitive confirmation of my suspicion that there, in the solitude of the hut, the wretched boy did in fact speak—I noticed a rather ethereal body moving swiftly around in the undergrowth, keeping just behind me.

When I turned around, startled, I could see nothing; but I felt the leaves brushing against me, and shortly afterward, my ear drum was nearly pierced by that terrifying noise, like the shriek of a stupid, unfeeling bat. Again it was as if a goad had been stuck into me; an incredibly shrill note was drilling into my head. I turned around again and saw Tito nonchalantly standing there, cradling the chicken in his arms, smiling at me, then biting his nails in that irritating way, not raising his finger to his mouth, but lowering it, the palm of his hand facing me, his elbow lifted, as if performing some act of thanksgiving.

"Was it you who made that noise?" I asked, still trembling. He gave an odd lunge toward me and tried to bite my ear. "Was it you who made that horrible, savage, monstrous noise?" I asked again.

Tito exchanged his smile for a far less innocent expression, which I would describe as extraordinarily somber. He began sending me strange greetings from the depths of his sinister soul. He began giving me the horrific look that he used only on certain occasions and which was always accompanied by a terrible twitching of the eyelids.

That aggressive, flickering look was most unpleasant, and, knowing what it meant, I felt even more terrified. It was the extraordinarily aggressive stare that he reserved, for example, for any visitors we had—relatives and friends who would ask him, Why won't you speak? Why so silent, sweetheart? That is what they used to say at first, but then they lost interest and their visits became less frequent. I suppose they grew tired of feeling like perfect fools in the eyes of the silent child who was always standing at the door of the room, scornfully observing everything from some corner in the shadows, standing impertinently still in a doorway, staring fiercely at the visitors, who began to feel more and more uncomfortable about coming to see me because they knew very well what awaited them: apart from the pleasure of fussing over poor, sweet Inesita, there would be the unbearable ferocity of the little dumb tyrant, who seemed to be regarding them as if they were poor, misguided cretins.

It was a real mystery how, once those relatives and friends had left, he could switch, in a matter of seconds, from that terrible, ferocious gaze to a blank stare that was lost in the most absolute of voids. But the greatest mystery of all remained why he would not speak.

I soon reached the conclusion that no one and nothing could help me. No one and nothing, and I began to feel more alone and more anxious than I had when, as a very young woman, I had gone to Madrid to study. More alone and more anxious than in the now far-off days when I met the man who would become Tito's father.

I remember almost every detail about the morning I met him; I know that I will never forget it. I had gone into the student café of the law department, aware, yet again, that I must get myself a boyfriend as soon as possible. My family was on a downward slide financially and had sent me to Madrid in the vague hope that I might find my own solution to the grim future awaiting me. That morning, as on every morning since I had enrolled for a degree I knew I would never finish—I would rather have been a nun than a lawyer—I went into the law-department café not expecting to have any more luck than on previous days. I was with a poor, incredibly ugly girl, who knew nothing about life and nothing about me, and who, out of sheer ignorance, had failed to notice what everyone else in my class had: that I was looking desperately for a boyfriend. There were many others in my situation, which was at once a consolation and an annoying source of competition.

I ordered the usual hideous sandwich made out of disgusting, thin bread, with poor-quality cheese spilling out on all sides, threatening my carefully painted fingernails. As happened every morning, I had the clear feeling that I was wasting my time and that I would be better off enrolling in another department; after one term, I had got everything I could out of the law department: four outings with a boy who sang in a group with other students, including picnics by the river, and really very little else—an extremely poor result. I had pretty much seen how the land lay and I knew that my hopes of progressing in life went no further than that awful café full of bored would-be lawyers.

We were eating our pathetic sandwiches with our overcoats over our shoulders because it was always freezing in that ghastly café, and staring vacantly at the ponderous volumes on criminal law that I knew I would never read, our lips lightly shaded by some none-too-seductive lipstick, me on the hunt for a boyfriend, my ugly-as-sin friend on the hunt for nothing, when the waiter suddenly brought me a note from someone at a distant table. He explained—to make things quite clear from the start—that the note was intended exclusively for me.

"Who's it from?" I asked, feigning indifference.

He pointed to a young man I had never seen before and who was smiling at me in the most cheerful and shameless fashion. He looked like a fourth- or even fifth-year student, possibly even a graduate, but at that moment—in those days I already always thought the worst and now I do even more, though that's less surprising given my circumstances—it occurred to me that the note might be part of a bet between two male students or some stupid trick of the kind I had seen in a movie called *Calle Mayor*, and perhaps they were just making fun of my abject, provincial misfortune. Nevertheless, pretending to be greatly put out by such boldness, I opened the envelope and found a brief message, which, in time, seemed to foreshadow the tragedy Fate had reserved for me, and which, at that moment, I even read out loud:

"Greetings from Dante."

I looked at him as if to say I'm not that kind of girl, and, what's more, your name isn't Dante, or do you take me for a fool? Dante's the name of a poet! He gave me a studied smile, learned—as I now know—from actors in art movies; he kept smiling at me seductively from his distant table, and I began to find him interesting—different from other people, as a song by the Cinco Latinos put it. I was glad when he came over and provided us with documentary evidence that his name really was Dante; he explained that his mother was from Málaga, but that his father had been born in Bellagio, on the shores of Lake Como, in northern Italy.

"Italy," I said, filled with fascination for the word and for the country. I always felt an immediate fascination for anything I didn't know, which meant I was fascinated by almost everything because I knew almost nothing apart from the overwhelming tedium of my home town of Salamanca and a few bars in Madrid that served potato omelettes and whose floors were strewn with discarded prawn shells and toothpicks.

"Yes, Italy," he said triumphantly and began to talk nonstop. He had only four more subjects to complete his degree. His main *hobby*—an English word I hadn't heard before—was pop music, and the Beatles were his favorite group. He loved reading too. Kafka, he said. One of his stories is about an insect, he explained to us, and the Beatles, translated into Spanish, are a kind of insect. Kafka and the Beatles were the greatest figures of the twentieth century. The century of the insect, he concluded, as if he were being terribly witty. But neither my friend nor I had understood a word of what he was saying.

"And what do you really like best?" I managed to ask him.

"I can tell you what I like least. Beaches. Or, rather, the people you see on beaches, with their convex figures and dark bellies. The summer's an absolute nightmare."

It seemed to me he was trying very hard to be original. I laughed. When I think of that day, what I remember most of all is how much Dante talked, which is why I find it so hard to understand why his wretched son finds it so difficult to do likewise.

"What I hate," Dante went on, "is seeing those people all vulgarly crammed together like sardines on beaches that are not only filthy, but utterly repellent."

And since he couldn't stop speaking, he explained that if he lay still on the burning sand with the sun beating down on him, he ran the risk of exploding like a bomb.

"There comes a point," he said, "when I just have to get up and go plunge straight into the water. But since I don't know how to swim, I immediately sink. I put my feet into the water and it feels like ice, the water creeps up to my knees, and when it reaches my belly, it's just terrible. The worst thing, though, is all those people watching you and laughing to themselves, thinking you're just a common little coward. That's enough to make me walk straight back up the beach, scorching my feet on the sand. I shut myself up inside my beach hut, and feel like bursting into tears."

He loved to talk, and he especially liked to say things that seemed unusual; this was a time when it was considered very important to be original. He liked to talk and, at first, it seemed that he was only capable of uttering banalities; but soon, that same morning, when we had got to know each other a bit better, he showed that he could also be quite metaphysical. I remember—probably because it seemed to foreshadow something that would affect us later on—the long speech he made about how we humans are all carriers of inner devils, of poisons, that can undermine our marvelous achievements.

My girlfriend eventually left us alone. Maybe Dante's transcendental tone of voice frightened her. But he and I quickly became close friends. He told me all about his family, focusing especially on his father, a Fascist who had died at the end of the war trying to help the Duce to escape. His father filled him with disgust, he utterly rejected his illiterate ideas and, perhaps because of that, he was more and more in favor—and he said this cautiously in a half-whisper—of allowing the wind of freedom, as well as ideas of a democratic nature, to sweep through this university.

He talked and talked for a long time. He said the day wasn't far off when the whole university would rise up in revolt. He said this very close to my ear, which he took the opportunity to kiss; this really shocked me, because I had no idea that ears were kissable. He said that he believed—and he spoke in very lofty tones—in an end to man's exploitation of man and he told me about the Council that had taken place in the Vatican, about a march by black Americans in defense of racial equality, about a Catalan abbot who had come into conflict with the dictator. Everything I was hearing seemed new to me, and this continued in the days that followed; the novelties kept multiplying, thanks to this person who, with great dedication, was inculcating me with all these very advanced ideas which were gradually turning me into a new woman—modern some might say—a woman bewitched and in love with this man whom I knew right from the first moment would be my husband.

We got married in Madrid. Dante wore jeans and no tie and I—oh, scandal!—wore a miniskirt—a very modest one, but a miniskirt nonetheless—from Carnaby Street. Inesita was born nine months later, and a year after that came the monster whom we, caught up in the foolish thrill of parenthood, immediately called Dantito. After four years in Madrid, in Costanilla de Santiago, we moved to Salamanca, to the house in Plaza de San Boal where the boy first began to show an inclination toward mutism and malice.

Until the appearance of those first alarming symptoms, our life was fairly happy. It was, I think, the life of a couple trying to make the most of things in difficult times, the life of a progressive couple, cheerful fornicators, keen on the cinema and opposed to the dictatorship. Who doesn't remember the days when they were happy? I think that period lasted about five years, and, during that time, my relationship with Dante was, without a doubt, like a great dream. Alas, that period will never again return, however close—perhaps very close—poor Dante's freedom might seem, however close the amnesty that will allow him to return home, not to the house in Plaza de San Boal, which, sadly, I had to leave, but to this apartment building in Avenida de Portugal.

Now, nothing can ever be the way it used to be. Today, Dante is a broken man embittered by his years behind bars, and, above all, by his silent son, who was, at first, his obsession and then his perdition.

Our appropriately named Dantesque road toward Evil began when the boy, quite apart from his obstinate silence, began to reveal a great talent for domestic terrorism, that is, when he began sending out signals as sinister as they were perturbing, in addition to that habitual and barely perceptible twitch of the eyelids.

Aside from that shriek that seemed to come from some particularly stupid and unfeeling bat—I've never known for sure if it came from him or from myself, from the tormented soul of a desperate mother—these disturbing signals took the form—and they still do—of such actions as: destroying every living creature in the fish bowl, smearing India ink over his poor sister's dolls, biting my ears, stealing from the building superintendent, sticking pins in the maid's cheeks, and making endless drawings of tanks and pistols.

It is all so sad that sometimes—I suppose in order to escape such horror—I dream that I am with my son, feeling wildly happy, sitting smiling on a train, both of us leading a happy, normal life.

In the dream, Dantito turns his head to look at someone, but because I don't like him to do that, I say to him:

"Why are you looking at that man?"

"Because I can see him talking to himself," he replies, for in the dream my son talks.

"Well, stop it. No one else is looking at him."

"I know, poor thing, that's why I'm looking at him."

"And what's it got to do with you? It's his business. There are lots of mad people who talk to themselves on trains."

Usually, after I have made some such remark, the child bites me savagely on the ear or starts talking to a gigantic red hen that he ends up eating, or else he makes horrible clicking noises with his tongue, and then the dream ends abruptly and I return to reality.

The reality is that, up until yesterday, fool that I am, I have always treated Tito like royalty—or like a tyrant, which comes to the same thing—taking him his breakfast in bed, cutting up his meat for him at mealtimes, reading him instructive bedtime stories, and hoping, at some point, that he will finally be infected by the human word, and I will forgive him all his diabolical actions—in short, doing everything possible to make him happy and return him to the straight and narrow, loving him because he is my son, loving him as only a mother can, clutching at his soul with my pain and anxiety, always trusting that one day he will change, through his mother's limitless love.

"You're spoiling that child," Dante often warned me.

One night, after making precisely that comment, he added:

"He's not our son."

"You know perfectly well he is."

"I mean, he is," he said, "but I wish he weren't."

Because Dante has always loved to talk—though now he likes it less—I assumed he was just saying that, but I soon realized he was extremely worried, and with good reason.

The child's hostility toward his father had reached new heights that day: Tito had been throwing lighted matches at him, emptied the fish bowl over him, smeared oil all over his pants, bitten him on the leg, and he had used him as a target for his latest and most effective slingshot, the fruit of his malign ingenuity.

"Have you ever noticed his left eye? Of course you have, you've just never wanted to mention it," he said, looking ever more somber and anxious.

"Of course I've noticed."

"His left eye is really strange."

"It's smaller than his right eye."

"And sometimes it twitches."

"I know what you're going to say. For some time that twitching has been getting worse and now it's much more noticeable."

"Ever since he's had that twitch, he's been making my life even more of a misery. He wants me out of this house, I'm sure of it. What happened today was just intolerable."

"Don't worry about it, just forget it."

"I'm sure he knows how to speak. He's a monster."

"Don't worry about it," I said again.

"I can't help it. You see, that physical tic … And it would be just that, a twitch, a physical tic, if it weren't for the fact that my father had it too."

"What do you mean by that?"

"I think his evil tendencies are intimately bound up with that small physical tic."

"I'm not sure I understand."

"I'm talking now about something terrible that lies in the very depths of the human soul."

We were silent for a moment.

"I think I understand," I said.

"I'm talking about poison in the blood. That twitch and that ancient poison are intimately linked. It's exactly what used to happen with my father. Unfortunately, it's not a new experience for me. It's an irregularity of the spirit which is painfully familiar."

"Now that I think about it, it does seem to me that when his eye twitches like that"—and I almost trembled as I said this—"he's sending us some sort of greeting from the depths of his silence."

"From the depths of his dark, black consciousness," added Dante, and he remained plunged in a sadness and sorrow from which he would never emerge.

During the days that followed, the child's hostility toward his father increased. He kept sticking out his tongue at him and parading the fact that he was putting the finishing touches to a slingshot that would be at once definitive and sublimely criminal. There was a point where it became very clear that, behind the shield of his silence, his one aim was to drive his father out of the house. If that was his objective, he fully achieved it, and he did so, moreover, in exchange for a great many slaps and periods spent in dark rooms.

Tito achieved his objective, for his father went out of his mind, and committed the unforgivable folly of openly distributing some clandestine propaganda. Throwing himself into his task with such excessive zeal—I'd like to think he did so out of pure despair over his savage, silent son—he had the brilliant idea of shouting out the most subversive ideas contained in his pamphlets in the middle of the Plaza Mayor, and that led to his confinement in jail where he continues to rot, even though, with the death of the dictator, he now has some prospect—not exactly promising, but a prospect nonetheless—of being granted early release and being able to walk the streets of Salamanca again and seeing the apartment where we moved after having to sell the house in Plaza de San Boal. We live in a rented apartment now, scraping a very precarious living since Dante went to prison.

By the way, I tried to make sure the boy received his proper punishment. On the day we were due to leave the house in Plaza de San Boal, I chopped off our chicken's head and made Tito eat the chicken. It was the last lunch we had at the oak table, which I had inherited and would have to sell along with the house. Imagine my surprise when the boy not only happily ate the chicken, he also wiped his plate clean, blithely asking for seconds. He seemed delighted to be eating the one living creature with whom he had ever spoken.

When he had finished, he sat there, looking angelic, waiting for dessert. Such was the innocence in his eyes that the atmosphere in the room grew strangely calm, the kind of atmosphere one expects to be interrupted by a bomb exploding or by some grave event. I thought that, at any moment, there might be a recurrence of that awful bat shriek that had already pierced my eardrums on two previous occasions, but there was nothing like that. Perhaps I had imagined that shriek. The boy was looking across at me as if he had never broken a single plate, belching contentedly after having just eaten his best friend.

He is a small, unbearable tyrant, but my relatives and friends—the few who still have the courage to come here and endure the boy's disquieting gaze, as he sits on the throne he himself has placed at the door of the living room—they know only his resolute silence, thinking that his resolute mutism is all that has tormented me for the last ten years. In an attempt to soothe my anxiety, they assure me that everything is fine.

But they don't know what happened yesterday.

The dictator's funeral was being shown on television. Franco's coffin was just about to be lowered into the deepest, blackest hole in Valle de los Caídos. The boy was watching all this with a strange mixture of fascination and concern. "At least he's quiet," I thought, speculating at the same time on the possibility of an amnesty that would return my husband to me. These speculations gave me such hope and strength that, filled with sudden optimism, I even sang a song by Serrat. I started singing it in the kitchen, assuming that the boy was still sitting quietly in the dining room in front of the television. Suddenly I heard a strange noise and thinking—with utter terror—that it might be that terrifying bat again, I slowly turned around, prepared for the worst. Behind me was the boy with his slingshot in his hand and a look of deep displeasure on his face, a look directed—at least this is how I interpreted it—at what he had read in my thoughts: my happiness at Dante's possible return home.

"Don't you want to watch the TV anymore?" I asked.

Wearing his usual impertinent gaze, he stood absolutely still in the doorway, as if reproaching me for hoping that Dante would soon recover his freedom.

"Weren't you enjoying what you were watching?"

I noticed that he was covered in goose bumps, like a plucked chicken. Just as, during Franco's lifetime, it became clear that the dictator somehow took on all the stupidity of his admirers and supporters, so my small tyrant—the sad fruit of my womb—seemed to have taken on the flesh of the many chickens he had eaten before and after he had so enthusiastically devoured his chicken friend.

"Come on, don't be silly," I said. "It's time for supper now. Your meal's all ready. I hope you've no complaints on that score."

With all the love of a selfless mother, I served him and Inesita steaming hot soup and chicken croquettes. Since I wasn't hungry, I simply watched them eat, at the same time distractedly following the steps taken in burying the late dictator in the darkest of dark holes in Valle de los Caídos.

When it came to dessert, the boy suddenly shot me a terrible look of protest and defiance.

"Now what's wrong, may I ask?" I said.

He overturned his plate onto the linen tablecloth I had inherited from my mother.

"Whatever's wrong?" I shouted indignantly.

"This crème caramel is an absolute disgrace," he replied.

I was utterly stunned, amazed.

"I see," I said, once I had recovered. "So you can talk after all. You've been deceiving us all these years, haven't you? But why have you waited until today to speak?"

"Because up until now everything was perfect," he said, fixing his gaze on Franco's coffin.

Then his left eye twitched, and he sat there sending me sinister greetings from the very depths of his dark, black, repellent soul.

SALAMANCA, 1975

IDENTIFYING MARKS

America is basically a big circus.
— Walter Benjamin

I remember nothing of that year except that elections were held, and someone, on a night that seemed to me interminable, swore blind that I was Catalan. I continued on my way. I turned a corner. The north wind was blowing hard, and I remembered that, in my youth, I wanted to be many different people and from many different places at the same time, because being only one person seemed too narrow somehow. When I turned another corner and the wind beat against me even harder, I finally understood something I had suspected for a long time. We are too much like ourselves, and the danger is that we end up resembling ourselves too closely. As one's life progresses, the same obsessive, insignificant character takes root. I turned another corner and have still not woken up from the nightmare of waking up from a nightmare and finding that I'm still working in a circus in Oklahoma, and there is no way out.

PORT DE LA SELVA, 1977

THE BOY ON THE SWING

I

An employee of my father's who works in an office very close to mine—a man who is held by everyone to be the most boring and most ordinary person in the world—was unfortunate enough as a young man to be sent to Melilla to do his military service, and there he had what, for him, was an extraordinary experience, which he never tires of recounting, as if nothing else had ever happened to him in his entire life. Since he has never told any other story, the whole office thinks he has no other stories to tell.

He was sent to Melilla and, far from being upset, the Unknown Soldier—that is what I'm going to call him because he has an unspeakable surname, as odd as it is frankly ridiculous, Parikitu, which, according to him, is Czech in origin and which, as well as being ugly (in Catalan, it means "parakeet"), has, I think, affected him his whole life—he took the attitude that what won't kill you makes you strong and that his journey to Melilla might be his chance to live out a passionate love story of the kind he had so admired in the movie *Morocco*. In the last scene of that movie, Marlene Dietrich—who in all her other movies had always been cast in the role of maneater—kicked off her expensive shoes to pursue the handsome legionnaire Gary Cooper in order to share with him, like a humble Bedouin woman, the dangers and discomforts of the desert.

Or so reasoned Soldier—I'm going to call him that for short—when, with admirable optimism, he set off for Melilla, convinced that, far away from my father's gloomy office—he has worked for him for forty years, and no one will be surprised to learn that, in only a few days' time, this slave will be retiring—a love story awaited him in which, for his sake, a beautiful, arrogant woman would end up groveling in the desert dust. However, as soon as he arrived in Melilla, after an absolutely ghastly voyage, he realized that he could expect nothing good of that godforsaken town. Indeed, the sea crossing between Almería and Melilla had already demonstrated to him, with absolute clarity, the gulf that exists between the movies and life, between the cinema and the Spanish army. The voyage was simultaneously calm and rough. Calm because Soldier was the only one on board who had taken seasickness pills and thus remained in a state of perfect beatitude and inner wellbeing, agitated only by an abstract feeling brought on by what was happening around him, that is, the anarchic serial vomiting by officers and men during the whole of that unforgettable night in which he found it impossible to sleep, distracted as he was contemplating the "silent movie" amiably provided by the vomiters (the pills had left him in an excellent mood, but also deaf), and which, albeit spectacular, constituted a depressing prologue to the other movie supposedly awaiting him in Melilla, in the kingdom of Morocco.

Shortly before disembarking, he was overwhelmed, almost to the point of despair, by the sight of a few legionnaires in the town (none of whom bore any resemblance to Gary Cooper), or, rather, by the sight of a collection of scrawny human flotsam, bald and toothless, who were doing their best to provide a warm welcome with a rendition of traditional Spanish music played on fairground trumpets which they would occasionally toss into the air, catch, and then nonchalantly continue with their version of *España cañí*.

Soldier saw at once that he was lost, for to make matters worse, each scrawny legionnaire had thought fit to turn up at the port partnered not by Marlene Dietrich, but by a nanny goat, probably of the wild variety, each decked out in its Sunday best. A nanny goat, said Soldier to himself, and he immediately began thinking about how he could escape. My father's office must, at that moment, have seemed to him a truly marvelous place.

A nanny goat, said Soldier to himself, feeling utterly confused and terrified. And that gave him an idea. In the days that followed, he devoted himself to acting the giddy goat, but as if to indicate that he was a goat for feast days only, not your average workaday animal. He began committing small but noticeable acts of madness each day, for example giving the Arabs he was assigned to search as they crossed the frontier a quick kick in the ass, thus laying the groundwork for his final, carefully planned (and, for him, very painful, because he was always very proper) display of dementia in its purest form, which, if it did not get him expelled from the army, would at least allow him access to a kind of health spa with a formal garden—the military insane asylum in Melilla—and preserve him for some considerable time from the long period of training awaiting him and from the nightmarish barracks known as the Engineers' Regiment, where each morning he was forced to carry out the exhausting task of placing his rifle on his shoulder.

He had already earned quite a reputation for madness when, having gradually increased the number of kicks he dealt out to Arabs crossing the frontier, he decided that the moment had come to mount his spectacular act of total dementia. On that day, he got up an hour earlier than everyone else and, hiding in the barracks pigeon coop, he washed down several seasickness pills with a whole bottle of pernod and smoked a large amount of marijuana, so that by the time military training was due to start, he had no need to pretend to be mad because he was. In that strange, demented state, he had no difficulty at all, right in the middle of the training session, imitating a crow and hurling his rifle at a sapper who was engaged in the daily exercise of singing and marching toward the humble trench.

There was general consternation. Eyebrows were raised, eyes rolled, both on the part of the captain of the company and his long-suffering colleagues.

"Pacaritu!" the captain yelled indignantly.

"Parikitu," Soldier gently corrected him, with the strange, bitter laugh of a nervous, old man, as if there were some mysterious connection between his difficult Czech name and his madness.

"Yes, of course, Parikitu. I want you to pick up that rifle right now," the captain said, somewhat perplexed.

Then, speaking slowly and calmly, Soldier uttered the words—the very simple words—which he had so often practiced in front of the mirror.

"Sir, oh, sir, I'm mad."

And he took one step forward. The captain took two, walked straight over to him, looked him in the eye, as if scrutinizing his mental health, and concluded:

"Mad people never say they're mad."

"That's because they're not as mad as I am," Soldier replied rather haughtily, and was quick to realize that he shouldn't have taken that attitude or given that hasty, entirely unrehearsed response.

He humbly lowered his eyes, then, suddenly, almost like a miracle, a strange trembling shook his body and, at the same time, an even odder phrase came into his head—both things doubtless the result of the explosive mixture of marihuana, fear, pernod, and seasickness pills. The phrase struck him as being truly inspired, though quite why he didn't know, since he had no idea what it meant; from within his genuine madness, it made him weep real, convincing tears as he said it:

"We all know Hong Kong."

Whether inspired or not, there was something very touching and persuasive about the phrase, or about the way he trembled or, quite simply, about the way he said it. The fact is that Soldier was quickly led away to the Military Hospital, to the so-called Annex for the Mad, and there they left him in the care of a second lieutenant, who was studying psychiatry, and a nun, who offered him some cookies.

When the second lieutenant and the nun invited him into the annex, he refused. By then, he was barely aware of the effects of the explosive mixture, but he continued to pretend that he was mad, because he knew it was only his madness that prevented him being sent straight back to the barracks. They decided to leave him at the door of the annex and bade him goodbye, saying they would return.

"Goodbye," said the nun, giving him her last cookie. "You just stand here nice and quiet in the sun. And when you get tired of standing by the door, just remember that inside you have your new home and your new family. You'll find your new friends are all good, kind people."

Soldier wondered if the nun, with her strange way of speaking, wasn't madder than the crazies she cared for.

"Goodbye," said the second lieutenant. "I'll come back in a while, and you and I can have a good chat, all right?"

Soldier, in his role as madman, decided to surprise the future psychiatrist with his reply.

"Goodbye, stupid fly!" he said, brushing away a fly that had conveniently landed on his nose.

They left, looking at him strangely and with real distrust out of the corner of their eyes. Goodbye, second lieutenant, goodbye, nun, and I hope they box your ears on your way down to hell, thought Soldier. And he stayed there in the sun, delighted with life, beneath a perfect African noonday sky, gazing out at the sea beyond the palm trees and at the splendid formal garden.

Around mid-afternoon, he decided to inspect his new home and he saw that there were only five other inmates. Five men with fierce expressions who, the moment they saw him enter, immediately turned away and stood grouped around the window at the far end of the annex, staring with false, forced melancholy at the wall of the brief cul-de-sac outside.

They're a bunch of pretenders this band of madmen and criminals, thought Soldier. But shortly afterward, he saw that they weren't a band at all. For they soon moved away from the window and, as they dispersed, they ceased to be a compact group—madness always tends to difference—and, in keeping with their condition of lost souls, of madmen who could, when they chose, distinguish themselves one from the other, they resumed their fierce expressions.

Soldier's attention was first drawn to a man known as Gin. He was a fellow in his fifties, a sergeant in the legion, whose alcoholic nickname came from his old habit of mixing milk with gin and drinking six or seven liters a day of this singular and intoxicating brew. This man always wore six watches—three on each wrist—and he would wear them all day, striding around inside the annex, from which he never stirred, not even to take the air in the garden, and this despite the fact that he greeted the coming of each new day with great enthusiasm, for when he heard the nun ringing the bell for breakfast, he would comment out loud on how marvelous the light of day seemed to him, and he always did so with the same words:

"What a beautiful morning! Have a good day, sir."

The last phrase was spoken exclusively to himself, the former was addressed to the whole annex. It made no difference if it were hot or cold, or sunny or if the skies over Melilla were cloudy. He always said the same thing and then immediately sat up in bed, and while the nun and her assistant, a very thin, young Moroccan girl, were serving breakfast, he solemnly consulted his watches.

"Let's see what time it is."

And he would sit gazing ecstatically at his six watches, none of which had minute hands.

Soldier used to wake each morning—I know every detail, as you will have noticed—to Gin's watches and the comical remarks made by a Galician called Senén, who was the consummate writer of brief, mischievous messages that would turn up hidden among the breakfast cookies and the glass of milk that were served punctually by the nun and her thin Moroccan assistant.

It occurs to me that any reader who has got this far must be wondering how it is that I know even the most insignificant details of this story, which, by the way, is not, contrary to appearances, just one of those silly adventures belonging to the clichéd world of military service and which are always so over-rated by their protagonists. Well, the answer is simple. I know this story by heart because I've had to listen to it hundreds of times in the office, which means that I cannot only reconstruct it with absolute precision, I can even improve on it; for the fact is that I tell the story—and forgive my immodesty—far better than that slave of my father's, who, until only a short time ago, I believed—as everyone here in the office continues to believe—had no other stories to tell, which was why the poor man always told us the same one. And why do I bother to reconstruct it or improve on it? That's easy enough: it's because, since that wretched supper for four the other night, I am now the one obsessed with the Melilla story, and, believe me, I have good reason to be.

II

I return to the Galician Senén and to those finely honed, mischievous messages that he slipped in among the glasses of milk, the dawn rosary, and the breakfast cookies. One message that Soldier remembers most clearly is this: "Would you be so kind, Señor Parikitu, to grant me an interview, or perhaps you would prefer to receive a daily Slovakian whistle and, with a titter, include it in your innovative treatise, the subject of which no one here understands or ever will? Yours sincerely, Apprehension, for that and no other is the real name of your neighbor in the next bed and in despair."

Senén was, indeed, very apprehensive. But when he wasn't seeing frogs everywhere or feeling excessively apprehensive about the other madmen in the annex—especially the one whom the others called Screwball, who was a real gem, as well as being stupid and profoundly epileptic—Senén was quite a reasonable fellow. He had found a way of enjoying himself, which was, I think, both original and intelligent: writing cryptic messages, all as enigmatically phrased as the one I reproduce above and which, as you can see, even I, by dint of hearing it over and over again, now know by heart.

Senén was the only madman in the annex that one could talk to. He had his eccentricities like everyone else—for example, he thought he could control all the madmen simply by pronouncing in a loud, affected voice the name of some famous composer—but, on the whole, he was perfectly reasonable, and on many unforgettable evenings spent looking out over the garden, Soldier had long, involving conversations with him about life and death.

Soldier even became Senén's staunch ally in the latter's attempts to achieve the near impossible—in fact, he did achieve it once, albeit more by luck than judgment: lulling the wild beasts to sleep, soothing their fevered brains when it was time to turn out the lights in the annex and go to sleep, although there no one slept. It was the same every night. The nun would appear accompanied by her skinny female assistant and, after a hasty Our Father muttered by the inmates, she would turn out the lights. Then a kind of theatrical performance would commence. When the footsteps of the nun and her female assistant were only faint echoes in the distance, the darkness grew even blacker and denser than usual and then one could hear even the weakest beat of the most irrational of anxieties: wild cries, people running up and down the corridors, buckets of cold water being thrown over the epileptic, grunts, songs sung by Bobby Solo (the alleged name of one of the other inmates), heartfelt laments, hysterical hymns (*The Bride of Death*, for example), and other symphonic nightmares that took an eternity to die down.

An unbearable nightly horror, to which Senén managed to put a stop only once —and that was, I think, by pure chance. Taking advantage of a pause in that particular night's intolerable racket— a vile, clamorous game consisting of Bobby Solo being violently beaten at sudden, unpredictable intervals—Senén adopted a loud, affected voice and said very slowly to Soldier, who was in the next bed: "Friend Parikitu, what do you think of Richard Wagner?" And then something strange happened, because it was if his voice rang out in the annex with absolute authority, leaving the wild beasts utterly perplexed, convincing Senén (he said as much to Soldier on innumerable occasions) that the wild beasts couldn't cope with hearing the word "Wagner." I tend to think that, by the same rule of three, it could just as easily have been the word Parikitu, but never mind. They were so terrified by the sound of that intensely musical name that, filled with a sudden fear, they were, in turn, lulled into the deepest of sleeps and soon ceased to be a nuisance that night.

That trick—always supposing it was one—only worked once. But Senén refused to accept this. He became obsessed with the idea that the names of composers might allow him to become the emperor of the annex, the artificer and jealous guardian of the most civilized of nocturnal silences. It was sad to see this otherwise intermittently intelligent, decent man wearing himself out on certain nights by pronouncing the names of all kinds of famous and not so famous composers (in his madness he even mentioned an accordionist from his own village) without achieving anything like the success of the triumphant night of Richard Wagner. Often, when he was in the grip of this obsession—one shouldn't forget that such obsessions have led many to the insane asylum—Soldier tried to help him by revealing to him that behind that senseless obsession lay a cul-de-sac.

On those occasions, Soldier recalled what the fans of a great bullfighter used to sing whenever he temporarily forgot his mastery and made eccentric passes before the bull; Soldier would sing this same song to his friend and neighbor in the dormitory by way of a serious warning with the words: "Senén, Senén/there you go again." But that had no effect, because Senén, the pigheaded creature, clung stubbornly to his obsession, calling out the names of famous and not so famous composers and musicians in the midst of the general, uncontrollable hubbub.

And with each day that passed, Soldier felt happier and happier, and there is no reason to doubt this, since the prospect of returning to the barracks was far worse. The formal garden, the evenings, the dawn rosary (so comforting from the religious point of view), his amiable conversations with Senén, his own extreme idleness … He felt so happy that he began to worry that it might not be long before they discovered he wasn't mad at all, and, given that he wasn't the same man who had made the comment about how we all know Hong Kong, he worried they might return him to the barracks. For each morning, with barely enough time for him to affect a state of profound dementia, they would all be lined up at the door of the annex, and the apprentice psychiatrist would review the madmen, that is, he would review the mood of each inmate by asking, always in a slightly different way, how the patient was feeling that morning. "Are you feeling better today?" he would ask, and it was as if in reality he were asking: "Still as mad as usual, are we?"

Gin would respond: "Much better, sir." Then he would let his gaze wander down to the six wristwatches minus their minute hands thus revealing that he was, in fact, mad and that his madness was incurable. Screwball would say: "Much better. And the proof is that I got here on time." Everyone there knew what Screwball meant; they all knew he was one of those people obsessed with punctuality and, indeed, he demonstrated this each day by always sitting down at the lunch or dinner table before anyone else did.

As soon as Bobby Solo heard the question, he would move his lips as if he were about to burst into song, then, simulating an attack of the hiccups, he would end up saying: "Per-fect." All the inmates said they were much better. Senén would say: "Superlative, sir." "Feeling more cheerful every day, sir," came the reply of the fifth madman, whose real name was Rick, but who was nicknamed Kick because of the way he always kicked the epileptic Screwball.

Everyone said they were much better, all except Soldier, who even then was the most ordinary of men, and who, therefore, experienced serious problems having to pass himself off every day as mad. His common sense told him that if, like the others, he said he was feeling much better, he would be sent straight back to the barracks, which led him to be prudent and to remain anchored to what, from the very start, had proved to be a remark as fortunate as it was mysterious and which had instantly opened the doors of the asylum to him.

"We all know Hong Kong."

Soldier, however, soon came to realize that by repeating that phrase, he risked bringing about his own perdition, because it simply wasn't enough to repeat it every morning unless the words were accompanied by a fiery glance, by strange bodily writhings, general delirium, and with pernod and pills in his belly.... And even then it was hard to imagine that, day after day, such an ordinary man could convince the apprentice psychiatrist when he asked him:

"Are you feeling better today?"

"We all know Hong Kong."

When he began to consider changing the phrase, it was already too late, because the madmen had learned it by heart, and when it was his turn to answer the question during the morning review, his companions would beat him to it, and, as if they all wanted to denounce what, for them, was his obvious sanity, they would all chant together in merciless parody: "We all know Hong Kong." (Here in the office he's seen as the least mad man in the world, as a poor unfortunate, the most ordinary person one could ever hope to meet; everyone sees him like that apart from me, because since his phone call to me last Sunday, I know exactly what my father's poor wretched slave is like.)

And since everything in this world comes to an end, the day arrived which turned out to be Soldier's last day of marvelous exile from the barracks. The apprentice psychiatrist asked him the usual question, and, as had become the norm, the madmen answered for Soldier, saying they all knew Hong Kong.

There was nothing new about this, but what was most unexpected was the reaction of the apprentice psychiatrist, who, turning suddenly to the chorus of madmen, said:

"Of course, lads. We all know Hong Kong intimately. We all know its harbor"—just then he burst into loud guffaws—"its junks, its modern buildings, its sampans, the good Chinese and the bad Chinese. Isn't that right? We all know Hong Kong, don't we?"

Soldier went pale with horror. The apprentice psychiatrist was mad too. And he wasn't alone. The nun and her thin female assistant also began laughing wildly. Everyone there was mad but him. Gin began blithely bumping against the walls. Screwball rang a small bronze bell, as if announcing to him the imminent end of his stay in the annex. Bobby Solo and Kick sang a tuneless calypso. Senén and the apprentice psychiatrist, gripped by a strange fever, wept, laughing at the nun, who had dropped several cartons of cookies on the floor. In the midst of this clamor, Soldier realized he was lost, for there was no room there for an honest, decent man.

Desperate, and in a final attempt to calm the wild beasts of the annex, he even resorted to Senén's obsession.

"Wagner! Richard Wagner! Chopin! Mozart!" he cried.

But no one heard him. The place was in a complete uproar. When all this had died down slightly, the apprentice psychiatrist came over to him and said:

"I'll ask you the question again. And all you have to do is give your usual answer, but I just want to hear it once more. All right?"

"All right," said Soldier, knowing this was the end.

"Are you feeling better today?"

"We all know Hong Kong."

More bumping against walls, more frenzied ringing of bronze bells, more tuneless calypsos and roars of laughter. Complete pandemonium. And an hour later, Soldier was back in the barracks.

We've heard this story thousands of times in the office. Everyone considers Soldier a pathetic creature, one of those gray, almost leaden beings, who, out of an utter lack of experiences to recount, is always repeating the same story from their days doing their military service.

"Go on, tell us again what happened to you in Melilla."

That's how we usually pass the time in the office at that awkward hour when the day's work is done, but we still have to wait for my father to come and tell us we can go home.

Since he is always in the same mood, our man never minds repeating a fragment of the story at random and recounting it exactly as he always has. We listen fairly attentively at first, and then, since we already know the story by heart, we start to make a lot of noise and to fall about laughing. That is how the day's work often ends. Some bump against the walls, others sing tuneless calypsos, and there are even some who pretend to be ringing small bronze bells, and so on until my father comes and gives us permission to leave. It's often like that. Yes, many days at the office end like that.

"Go on, tell us about saying goodbye to the garden."

And Soldier goes and tells us all over again, he tells us the story in those awkward hours, which are like a transitional passage into the void, always at the end of the working day, and every time he tells it to us, we kick up a tremendous racket and roar with laughter and call him Hong Kong.

III

For me, he was Soldier when he told us about his time in the asylum in Melilla. He was Parikitu when I saw him as a poor unfortunate, for forty years my father's most loyal employee. He was Hong Kong when I thought of him as one of those very ordinary people, who, for lack of other experiences, always tells you the same story. Then last Sunday—on one of those awful evenings that seem to drag on forever and which you spend slumped on the sofa knowing that no one, absolutely no one, is going to call, and if, by chance, someone did, your pulse would quicken imagining that something very bad had happened, and you would hurl yourself at the phone believing you were about to hear an announcement of the end of the world— I did, in fact, receive a phone call.

"You get it, will you?" shouted Alicia from the bedroom. "It's bound to be for you."

"Why should it be for me?" I protested, feeling equally disinclined to leave the bedroom I had improvised for myself in the living room.

Both of us, Alicia and myself, were suffering from bad hangovers, because we had spent the previous night desperately celebrating my fortieth birthday with some friends.

"You get it," insisted Alicia.

"Hello," I said, timidly picking up the receiver.

"Is that Señor Esteva?"

It can't be, I told myself. I obviously didn't hear properly. I thought that maybe my hangover had seriously damaged my brain, for I had just heard Hong Kong's voice.

"Señor Esteva?" the voice said again. It was him, there was no doubt about it. It was Hong Kong. I remained floating on a cloud of astonishment and incredulity, filled by a sense of profound embarrassment, a bit like the unease I feel sometimes when I'm walking along and bump into a waiter out of uniform, whose face is familiar but whom I can't place in any particular bar.

"Hello," I said again in the vague hope that it might be a joke, that someone might be pretending to be Hong Kong.

"Who is it?" yelled Alicia from the bedroom.

"It's Parikitu," said the voice. "Your father kindly gave me your phone number. First of all, I wanted to apologize for not wishing you a happy fortieth birthday yesterday. I'm calling with your father's permission."

This wasn't a joke, it was real. Hong Kong himself was phoning me, because, as far as I knew, no one in the office had ever even bothered to imitate his voice. I decided to remain calm and pretend not to be in the least surprised.

"So, Parikitu, is there some emergency?"

"I expect you're surprised that I should presume to phone you ..."

"Not particularly, Parikitu. But why exactly are you calling?"

Despite all my efforts, he could tell I was a bit put out. "The office hasn't burned down, has it?" I joked. "Of course it hasn't. Though it would certainly be funny if it did." (My father's business was fire insurance.) "Now, tell me, Parikitu, what can I do for you?"

It really was extremely odd that he should call me at home. Especially saying that he had my father's permission to do so, because that, I thought, was what he had said.

"I discussed it with your father first," he said, "and he was all for it. Indeed, he said he thoroughly approved of such an initiative, because he's always in favor of improving relations among his employees."

I had no idea what he was talking about, but I felt obliged to clarify one point.

"I'm not just one of my father's employees," I said.

"Who is it?" Alicia yelled again from the bedroom.

"I know that, Señor Esteva. Perhaps I didn't express myself properly. One gets so nervous making a phone call like this.... Now, as you doubtless know, I will be retiring in four days' time. After forty years of service to your father and, of course, to you as well, I would not want just to walk out of the office door. I mean, I don't want to simply retire and feel that's an end to it, that one closes the door for the last time and that's it. For this reason, my wife and I would be most honored if you and your wife, if you ..."

He had run aground, and I helped him out of the mire.

"Calm down, it's all right."

"Well, what I wanted to say was that we would be very pleased if you would accept our warm invitation to dine at our house on a night of your choosing, any night from tonight on. Whichever date suits you best. I know how busy you both are, the first free night you have, any evening would suit us fine."

Callously, I hung up. I was too stunned to say anything. I pretended we had been cut off in order to give myself time to respond and at least have a few seconds to think. I was utterly confused, and my hangover only compounded the feeling. Hearing the sudden silence, Alicia returned to the charge from the bedroom.

"Look, who is it? Is something wrong?"

The telephone rang again. I hadn't had a single second to think.

"It seems we got cut off, Señor Esteva. Anyway, my wife says that you don't have to give us an answer now. We very much hope you will say yes, but I know you have a lot of commitments, so just give me your answer when you can. I just wanted you to know that in our opinion ... I mean that we can think of no greater honor ... In my view, it would be a fitting end to all those years in the trenches. But don't worry, don't let the military metaphor fool you," he said lamely. "Old Hong Kong isn't about to tell you the Melilla story again."

"What the hell is going on?" said Alicia coming into the living room.

"My wife isn't at home right now," I said. "I have to consult her first. She has a lot of work commitments." Alicia has never worked in her life. I was lying through my teeth, but my hangover was giving me wings to try and escape from that situation. "You know, business suppers, meetings, all the usual things you'd associate with the fashion industry."

"Of course, I understand. But as I said"—his voice sounded slightly troubled—"you needn't give me an answer immediately. I just thought it would be best to ask you over the phone, because it's always a bit awkward in the office. It's awkward enough over the phone."

He seemed a bit hurt, not because he thought Alicia was at home, but because he sensed no enthusiasm on my part. I tried to change the subject and inquired about the thing that most intrigued me. I asked if I had heard correctly, if my father really had been pleased about this initiative.

"Yes," said the voice, incredibly sure of itself this time. "Your father wants to usher in a new era of employee relations in the office."

"There you go again," I protested. "I've told you already, I'm not an employee."

I began to wonder if behind all this lay some grave, treacherous act of provocation. On the eve of his retirement, having put up with my father for forty years and with me for twenty, the man wanted his revenge. The way he kept apologizing over and over calmed my suspicions, but did not entirely put my mind at rest. I was agitated, because deep down I knew that, however I tried to deceive myself, I had been my father's employee all my life. Wasn't that what Alicia was always saying whenever she got drunk and started hitting me?

"Who the hell is it?" she shouted, this time standing right by the phone, so there could be no doubt that she was at home.

I thought of telling Hong Kong that my wife had just got back, but then I would have to give an answer to his invitation and I didn't want to do that at all, it would be best to keep putting it off until the man retired and disappeared from sight.

"Señor Esteva, are you there?" I heard him say.

I hung up. With a bit of luck, I told myself, he might think I'm angry with him for calling me an employee, and that way I'll avoid the bother of having to talk to him again. Shortly afterward, the phone rang.

"Goodbye, Hong Kong. No one calls me an employee, least of all you," I said, and hung up again.

Now, I told myself, now he will think I'm angry with him and he won't call back. I felt very pleased with myself for coming up with this excuse and a way out of that embarrassing situation. But the phone rang again.

"Look, Hong Kong," I said, slightly shaken, "don't you understand? You call me an employee, you insult me when I'm sitting comfortably in my own home, and you even suggest that my wife and I should pay you a social visit. I've got just one thing to say to you, Hong Kong: that isn't how one goes about things, do you hear? That isn't how things are done. So if you don't mind ..."

I didn't even give him time to respond. Again, I put the phone down, thinking this will be it, I don't believe he'll bother me again. I was right. There were no more phone calls. Shortly afterward, I told Alicia who I had been talking to. I just told her the name of the caller, nothing more, but that was enough for her to look at me, incredulously of course.

"Good God," she exclaimed, then announced she was going to put a cold compress on her forehead.

"I'm not in the mood for any jokes from Daddy's little employee," she shouted, from the toilet this time. I guessed she had started drinking again.

After lunch, when I least expected it, she returned to the subject.

"Did I hear you right? I thought you said something about that employee of your father's, about that Perroquet fellow. You did tell me," she said, looking at me with deep distrust, "that his name was Perroquet, didn't you? You said that your ancient father's ... I mean your father's ancient Czech employee called. Isn't that right?"

That was the last straw. She was going to hit me, and I would have to defend myself and, as always, try not to hurt her; because that would be worse, much worse. And it was all the fault of that wretch, Hong Kong. I furtively grabbed a silk cushion so I could fend off the first Chinese vase that came flying in my direction. I armed myself too with a great deal of patience. I did my best to avoid a fight and said:

"I wasn't lying. Perroquet did call." In the circumstances, there was no way I was going to tell her his name was actually Parikitu. "And if you'll just calm down, I'll tell you what he wanted, because it's interesting actually. Apparently, my father"—and I said this very grandly—"wishes to introduce a new style of relations between me and his employees."

"You, you say. Well, that really is the limit. Are you trying to provoke me?"

"No, on the contrary, I just want you to calm down." I was using my most persuasive tone of voice; I was telling her this story about Hong Kong in order to distract her. "You're going to like what I'm about to tell you. I gave a flat 'no' to my father's idea, to the idea that Perroquet put to me. I'm against my father's idea of introducing newfangled ideas about employer-employee relations in the office."

"Are you telling me you said 'no' to your father?"

She seemed calmer and even rather pleased.

"That's right. I said 'no' to Perroquet's invitation to dine at his house. Because he invited us to have supper at his house. Both of us. He invited us. To have supper with him and his wife."

She got up from the table. She was clearly undecided whether to throw a vase at me or to go get another cold compress for her forehead. She sat down again, as if overwhelmed by astonishment.

"This is too much. I've never heard anything like it. The Perroquets have invited us to supper? Is that what you're trying to tell me?"

Her sheer perplexity actually helped to calm her. Assuming the threat of a fight was over, I turned on the television. They were showing a documentary about the not very fascinating world of nightingales in captivity. The program plunged Alicia into a state of even greater confusion and perplexity and, gradually, with the inestimable help of alcohol, she fell asleep on the sofa. I seized the opportunity to phone my father. To my surprise, he told me:

"You've got to go to that supper. That man has been loyal to me for forty years. And it would be unforgivable of you to scorn honest Parikitu just because that wife of yours—because I know she's behind this, you can't fool me—just because Alicia is a lazy slob or thinks it's somehow beneath her to visit a modest home ..."

"But you've never shown him any respect ..."

"You must go," he replied in a fearsome tone of voice, at once severe and deeply enigmatic. "There are plenty of reasons why. There are moral reasons, for example. Do you know what morals are? No, of course you don't. You're corrupt and superficial. But you'll go to that supper, because I'm ordering you to. Yes, I know you're forty years old, that you're grown up now, but I have the right to give you orders in serious matters like this. And don't ask me now why this is so serious. You should have realized by now. You've had the odd clue, and, besides, if I say you're going and that I want you to go, that's enough. You'll go, all right? Yes, you'll go!"

IV

I *am* corrupt and superficial, and it really doesn't bother me at all. What does bother me is that my father isn't aging at all well. On Monday morning, when I went into his increasingly gloomy office, I found him wrapped in a blanket, lying on the hideous sofa he's had installed next to the heater, and with the blinds drawn (he's suddenly taken against the Sagrada Familia and can't stand the sight of it any more). In short, he was in a very strange state altogether, bordering on the unhealthy I think, wallowing in what he describes as his terrible loneliness and pain since Mama died.

"Come in, son, come in," he said, comically covering his head with the blanket I'd given him as a present on my return from my honeymoon in Scotland.

"A blanket," I felt obliged to tell him, "is hardly a suitable thing to have in an office."

"Anyone would think you were already running the business, boy. You're not even prepared to wait for me to die first. You're itching to be in charge of the whole thing, aren't you?"

There was an unbearable smell of pipe tobacco, Scottish blanket, and mustiness. And there was a smell, too, of senility.

"How long is it since you let anyone clean up in here?" I asked.

"I don't intend to let anyone clean my tomb from time to time either. And now, my little tadpole"—that was his way of showing some slight affection for me—"listen to me, listen to what your father has to tell you. Come over here, come on."

I stood stock-still in the doorway, not daring to go in. I stood there studying that old man who seemed to be enjoying his decrepitude. I told myself I would never end up like that.

My motionless stance in the doorway must have annoyed him.

"Come here!" he shouted suddenly, hurling the blanket at the blinds.

Feeling troubled, I approached. I felt uneasy. I saw him get up and lean on the desk.

"I suppose you thought I couldn't stand up any more."

I didn't reply.

"Well, as you see, I can. Your father has still got strength enough to tell you a few home truths, whether you like it or not. Because you came here with the idea that I might change my mind about supper at Parikitu's house, isn't that right? You'd like it if my strength had ebbed away completely, and I'd collapsed on the floor, been wrapped up in your wretched Scottish blanket, and carried off to the cemetery. That's what you'd like. But, as usual, I can read your thoughts. So watch your step. I'm still the stronger of the two of us. And you're going to have to go to that supper."

"I just don't understand why," I said.

"Yes, you do, and you're worried about having to tell Alicia that you both have to go. That's all you're worried about, because you know she'll tell you to go to hell. It's shameful how little authority you have over Alicia. No one would think you were my son. But I do have authority over her, and I promise you she'll go to that supper. Tell her if she doesn't go, I won't pay for her expensive little caprices. Tell her if she wants to go on spending more of the allowance you give her for clothes and visits to the hairdresser's, then she knows what she has to do. She'll go to that supper, my little tadpole, you'll see."

Feeling once again profoundly humiliated by my father in matters of money, I bit my lip and lowered my head. I protested timidly, but I protested nonetheless.

"Is this your way of reaffirming your authority? What exactly have you got against Alicia anyway?"

"Everything," he said.

"Is this your way of feeling you're still in charge? By forcing my wife to go to a supper that's of no importance, even to you."

I saw that my father was worse than I had thought, because his reply wasn't just that of a senile old man, it was both crazed and violent.

"Feeling as if I were still in charge? You listen to me, you little wretch. Just because she opened her legs, just because she lifted up her skirts, that filthy sow, that stupid drunkard, you surrendered to her like a fool! And in order to be able to screw her in peace"—he began emphatically stabbing the air with his index finger—"in order to fuck her at your leisure, you profaned your poor mother's memory and lay your father out on this sofa so he couldn't move. Well, perhaps he can move. Your mother dies and your poor father's left a widower with only you to console him, not realizing that you were a traitor and would always behave like one. Your father could never have suspected that only a few days later, because some woman was prepared to spread her legs for you, you would simply abandon him, leaving him entirely alone, hoping that he'd cash in his chips as soon as possible. Is that any way to treat a widowed father? You get married, and all he gets is a rotten Scottish blanket. You strut around Barcelona closing deals that he set up in the first place. You're so full of yourself, you stand before him wearing the enigmatic expression of a man of importance. Is that any way to treat a widowed father, by buying him off with a Scottish blanket? Is that filial love? Get out of here, you wretch, get out of my sight!'

I retreated to the door.

"No, stay," he said. "I need you to be my ally. Be my friend at least in this and I'll forgive you. Go to that supper, make her go with you. Be a man for once and not the puppet of a silly perfumed woman."

He kept leaning forward, stabbing the air with his ridiculous finger, and all I wanted was for him to slump down onto the sofa again after all that leaning forward. I suddenly raised the blinds. The Sagrada Familia reappeared in all the splendor of that February noontide. My father cried out in pure horror at the sight. I lowered the blinds again.

"Fine," I said, "sit in the dark if you want. But I'm telling you, the employees are getting restless. Do you think they like having to come in here and do business with you in this state? If you carry on like this, sitting in this gloom, you're going to end up with a mutiny on your hands."

"And they'll make you their boss, will they? I doubt that very much since they have no confidence in you whatsoever. You're always hoping for a coup d'état. But I'm still the stronger of the two of us, and don't you forget it. Even lying here in the darkness, I'm much stronger than you. It makes me laugh to see you so pale and thin. You haven't turned out like me at all. Do you realize that? You're not a bit like me, and yet you still think you can succeed me. To top it all, and without your knowledge, I've got all your new clients in my pocket."

I looked at his ridiculous pocket, but I still couldn't quite bring myself to laugh at him, not even under my breath. That's because I suddenly remembered his terrible fists when I was a child, those clenched fists that he would thrust into his pockets when I was on the swing. I remembered the equally terrifying iron swing he built for me in the garden of our vacation home. On it, tragically swinging, I had let the iron hours of childhood pass.

"Don't worry," I said, leaving the office, "we'll have supper with your model employee if that is your gracious will."

As I closed the door, I saw Hong Kong himself coming slowly down the corridor, carrying, as always, some enormous files, and heading, with his usual resigned step, toward the office I had just left. Here's the man with only one story, I said to myself. Then I softened. Life hadn't been exactly kind to that poor wretched pensioner-to-be either, I thought. And as I thought that—overcome by a sudden sympathy for the sad, touching figure of this man with only one story—I cursed the whole of humanity, doing so above all because that same humanity invented both slavery and those fire insurance policies, which, along with that terrible childhood swing—on which, by the way, even while I'm saying this, I am, believe it or not, still tragically swinging—have, to put it mildly, destroyed my life.

For a few moments, I wanted everything to go up in flames, but I continued walking calmly along the corridor, until I came level with Hong Kong, who said a reluctant "Good morning" to me as if upset by my treatment of him over the phone the previous day. I looked him up and down as insolently as possible, putting on a very superior air. This was my usual way of getting out of a tight spot like that, of covering up my timidity—and, in that particular case, of ridding myself of a vague feeling of shame, remembering how often I had hung up on him.

Normally, in cases like this, and again out of pure timidity, I end up inflaming the situation still more by responding sourly—in that respect at least I am like my father—by saying really terrible things, whatever comes into my head. But that morning, when I saw Hong Kong, I felt so touched and disarmed that I reacted completely differently.

"You do forgive me, don't you?" I said. "You're a kind man, I can see it in your eyes. It was very rude of me to hang up on you like that. Something just got into me, as it did with your friend in Melilla," I joked rather awkwardly. "You know: 'Senén, Senén, you're doing it again.'"

Hong Kong smiled diplomatically.

"I must tell you," I said, "that my answer today is a resounding 'yes' to your kind invitation of yesterday. Would tomorrow suit you?"

The sooner, the better, I thought. And I said to myself that Alicia would agree with me, for I knew perfectly well that when I told her

147

of my father's threat, she would be the first to demand—after first insulting and trying to hit me—that we go to that wretched supper and not run any foolish risks; because she was, and is, more and more convinced that my father is looking for the slightest pretext—an arbitrary order that I might neglect to carry out, for example—to disinherit me.

"Tomorrow would suit us fine," said Hong Kong. "And say no more about it. It will be a great honor."

He proceeded toward my father's office, and I knew that the smell of pipe tobacco, Scottish blanket, and obstinate mustiness would invade the corridor as soon as he opened the door of that dark cave.

As usual, I saw Hong Kong dozens of times during the day, which is hardly surprising since he spends the day carrying back and forth files containing his measured but implacable reports on presumed arson attacks (his particular specialty). He spent the day giving me enigmatic, knowing smiles that began to bother me when I realized that sooner or later the other office workers would notice this new and unusual communication between us. Hong Kong seemed determined that this should happen and kept smiling at me. My standing in the office was clearly at stake, and, as the day progressed, I reciprocated with increasingly chilly, indifferent looks, which he ignored, bestowing on me instead beaming smiles worthy of a Chinaman, as if wishing to do belated justice to his oriental nickname.

At about seven in the evening, the man who brings around coffee announced, between jokes, that there had been a coup d'état in Madrid. At first, everyone took it for another of his jokes, but as he provided us with more facts, it became clear that it couldn't all be a mere product of his imagination, which was, anyway, pretty minimal, and that what, according to him, was being reported on the radio was probably true.

Some terrorists disguised as civil guards had just stormed Parliament. We were astonished. A coup d'état, everyone kept saying. Even my father showed some interest and, leaving his gloomy office, he ordered someone to buy a radio from the store downstairs—the cheapest one possible—in order to be able to follow the course of events.

A battered radio was brought up and everyone had to listen hard to try to find out what the hell was going on in Madrid. Everyone except me, that is, because I experienced a sudden wave of relief, realizing that this gave me the perfect excuse for not going to that boring supper at Hong Kong's house. Such was my relief that, without realizing it, I got rather carried away and, oblivious to the atmosphere of general consternation, I began gleefully retelling out loud the case of a civil guard who used to traffic in cheese and sugar and whom I followed one afternoon through the streets of Ceuta, curious to know how he spent his free time when he wasn't engaged in trafficking, only to find out that he was happy just to find a bit of shade beneath a vine trellis where he could sit quietly and drink a glass of water.

"A bit of a shady tale really," I concluded. At that precise moment the radio stopped working completely, and I became the focus of the anger and agitation of all the others, who, accusing me of being stupid and inconsiderate, and looking at me as if I were a Chinaman, began addressing *me* as Hong Kong, to my inevitable distress.

V

When I woke up the following morning, the coup d'état was over. Since I had spent the entire night carrying on my back, throughout a prolonged and ghastly nightmare, that wretched iron swing from my childhood, I woke up feeling somewhat stunned and anxious. Alicia told me the rebels had surrendered and remarked:

"So you see, my dear, now there's no coup d'état, we've lost our splendid excuse. We'll just have to go to that supper."

And trying hard not to laugh, she added:

"You'll just have to resign yourself, my dear."

She then burst out into that obscene, erotic, melodious, magnificent laugh of hers.

So early, and drunk already, I said to myself. But at least she was happy, and that was what mattered. It's better this way, I thought. Perhaps my father's threat had had an effect. But that didn't seem to be the only reason why she was unconcerned about going to Hong Kong's house. Another reason soon became clear.

"I've been thinking about it," she said, "and I think it might be quite a laugh. It could even be positively amusing, you know. You and me with Mr and Mrs Wallpaper."

"What do you mean 'Mr and Mrs Wallpaper?'"

"I don't know, that's just how I imagine them. I bet all their walls are papered"—she gave another fascinating ripple of laughter, followed by a hiccup, which I found both highly erotic and rather repellent—"with that paper with tiny flowers on it."

"Yes, I think it might be quite fun too. Besides, I don't intend to spend much time there."

"What would we have done tonight anyway? Just bored ourselves silly at the Nautilus, listening to the same stupid conversations."

The Nautilus is the place where we usually meet up with our friends. I explained that we wouldn't necessarily have to give up our visit to the bar. And I told her my plan: to eat as quickly as possible with no seconds (however good the food), have a coffee and a liqueur, half an hour of after-dinner chat, and out. The shortest supper of the year. And enough—just enough—to please Hong Kong and, above all, my father. And we would still have time to ease our friends' boredom by surprising them with an account of what promised to be a most singular supper.

"But," I said, "you're quite right. It will be a bit of a laugh. Because as you'll see"—I would say anything to encourage her to attend the supper—"it's very easy to make fun of poor Hong Kong."

"And why would you want to do that?"

I smiled faintly. I didn't really know the best way to answer her.

"Don't you do that anyway every day in the office?" she asked mischievously.

We laughed rather conspiratorially while distractedly watching the television, which, at that moment, was showing the first statements being given outside Parliament by the recently freed deputies.

"I had a far worse night than they did," I remarked.

"How come?"

I insisted on regaling Alicia with every tiny, apparently unimportant detail of my awful nightmare about the iron swing with which, for some time now, I have had to do battle in my sleep and in real life.

She, quite rightly, couldn't be bothered to listen and vanished, going off in order to continue drinking behind my back, the same long-suffering back that has had to carry that swing in my dreams.

"Darling," she said a little while later, when I was having my breakfast in the kitchen, "isn't it time you forgot all about that wretched swing? You're worse than Hong Kong and his one story about the asylum in Melilla."

I was being compared to Hong Kong yet again, and I didn't like it at all.

"I wonder what his wife's like," she remarked suddenly.

She had caught me unawares.

"Whose wife?"

"Whose wife do you think? Hong Kong's of course."

"I don't know. I imagine she'll be very ordinary and shaped rather like a meatball. What do you want her to be like?"

'I want her to be like you,' said Alicia, accompanying her remark with her most melodious and erotic laugh that revealed, nonetheless, that she was indeed in an advanced state of drunkenness.

She wouldn't stop laughing, and, in the end, I had no alternative but to stick her head under the shower. And there we made love.

"If we're going to this supper," I said shortly afterward, while I was lovingly drying her hair and she was looking at me half-confused and half-furious, "it would be best if you didn't drink anymore, especially not at this hour in the morning. If you carry on like this, I hate to think what state you'll be in by the time you get to Hong Kong's house."

When I was about to leave for the office, she came with me to the front door. She gave me my briefcase and a kiss and seemed to have calmed down a little.

"You're quite right," she said. "I shouldn't drink. But speaking of drinking, do you think we ought to take them something? I think a bottle of wine would be enough. Or perhaps it would be better not to take anything. Oh, who cares. Anyway, do you think people like them drink wine?"

"I wanted to talk to you about that. I don't think they'll have a drop of alcohol in their house. And if that's the case, we might die of boredom. I think that's reason enough to take them something. But you've got to promise you won't drink it before we go to supper."

She promised.

"Just in case," I continued, "I'd take a bottle of whisky as well. Just in case. Imagine getting there and finding nothing to drink. It would be like a funeral. Two hours with no alcohol could be a bit much. Let's take two bottles of wine, one for each hour we're there, *and* a bottle of whisky. It's best to be prepared for all eventualities."

I made her promise again that she wouldn't drink anything until that night, and, not at all convinced she would keep her promise, I set off for the office, where Hong Kong received me with open arms. I couldn't stand the man. I asked him what date exactly he was due to retire. All I wanted—though now I'm not so sure—was to have him out of my sight.

"In four days' time," he said.

"I asked you for the exact date," I said, raising my voice.

"And I told you," he replied, somewhat startled. "The twenty-eighth of this month. It's the twenty-fourth today, so, as I told you, in four days' time."

I had to bite my tongue and said nothing for the rest of the day. I took no part in any of the dreary conversations about the failed coup d'état. I said nothing when the people from the store downstairs had the nerve to demand payment for the broken radio. I barely spoke to my father either, except to tell him that we were dining with Hong Kong that night and to ask him if he was pleased to have got his own way. As for Hong Kong, I didn't even say anything—much as I wanted to—when, at the end of the day, he waxed even more repetitive than usual with his Melilla story, and feeling sorry for him and more out of habit than anything, we laughed halfheartedly and called him Hong Kong.

As we were leaving, though, I had my first big surprise of the day.

Hong Kong came over to me and, apropos of the failed coup, though without my quite understanding the connection between the two things, he told me that there were times when he felt profoundly Czech, which was hardly surprising since many of his ancestors had been Czech. He said that he was telling me this because he wanted to put an end to the idea, once and for all, that the Czechs give in easily to their enemies.

"Because it isn't quite like that," he explained to my stupefaction, without my asking for any explanation, "it's just that our own peculiar vision of life means that we consider all acts of force to be ephemeral."

That, I think, is more or less what he was saying. That is what I seemed to hear him say, and, as is only natural, I felt both sad and very surprised.

"Where did you read that?" I asked, just to say something, because I was feeling mightily confused.

"I didn't," he said calmly. "It was something I realized when I finally visited Prague for the first time last summer."

"You've been to Prague?"

"Yes, and there I encountered that peculiar vision of life which all Czechs, or, rather, which *all we Czechs* share. It's what you might call a metaphysical vision, if you see what I mean."

"You've really been to Prague? And I'm sorry, but did I hear you correctly, did you just say 'metaphysical?'"

"Oh yes. I can talk about other things than my military service, you know. I said 'metaphysical' and I've been to Prague," Hong Kong said with his most oriental smile.

The second surprise, again of an almost metaphysical nature, awaited me at home. When I arrived, I found Alicia serenely preparing a lemon cake. In a bag were two bottles of white wine and one of whisky.

"A cake for the Perroquets," she said, giving me a kiss. "There's no reason why it should be such an awful experience going to their house. If we choose, we could even enjoy ourselves. After all, the Romans used to amuse themselves with their slaves."

It was truly amazing. She was in an extraordinarily good mood, and I had no intention of contradicting her suggestion that we were like the Romans. I hadn't seen her so happy in ages, although I smelled a rat, and it didn't take me long—after a rapid inspection of her sanctuary, that is, the bathroom—to discover that she was taking uppers again. I didn't mind that much. It was preferable to other things, for example, to her spending the whole day drinking. Pills and a good mood were definitely preferable. But I warned her, without any real hope that she would listen to me, that it was important not to mix pills and alcohol, because she might end up in a worse state than Hong Kong had in Melilla.

"And speaking of Hong Kong," I said, "the man with one story is not such a fool as I thought. He's a bit of a dark horse. He's been to Prague, you know."

She thought I was still trying to encourage her to go to the supper and protested:

"I'm perfectly happy to go to their house. I'm even rather looking forward to it. I think we'll have a terrific time at the home of those *parvemus*, the Perroquets."

"You mean *parvenus*," I said. And while I was correcting her on that point, I thought it might be an opportune moment to tell her that their name was not Perroquet, and so I did. Their real name struck her as enormously funny, almost too funny, and she said it out loud several times, then covered her mouth with her hand, and, shortly afterward, burst out laughing with a laugh that was as contagious as it was erotic and melodious. We made love right there on the sofa, which is our favorite place to do it. And she was still laughing half an hour later, when we reached the house in Plaza Rovira, in the heart of the Gracia district, where Hong Kong and his wife live.

Paquita, his wife, opened the door, asking at the same time if we had had any problem finding the house. She was very thin, with rosy cheeks and sandy-colored hair streaked with gray. She was from Andalusia, which I knew already, but one could tell straight away. Her dark eyes betrayed her, as did her accent. She wore a frilly white apron over her blue woolen dress. Her legs were encased in black stockings with a couple of holes on the knees, revealing white skin. To complete the effect all she needed was a little lace cap. She was dressed as a servant. I could find no reasonable explanation for her dressing like that in her own house. Why would she do that?

As with other questions I've been asking myself since that supper last night, I still haven't found an adequate answer.

"Do come in," Paquita said rather nervously, removing her apron. "No, you're not too early, not at all. We were expecting you. Oh, good gracious, you shouldn't have gone to the trouble of bringing us anything."

"It was no trouble," I said, as I watched Hong Kong approaching, also with the air of a servant, for, although he was wearing an impeccable double-breasted gray suit, he came toward us in the hallway bearing a white-china dish on which were arranged slices of cheese and some crackers, salami (Hungarian, he told me), as well as pickled cucumber cut into the shape of rather strange flowers (Czech, he explained), and plenty of smoked salmon.

By way of greeting, he bowed his head slightly like a butler, and when we had helped ourselves to hors d'oeuvres, he ushered us into the living room, where a slight mustiness, emanating from some ancient objects inhabiting the room suddenly reminded me of the smell in the dark store owned by a Hungarian Jew to which my father used to take me now and then when I was a child. And in a whirl of associations, possibly influenced by Hong Kong's Central European roots, it occurred to me that many interiors in the mysterious city of Prague must be just like this.

VI

I remember that despite the fact that there remained only the faintest echoes of something as enigmatic for a child as a war and the attempted extermination of a race, an invincible sadness still hung around the Hungarian Jew's store, a sadness that seemed to come from somewhere far back in time, and which he tried to attenuate by selling comics, old books, artifacts, and iron bedsteads in the midst of a sour smell that mingled with the evident whiff of suffering and fear that lingered there. Combined with that was a strong smell of incense, lacquer, and the aroma of distant lands and exotic merchandise, which I imagined lay hidden in the foreigner's inaccessible back room: rare books, models of ships, Meissen china, magical trunks, Bengal lights, old portfolios full of engravings and dazzling tales from Cochinchina.

It was in that very back room, on the express orders of my father, and in a matter of only two days, that the iron swing on which I would thereafter spend so many childhood hours was made. The skillful Jew built it with extraordinary speed, and I can still remember the day on which he handed the swing over to my father and assured him it was his finest ever work. That, apparently, is what he said. I was just a child—but that is what my father told me the exiled Hungarian said. I remember, because my father often repeated it to me. I remembered it too when I entered Hong Kong's house and my eyes fell on a detail that stood out amidst the otherwise hideous décor that was pretty much on a par with the proletarian aesthetic that rules in most humble homes. It was something, however, that seen in isolation could have been worthy of any bourgeois interior in the mysterious city of Prague. Two floor-to-ceiling display cabinets entirely crammed with music boxes from all over the world.

Apart from those cabinets, there was nothing else worth looking at. It was all plastic table cloths, flowered wallpaper, and the usual paraphernalia to be found in the home of that class of person. Alicia was so perplexed by the ghastly proletarian aesthetic of the living room that she didn't even notice those extraordinary glass cabinets and the music boxes, which, if one focused exclusively on them, allowed one to forget the vulgarity of the rest and to believe oneself in one of the most sophisticated of Central European salons.

Hong Kong indicated some bottles arranged on a tray on top of the television: vodka, whisky, gin and rum.

"We don't drink ourselves," he said. "We just keep some for visitors."

And he permitted himself what seemed to me a superior smile, as if he were perfectly well aware of how much the two of us, especially Alicia, usually drank. Alicia was oblivious to everything. She had not seen the glass cabinets. And although she had handed over the bag with the drinks in it, she was still nursing the lemon cake in her arms.

Paquita saw this and finally relieved her of the cake. She looked at it as if it were the first cake she had ever seen in her life.

"How very kind of you," she said.

She raised the cake to her face and sniffed it.

Alicia made a grimace of disgust. I pointed out the glass cabinets to her.

"She made the cake herself," I said to Paquita.

Paquita nodded and again sniffed the cake. Again, I became aware of the sour smell in the living room that reminded me of the Hungarian Jew's back room, where they crucified me with an iron swing. Paquita withdrew to the kitchen with the cake.

"What would you like to drink?" asked Hong Kong.

Alicia and I flopped down on the sofa. I got out my cigarettes. "Whisky," we both said, and Hong Kong brought us an ashtray.

"We've never smoked," he said. "But we don't mind other people doing it. The proof is, we've got ashtrays for our guests."

The glass ashtray was in the shape of a saber. I lit my cigarette and dropped the match into the saber hilt.

"It's from Japan," said Hong Kong.

"The Philippines," Paquita said, returning from the kitchen.

"Oh, that's right. I always get confused. Some friends brought it back from Manila, along with two marvelous music boxes containing miniature dancers that whirl around inside the box."

We were clearly not going to be able to avoid a conversation about music boxes.

"You have quite a collection," I said.

"Do you like it?" asked Paquita, turning on the television.

"We're not going to watch TV," Hong Kong explained. "It's just that my wife likes to know which numbers won the lottery."

"Were you asking me," I asked Paquita, "if I liked the collection of music boxes or the television? Because they are, of course, two very different things."

Hong Kong reacted as if he had sensed a note of irony in my words.

"Whenever my wife asks a question, she always refers to two things at once. That's why it's so difficult to answer her."

Alicia couldn't suppress a brief burst of musical laughter. She had just knocked back a whole glass of whisky. For a few moments, I prayed to Providence to make Alicia notice the collection of music boxes and thus find at least one positive aspect to the personality of the owners of that house. If only she had my imagination or my resources and could imagine that we were inside some stately home in Prague. It was easy enough, I said to myself, you just had to look at those two great glass cabinets and forget about the rest. I was convinced that this would help us keep a grip on ourselves. But Alicia could still see only the lottery ticket, the flowery wallpaper, and her hostess raising the lemon cake to her face and sniffing it. She laughed again, this time because she had spotted a well-known bit-part actor on the television.

Hong Kong, perhaps to save the situation, said that he loved the movies. He told us he used to see so many movies a week that, over a period of many years, it was as if he were watching one continuous movie.

"I know all the actors, even the extras," he said, "and I pay special attention to the actors in the minor roles; it's always such fun when you spot one of them."

"Well, lately," said Paquita, "all those faces have started to seem faded, flat, anonymous. I get bored."

Alicia again burst out laughing. She had poured herself another whisky.

"Perhaps it's just that your eyesight's failing," she said and continued laughing.

Paquita seemed quite hurt.

"Oh, come on," said Alicia, trying to smooth things over. "It was only a joke. It's just my way of talking. People who know me, my friends, just ignore me."

"Well," said Hong Kong, "I owe you both an explanation because you belong to a different world and you probably feel a bit out of place here with us, it's only natural. So, first of all, I would just like to thank you for coming. You've made me very happy. You have done an old man a great favor."

"You're not that old, you've just reached retirement age," broke in Alicia, again rather inappropriately.

"I'm old," he said. "She's old. We're old."

"Now don't exaggerate," I said.

He went on: "There's a difference of social class between you and me. There's always been a superficial relationship; after years and years of working together, we hardly know anything about each other. There's nothing to be done about that now, but this supper might serve so that tomorrow, when you think of Parikitu, you will remember that he, too, had a heart. To put it another way, you won't just associate him with that story about Melilla that I often tell in the office."

"I've never heard it," remarked Alicia.

Oh God, I thought. I would have to do something to stop him telling it again. I knew the story by heart. I knew every detail, every blessed detail.

"Have you seen the display cabinets?" I said to Alicia, changing the subject and trying one last time to make her notice the collection of music boxes.

"What's there to look at?" she asked.

"Can't you see? Aren't you interested in music boxes?"

She went very quiet and serious, as if stunned. Whenever she puts on that look of puzzlement, I always want to laugh, but I controlled myself.

"Well, can you see them or can't you?" I insisted.

"We'll be able to eat in about ten minutes," said Paquita. "I've just got to finish making a couple of sauces. I'll go and have a look at them."

I tried to pour oil on troubled waters.

"You were telling me your reasons for inviting us," I said to Hong Kong, "but there's really no need. Believe me, I understand. If you must know, it's a great honor to be invited to celebrate your retirement."

"Yes," said Alicia. "It's a great honor for us that it's a great honor for you that we've come to celebrate your retirement."

Alicia realized she had slipped up again and once more went very serious and quiet. This time I couldn't control myself and laughed out loud. It seemed to me that, despite all my best efforts and my wish for a peaceful supper, things were beginning to go wrong. I tried to put things right again, but Alicia got in before me, and, in her eagerness to put things right herself, she made them even worse.

"Now that you're retiring, Señor Parrakitu, you can speak openly. What do you think of your boss? Don't you think that as both a father and boss he is unnecessarily authoritarian? Although, I must say, that, as a father, that pig is just blindly authoritarian."

After the initial shock, Hong Kong reacted with great aplomb.

"I didn't ask you here in order to speak ill of anyone; on the contrary, I want to strengthen relationships with everyone. Although I would add—and I say this at the moment of my retirement without the slightest rancor—that, as a boss, he is indeed somewhat authoritarian, he is and always has been. But that has fostered discipline among his employees, and the business has prospered. Besides authoritarianism is a sign of a strong character. I only wish I had had a bit more of it myself. I wouldn't be where I am today, not that I'm complaining. I like my collection of music boxes.... But, yes, speaking frankly, he is very authoritarian."

"You don't have to tell me that," I broke in. "He made me spend my entire childhood on an iron swing."

"He is, if you'll permit me to say so, a man of iron," said Hong Kong.

"My husband still dreams about that swing," remarked Alicia.

"It's like one long endless nightmare," I went on. "An iron up-bringing, an iron job, and that wretched iron swing. What a life! But let's not talk about that. I haven't come here to criticize my father either."

They announced the winning number on the television, but there wasn't time to write it down. A small drama ensued. According to Hong Kong, if Paquita didn't get the number, she would become hysterical. When she returned with the food and asked us to sit down, we had to invent a number and give it to her.

As I had foreseen, the supper was very difficult. In order to forget how much Alicia was drinking, I started to drink heavily as well. White wine, pear liqueur, and four whiskies with dessert. Indeed, by the time we reached dessert, Alicia's laugh was at its most melodious—not to say irritatingly repetitive—and she promised to be quiet only if Hong Kong would tell her the Melilla story.

He flatly refused.

"Ask your husband to tell you," he said suddenly.

He was obviously angry. We had doubtless tested his patience to the limit. Especially Alicia. But I had contributed as well with various sarcastic comments born of my amusement at the couple's utter sobriety—they hadn't touched a drop of alcohol. Then Paquita, who hadn't spoken for some time now, apparently wounded by our barbed comments, broke her silence to say that it was one thing, just as they had foreseen would happen, for us to laugh at them and their humble state (in that aside she included our obvious distaste for her onion soup) and quite another for us to continue to insult them without the slightest sign of letting up. She added, suddenly addressing me as "tú":

"You're hurting your father."

Alicia gave a loud guffaw, without knowing what she was laughing at, for, by that stage, she wasn't really aware of anything. That laugh must have angered Paquita still more, because she turned to me and said:

"Listen. You no doubt remember the Melilla story. A thin woman appears in it. The nun's Moroccan assistant. She seems to be a minor character, but she isn't. She could be me, but she's not. I'm thin, but I'm not Moroccan. When my husband was in the asylum, he got her pregnant. He had a child by her. I bet you can't guess who his son is."

"The Aga Khan?" I said jokingly, although I was trying hard to conceal my inevitable agitation.

"No, you're wrong. You are that son," Hong Kong said.

And to my complete amazement—accompanied by the musical backdrop of Alicia's melodious laughter—and as if trying to apologize, he added a remark that filled me with unending dismay:

"I sold you because I was poor."

VII

Sometimes I wonder if I should feel ashamed of the fact that I had always considered Hong Kong to be merely a minor character, just as I had the nun's thin female assistant in Melilla. I think I have been a complete fool. I see all my office colleagues as fools, too, when, even now, they ask about Hong Kong and immediately kick up their usual stupid racket, thinking themselves terribly funny as they chorus:

"We all know Hong Kong."

By this they mean that they all know Hong Kong the man, which seems, at the very least, utter foolishness, especially when I recall that curious moment at supper when—I remember it perfectly and will never forget it—the hitherto discreet Hong Kong saw fit to tell me:

"I sold you because I was poor."

He plunged me into a truly Hamletian state of doubt, with which I am still struggling, swinging back and forth on the most tragic of all swings.

"Your mother died in childbirth," Hong Kong told me. "She had no relatives, just the poor nun with her cookies and her dawn rosary. I can't tell you much more about her. And don't ask me for a photograph, because I haven't any pictures of her. I haven't anything of hers. But, in case you're interested, I can tell you she was a Berber. From a village south of Marrakech. The village had a small mosque with a minaret and a lot of storks nesting on its towers. That's all she told me about it. I don't know anything more. As you can imagine, I didn't love her. It was just a mistake, a complete mess. The nun looked after you initially, so your first steps in the world were taken inside that insane asylum in Melilla that amuses you so much."

I was following his words with incredulity but with dismay too, because I couldn't discount the fact that what he was saying might be true.

"When I was discharged from the army," he went on, "I caught the first boat back to Spain and took you with me to Barcelona, where all that was waiting for me was my job in your father's office. I must confess that more than once during the voyage I thought of throwing you overboard. No one would ever have known. But the profound Catholicism of my Czech ancestors prevented me. Because all I have ever had are my ancestors. That has been one of the most painful facts in my life. Only ancestors from a far-off country. But Czechs are intelligent people, as I discovered on my trip to Prague last year. Not in the least authoritarian, but with a metaphysical vision of life, which makes them consider any political coup d'état as purely ephemeral. Perhaps it's my Czech nature that has helped me get through all these years in which, slowly, I have grown fond of you, not that you have done much to deserve it."

He said that and then began scrutinizing my face, inch by inch.

"Now do you understand why we invited you to supper?" Paquita said.

I was too troubled and preoccupied to answer. I heard all this with a mind enveloped in a dense cloud brought on by the alcohol, and everything seemed to me slightly unreal. As if that weren't enough, I was doing my best to avoid Hong Kong's meticulous, inch-by-inch inspection of my face.

"Why *did* you invite us to supper?" asked Alicia.

"Because he wanted to say goodbye to you," Paquita said to me, "to see you one last time, or, with a little luck, to forge a last-minute friendship with you to have the chance to go on seeing you now and then, to go on seeing his son. He loves you."

"I don't understand one word of this, not one word," said Alicia. She had doubtless noticed that, for some time now, she hadn't been getting any moral support from me for her laughter, and she was making an attempt to rejoin the conversation to find out what the hell was going on, and why everyone was talking so seriously.

"Anyway, let's just leave it," Hong Kong said with a tragic gesture, surprisingly histrionic for a discreet, gray clerk. "There's no point going over and over it. You're my son, but even that means nothing now. Forget it. Look, I'm going to show you something."

He seemed to be on the brink of tears. Perhaps that's why he got up and went over to the display cabinets, possibly in order not to cry. He returned bearing a splendid music box, on the lid of which were miniatures of three famous Prague automata. In the eighteenth century, Hong Kong explained, a fine clockmaker lived in the city, the disciple of a famous Swiss clockmaker. The moving figures represent a scribe, a draftsman, and a harpsichordist. The music box was the pride of the city, but it got lost somewhere on one of the long tours around Europe of these masterpieces. But in Prague the people never forgot about the existence of those three sons lost in the world, and sometimes advertisements would be placed in local newspapers abroad asking for news of their whereabouts. At the beginning of this century, the music box was found and brought back to Prague. It is also said that the three sons had a life of their own, and that it was they themselves who wanted to come back to their homeland.

"I should also tell you," said Hong Kong, concluding what appeared to be a metaphor on the theme of the prodigal son, "that just like the original automaton, what the scribe on my music box is writing in eighteenth-century calligraphy are these words: 'We will never leave our homeland again.'"

Alcohol makes us sincere. It also makes us believe what others tell us. I was more and more convinced that, however surprising it might seem, Hong Kong was telling me the truth. I kept remembering my father in the office saying to me: No one would think you were a son of mine.

"Is that the most valuable piece in your collection?" I asked, simply in order to say something.

He nodded.

I was still going over everything he had told me before showing me that valuable piece from his collection.

"Did you really want to throw me overboard?"

"What was I supposed to do?" he said at once, clearly eager to continue talking to me about the drama of being a father.

"You don't know what it was like for him arriving back in Barcelona with you in tow," said Paquita.

"A single father then faced nothing but problems. I came back to a post-war Spain at its lowest ebb. Luckily, I had a job. Your father's office was there waiting for me. At least I had work, thank God. But everything else was a complete mess: madness, disaster, ration cards, depression. Preparing baby's bottles, you waking up crying in the middle of the night, my appalling reputation in the boarding house where I lived, having to conceal the fact that I was a father from people at work. One day, I just couldn't take it anymore and burst into tears in the office of the man you have always thought of as your father. Yes, I broke down in tears like a child. I told him what was wrong and, after a few days, he came up with a solution. He explained that his wife was infertile, that adopting children was very difficult in Spain and he offered to buy my son from me."

Hong Kong covered his face with his hands.

"Did I hear correctly?" asked Alicia. "Are they going to adopt a son?"

When she heard that, Paquita also covered her face with her hands. As if she were sniffing the lemon cake, a cake, by the way, that we had already eaten.

Damn Hong Kong, the man with only one story to tell. That is what I thought when I saw that he wanted to go on talking as if his life depended on it.

"I'll buy your baby. That's what your dear father said to me," he went on, becoming increasingly upset, especially as he reached this part of the story. "I told him my son wasn't for sale. 'Then you'll lose your job,' he replied. And he offered me a sum of money and the promise that I could continue working in this office until you were older. He even increased my salary. That was what decided it for me"—again he covered his face with his hands—"and I sold you."

I began—and who, in my place, wouldn't have done the same?—to drink like a fish. I punctuated each sentence uttered by Hong Kong with large gulps of wine. He would still occasionally carry out that inch-by-inch scrutiny of my face, or of the expression on my face, I no longer knew exactly what he was studying, but he was as meticulous in that as he was in telling the story.

"I sold you because I was poor. Eventually I came to regret what I had done, and the pain of remorse was compounded by the almost absolute certainty that I would never get you back, because I knew I couldn't risk telling you the truth, because that would have meant automatic dismissal. And life in post-war Spain was very hard. Besides, when you were seven, your father, or, rather, the Authoritarian, as I like to call him, renewed the contract. When you first started swinging miserably back and forth on that iron swing, he renewed the contract and bought my definitive silence with a very large sum of money which I needed at the time to pay off a dangerously large gambling debt, because, in order to forget my sorrows"—again he hid his face in his hands—"I had sought solace in secret poker games and lost money hand over fist, and, what was worse, I had lost you forever."

He broke into loud, convulsive—I would say spectacular—sobs. The Prague music box fell to the floor and a lovely melody began to play, a gypsy melody, or perhaps it was something Czech. And to put the final touch to what I, by then, was hoping against hope was pure fiction—nothing but a subtle act of revenge on the part of the Parikitus, at least that was what I was praying to divine Providence for—he said that life had been very bad to him, very bad indeed.

"Very bad," repeated Alicia.

Paquita put her hands to her head and then carried the plates out to the kitchen.

"Very bad indeed, Señor Parruqué," said Alicia. "Awful in fact. I mean you didn't even give us napkins."

I felt that the time had come for us to leave. I was still relatively lucid, and I thought it best to withdraw sooner rather than later. I left convinced—I needed to believe it was so—that they had simply been making fun of us. Yes, they had been making fun of us, and, later on, I would put the blame for that on Alicia. I remember that they accompanied us to the door. I remember everything about that night, and I tremble. I will never forget it. I remember how Hong Kong, standing out in Plaza Rovira, kept scrutinizing my face inch by inch. And the two of them innocently said good night to us when we had already got into the car. Hong Kong insisted on giving me the music box from Prague. He even said to me:

"Go back to your homeland."

As we moved off in the car, Alicia sat very close to me. We went straight home without stopping at the Nautilus and kept a rigorous, cautious silence. Arriving home, I looked in the mirror and saw my beard, and saw too my Berber face.

I still catch sight of that Berber face now and then, but I decided not to tell my father about any of this, because, if it turned out to be true, if I really were Hong Kong's son, I would automatically be disinherited. But if I weren't, and if I asked my father if he was, in fact, my father, he might disinherit me anyway for being so distrustful. Alicia says that everything I've told her about that supper is a lie and that the only thing she noticed was the Parruquets' uncontrollable drinking and, worse, their failure to appreciate her lemon cake. She also says my father has always been my father, and that's that.

I don't see it quite so clearly though. My two fathers have condemned me to go back and forth, in a permanent, eternal state of doubt, on the most uncomfortable iron swing in the world. Seated on this swing, I have spent two whole days telling myself, bit by bit, this story that is driving me mad. I can hear the tragic, obsessive creak of the swing even in my dreams.

Hong Kong retired today. He came and said goodbye to me a little while ago.

"I'm so sorry," he said. "Give my regards to your wife. Goodbye."

My colleagues asked me what the poor man was so sorry about.

They also asked why he had passed on his regards to my wife. I had to come up with something quickly, so I told them I had gone to supper at his house—they all froze—and that it was very boring and, apart from having to listen to Hong Kong telling the story of the Melilla asylum, all over again and with no variation, the onion soup had been absolutely disgusting. They made an enormous hullabaloo and rolled around laughing, some even bumped blithely against the walls, and all of them called me Hong Kong.

BARCELONA, 1981

AN IDLE SOUL

It's still dark in the room, apart from the faint glow from the white wooden shutters that Benito Robles is studying with a certain fixity as he lies motionless in bed, listening to his still-sleeping wife's deep, rhythmic breathing.

"Can you hear me, Olga?" he whispers.

There's no reply, nor is it clear that he wanted one. He looks again at the white wooden shutters. Just another day, Benito says to himself. No, now that he thinks of it, it isn't just another day, today is the first of May, I'd forgotten, International Workers' Day, yes, I'd completely forgotten. That is what he's thinking as he recalls the day he moved to Meudon, next to the Renault factory, close to Paris.

His first years as a political exile had been hard, and the hardest thing of all was not knowing if he would ever be able to go back home. He spent all his free time—which wasn't very much—envying those voluntary exiles, the rich kids he would see sitting outside the cafés in the Latin Quarter of Paris and who, should they ever be seized by a sudden fancy or caprice, could go back to Spain whenever they chose.

And what if fate had ordained that he should live forever in a country not his? Let's hope that isn't the case, Benito says to himself now. Let's hope. You can feel like a foreigner in your own country, but that isn't as bad as being a permanent foreigner in another country. That's really bad, thinks Benito, resuming his study of the faint glow emanating from the wooden shutters in this room. Olga's rhythmic breathing is beginning to punctuate his painful evocation of those years of enforced exile that were brought about by the feeling of dread that filled him when he realized it was highly likely he would be accused of planting a bomb in the offices of the right-wing newspaper *El Pensamiento Navarro*. A more than justified feeling, because Benito *had* planted that bomb. Even now he's surprised at his own sangfroid when he left the device in a washroom and walked out onto the Plaza del Castillo—a square whose name always reminded him vaguely of the town where he was born, Valderrobres, with its imposing castle looking out over the Matarraña valley—there he bought a magazine, ordered an ice-cold beer, thought fleetingly of his father, who had been a fireman all his life, thought bitterly of the plight of the workers, took a sip of beer, opened his magazine, and sat waiting, as cool as you like, for the offices of *El Pensamiento Navarro* finally to be blown to pieces, and when this happened, he calmly put away the magazine he'd been pretending to read, drank the rest of his beer, and, reluctant and resigned, set off toward the ever-enigmatic horizon of absolute exile. Since then—and that was twelve or fourteen years ago, I'm not quite sure, I seem to have lost track—he has been waiting in Meudon for the dictator to die.

Four months ago, a car bomb killed an admiral who used to praise the tyrant with the singular enthusiasm of the very devout, and Benito thought then that perhaps there would be brighter prospects for exiles like him; but nothing changed, and Benito's hopes have gradually been fading, as slowly as the glow from the white wooden shutters is beginning to dissolve in the diffuse light of this morning on the first of May in this—I would go so far as to describe as "dramatic"—bedroom .

Soon he begins to hear the first sounds of the awakening house. A door slamming shut, footsteps on the stairs, a door opening, someone coughing and wheezing, a tap being turned on, the water in the pipes, and it's as if the walls of the room were murmuring. Perhaps someone's turned on another tap, thinks Benito. The taps are always the first to wake up. A car drives along the nearby highway, heading for Paris. Then a truck passes, and Benito imagines—although he knows perfectly well it isn't true—that it's full of workers and red flags. He tries to time how long the tap has been left on, but stops to recall the splendid dream he just had during one of the most dream-filled nights of his life.

"What a shame I woke up," he whispers to his wife.

Olga turns over in bed, but otherwise barely reacts, and continues breathing deeply and rhythmically. The morning light is coming into the bedroom now with a certain authority, and Benito amuses himself studying the colors of the paintings that he one day hung on the wall opposite the bed: red and black on a misty gray backdrop, the blue of the Neva river, the grayish green of the sea, the vermilion of the palaces, the febrile bronze of the soldier saint who founded Leningrad, the gray of the narrow streets, the white snow on the Nevsky Prospect, the red flags.

"What a shame I woke up," he says in a slightly louder voice.

Olga stretches slowly, then asks:

"Pleasant dreams, Benito?"

"Pleasant? Oh, you have no idea. I was a scout. I had loads of work. And I was in Spain, working for a soccer club, for the Real Club Deportivo de La Coruña. I had a lot of work and barely a moment's respite. What a dream."

"You said it: a dream."

"Yes, but a fantastic dream."

"And what exactly is a scout?"

He looks at her as if to say, you know nothing, my love. Another truck goes by, and Benito imagines it full of shepherds and their sheep—knowing perfectly well that it isn't. She sighs and leaps out of bed, takes off her green pyjamas, and goes to the bathroom. He seems offended by her lack of interest in his splendid working dream.

We're not in Africa—as I said, this is Meudon—but the bed is protected by a mosquito net, a ridiculous—although, to me, rather charming—whim of Olga's. Charming because I *am* the mosquito net. Or, rather, let's just say that I am, because to be honest, I have no idea what I am, I never have. But I don't really know what else I could be, because if there's one thing I'm sure of—much to my regret—it's that I can't see beyond the four walls of this dramatic bedroom. What happens outside this room never enters my field of vision or hearing. It seems that what happens outside has nothing to do with me. I can imagine it, but I would never say what I had imagined, because that would involve describing something I had invented. Anyway, my point of view is definitely modest and limited; it could perfectly well be that of a mosquito net, why not, so let's just say that I *am* the mosquito net, which—however pleased I may be to have an identity—doesn't stop me asking a simple and—I think—logical question: What is a mosquito net doing in Meudon? They're intended for people going to sleep in Africa, not next to the Renault factory, but there's no accounting for tastes and, besides, I'm not about to throw stones at my own glass house, at my own existence, and demand my removal from Olga and Benito's charming home. So I say nothing.

Soon I will fall completely silent. When it rains—which won't be long now, because it'll start pouring down at any moment—when that happens, a red flag will get wet and its color will fade slightly. And then this story will end. In a few minutes' time, Olga and Benito will go out into the street, and it will start to rain. I'm sure that's how it will be. It always rains when they go out. The red of their festive flag will fade. And I won't be able to see it, because that will happen outside the house, and my point of view is very limited; it's the point of view of the humblest mosquito net in Meudon. It will definitely rain. I will then enjoy myself fantasizing about what might be going on outside, but I won't be able to tell you anything more than that. I will speculate and invent in rigorous silence. They say the imagination is a place where it is always raining.

Although I'm not even a poor anonymous citizen, I enjoy talking about what happens in this dramatic bedroom on the outskirts of Paris. I really do, I really love this job that I have created myself in order not to grow too bored, or too desperate. In fact, I adore work in general. Work is the best steed or carriage on which to escape from life. Work, work, work. In that respect, I'm just like Benito, who is mad about work. As a child in that magical town in Teruel called Valderrobres, his mother instilled in him a deep love of work. Work is everything, his mother used to say each night in the shadow of the town's enigmatic castle, pointing out to him, through the open door of a house, the worthy figure of a tinker, who, with a seemingly infantile gesture, was systematically beating away with a hammer.

I love working and, if I do nothing, I immediately fall into a state of quite understandable unease brought on by my sad condition as a mosquito net bought in the African spring of some Paris department store. The only thing that saves me from anxiety is my work transcribing what happens in this dramatic bedroom. Work, work, work. It's the only thing that counts. Escaping from the void. As if ceaselessly banging away with an invisible hammer, and then, when Olga and Benito go off to that May Day demonstration, allowing the silent rain to fall on the wild gauze of my imagination.

"Don't you want to know what a scout is?"

Olga is already in the bathroom putting on her shower cap and doesn't hear.

"Can you hear me, Olga?"

Two trucks go past on the highway to Paris. In the stairwell, there is a brief crescendo in the dance of the taps.

"Ah, just what I needed," she shouts, enjoying the water from the shower.

"I can't hear you. Shout louder."

Through the half-open door of the bathroom, I can see how Olga, after that first blast of hot water, is standing, looking out through the narrow bathroom window at the clouds piling up over the hills on the other side of the valley and beyond the Renault factory. She pinches her chin, comes out of the shower, whistles her favorite mambo, puts on a red dress, and returns to the bedroom.

"I had loads of work to do in my dream," he says. "I just couldn't stop watching keen, young players. I was constantly writing detailed reports about all the promising young players in our club. *Our* soccer clubs, Olga. Because I was in Spain."

She smiles.

"I like to see you happy, Benito."

"It was an endless job, the kind where you can't allow yourself a single break, but, as you know, I like that."

"You do. You must have been delighted to have so much work."

"Of course. Doing a job I enjoyed and being paid for it too. Yes, I had a very good time in that dream."

"I'm pleased for you."

"You were in the dream, too. You came with me to all the stadiums and pointed out the technique of some up-and-coming youngster. It was good to have the old saying confirmed that four eyes are always better than two. Besides," he pauses for a few seconds, thinking, "it was a proper job."

"Well," Olga laughs, "aren't all jobs proper jobs? What do you mean?"

"I mean a job where you can shine. The stars," Benito continues, "always shine, and a scout is a discoverer of stars and shines whenever he finds one."

"Doesn't being a carpenter allow you to shine?"

"Of course. That's another proper job."

I know that Benito, who is obsessed with work, has striven all his life to be a fine workman. What matters to him is being able to justify his existence with a job well done. He's interested in any job that allows someone to produce a good piece of work. Indeed, he'd like to have several different jobs at the same time.

"If I could," he says, "I would happily combine working as a carpenter with working as a talent scout for a soccer club."

"Don't be silly, I don't know, lately you're even dreaming about work, which is really funny."

"Why?"

"Well, there you are dreaming about all that work on the very day we're celebrating International Workers Day."

When he's reminded that it's the First of May, Benito looks suddenly downcast, his face somber. A tense silence follows, and I can imagine why.

"I enjoy working," he says at last, trying to dispel the tension. "I love the smell of wood shavings, the sound of the saw and the hammer. In the workshop, the days just fly by."

He says all this in a deeply melancholy tone, and it's clear that this workaholic wishes he were back in his beloved workshop right now. He's so like me, this man, except, of course, the kind of work we enjoy is very different, because while, for him, life is meaningless except when he's in his workshop, where he can justify his existence with a job well done, for me, his being at work is a real nuisance, it leaves me with nothing to transcribe in this bedroom, by which I mean that when he's working, I'm left high and dry. His wretched obsession with carpentry abandons me to the awful void of existence, or, which comes to the same thing, he not only abandons me to my incredible, rain-filled fantasies, he plunges me into a state of awful vacancy, in every sense of the word.

"I don't know why," says Benito, "but no dream is ever completely, perfectly, totally satisfying. The one I just told you about was magnificent, but it had its dark side."

"Not too dark, I hope," she says.

"No, not too dark, but it really upset me. One of my discoveries was signed up for the first eleven of Deportivo, but just when the season was about to begin, he told me he'd decided to leave soccer for good because he didn't want such a hard, disciplined life when he was only nineteen. He said the idea of starting another season was simply unbearable. He repeated the word several times—unbearable. And what upset me most was that he was my best ever discovery."

"It doesn't matter, Benito. It was only a dream. Why get so upset? Besides, not everyone likes working."

"Unbearable," Benito says again, sunk in grave thoughts as he slowly gets out of bed.

Standing next to the paintings of Leningrad, Olga smiles broadly at him and, attempting to divert him, she changes the subject.

"I had a rather similar dream," she says.

"Really?"

"In my dream, I was a manicurist at a big salon in the center of Paris. Everyone wanted me, and I was utterly contented. In the dream, I was very bright and intelligent, what you might call an egghead, yes, I was a real egghead. I had a different pre-prepared conversation for each of my clients. The economy with M. Dupont, politics with M. Morand, sailing with M. Blanchard. Doesn't that sound great? I had a lot of work to do in my dream too."

"Too much," he says. "Too much work and too many gentlemen. I feel quite jealous."

"Surely not! Hey, I wasn't expecting that. I thought you would be proud of me for being able to talk to anyone. Besides, you were one of my clients. You don't think I would have left you out of my dream, do you?"

"Thank you! And so what did I do? Did I have to line up in order to see you?"

"In the dream, I'd already decided that when it was your turn, I would talk to you about your two jobs and your love of work in general."

"Very nice, but while you were dreaming, you didn't know about my job as a scout. In other words, you didn't know I had two jobs."

"Didn't I say that I'd prepared all my conversations with my clients beforehand? And what could be easier for me than to prepare yours? Or have you forgotten the number of times I've guessed what you were dreaming about—just from sharing the same bed?"

"Really? When has that happened?"

"Lots of times. Anyway, in my dream, you were a man with two jobs. Don't you see? I didn't know what those two jobs were exactly. I just knew you had two jobs. I only remembered you were a carpenter when I woke up."

"Now you're making fun of me."

"No, you don't get it. I have never seen what you are as clearly as I did in that dream of mine."

"And what is that?"

"A man with two jobs."

"A man with two heads," he says and slumps back on the pillow.

The first few drops of rain begin to fall, some trucks pass.

Olga goes over to their second-hand dressing table and combs her hair.

"Yes, I'm glad to see you've finally figured it out," she says. "A man with two heads. I'll never tire of repeating that. And with two jobs, as many as there are women in your life. Your mother and me. When will I have you all to myself, I wonder."

I don't think I would be wrong to say that Olga is trying, once again, to question what, for her, is Benito's excessive love of work. I've often seen her try to show him that his obsession with work stems from the negative influence of his mother, who taught him that work is the only possible source of happiness. Olga feels that her husband is still living in his childhood, because he still carries within him the childish gesture of that tinker in Valderrobres, ceaselessly hammering away. The same tinker that his mother, the local schoolteacher, would obsessively point out to him every day.

For Olga, Benito's whole life can be summed up in the image of that gloomy, enigmatic castle of the Knights Templar in the Matarraña valley, on whose walls his mother doubtless projected the image of a future model worker. A possessive Communist mother, a fireman father, withdrawn and silent, a castle swathed in mist and the hard fate of a hard worker make up, for Olga, the main features of Benito's personality.

"What it is," Benito says after thinking the matter through, "is that you would really like to work in the center of Paris, preferably in the Champs-Élysées. You've never felt comfortable in Meudon. That's what your dream is about."

"And in your dream, didn't you make yourself a scout because you want to go back and live in Spain?"

"I didn't *make* myself a scout," protests Benito, and without realizing, he very nearly hits out at me.

Olga creeps slowly over to him and affectionately tweaks the end of his nose. They are soon reconciled.

"I enjoyed being a manicurist," she says, "but only in my dream. Can you imagine how awful it would be having to traipse over to the Champs-Élysées every day and not be able to help you in your workshop? I like the smell of wood shavings, the song of the saw, the sound of the hammer. I'm happy in the workshop, as well you know. Everyone in Meudon knows that. There's no one here who doesn't know that we work even on Sunday, every Sunday."

"Yes, but I don't think they understand us," says Benito, his head bowed.

He is, I suppose, referring to the fact that, in Meudon, people call him The Jap. Olga has always maintained that it's really an affectionate nickname, which is good for business, because they've acquired a reputation for being efficient and irreproachable.

"Anyway," Olga says, clearly determined to bring the conversation to a close, "remind me when we get back that I have to take a few things to the laundry."

I think she looked at me when she said this. I would almost swear she did. Benito shot me a furtive glance too. In fact, I think he can see me. Often, when he goes out through the door, he looks back and gives me a silent farewell look. I think he'd like to talk to me. Naturally, if he ever did, he would treat me—possibly because of the presumed, but only presumed, small size of my brain—as if I were a child.

"So," he would say, "what's your name?"

"I don't know."

"And where do you live."

"Here in this room. This is all I can see."

I'd say that and I'd laugh, the rather peculiar laugh of someone who has no lungs.

Olga is the person laughing now. She's laughing because Benito has just asked her, for the nth time in a matter of days, why, if she likes the workshop so much, is she always going on at him for being obsessed with his work.

She laughs, but suddenly her expression changes and she looks very serious and thoughtful, biting her lip. Benito trembles. He realizes that he shouldn't have asked the question. When his wife starts thinking and biting her lip, a storm is brewing. Benito trembles because he knows that she will soon address him clearly and plainly, in her characteristic, brutally pointed way.

"Your body is always busy," Olga says at last. "From work to bed, from bed to work. Admirable. Excellent in bed and excellent at work. A good job done every time. The Jap of Meudon is always proud when he's finished his job. Here, gentlemen, we have someone with a vocation. Perfection every time! A tireless, admirable man, a worker to his fingertips. Even when he's sleeping! He has impeccable dreams: correct dreams, work dreams. His body is always busy. I wonder if his soul is too. I would say not. His soul seems to me completely idle. You work tirelessly so as to avoid the moment when you'll have nothing to do and be obliged to think. Your body's always in frenetic motion, but your mind is motionless. There's a shameful inner void. You are an idle soul."

A silence falls in this dramatic bedroom, the tensest silence I've known recently.

"You'll never change me," Benito says at last, putting up a degree of resistance with his absent soul.

"And I won't try to."

"Do you remember the day of the general strike? The people who weren't working wandered about as if they were lost and confused, taking their children or their dogs out for walks. There were more suicides then than in the whole of the rest of the month. The boulevards were so noisy, and yet, they were also more silent than usual. I saw one man looking simultaneously idle and anxious, who kept straightening things up for no apparent reason. He had a pen in the corner of his mouth. Could he be the owner of a restaurant, or perhaps the manager? I decided to follow him. He kept using his finger to remove the dust from the tops of door frames. He simply didn't know what to do. I left him on a bench, picking his nose."

"Come on, get dressed," she orders.

"That's why I never tire of telling you that doing a good job is the only way we can justify ourselves in the face of death."

"Look, you just can't accept that your mother was a negative influence on you. The poor woman had her good points, but, on the whole, she did you a lot of harm. The one good thing she taught you was a feeling of solidarity with the misfortunes of ordinary people, but otherwise she turned you into a poor wretch, perhaps to ensure your solidarity with other poor wretches."

"I don't mind you calling me a poor wretch. After all, I am."

"Come on, get dressed, will you?"

"You shouldn't say things like that about my mother. There are some things that shouldn't be taken for granted."

"Like what for example?"

Benito pauses to think.

"Come on, hurry up," she says. "They're expecting us in Paris. Quick. Don't start thinking now."

"We shouldn't, for example, take for granted our feelings about buttons being sewn on for us by someone else. I will always be grateful for the buttons she sewed on for me when I was a child."

"Good, I see that your soul isn't quite as idle as I thought, but, please, get dressed."

"You think you're superior to me, don't you?"

"You do make me laugh sometimes. You're so absorbed in your work that I realize I can say absolutely anything to you."

"Anything?"

"Yes. You're so absorbed in your work …"

"I'm not at the moment."

"Finish getting dressed, will you?"

"You think you're superior to me, don't you? You think your soul is less idle because you work less than me. Come on, get dressed, you say, but I need to get undressed in order to think."

"All I know is …"

"All I know is that there are some days when I'd rather be dead. Every year when this wretched day comes around, for example."

The energy with which they're arguing makes me think that they hadn't really woken up until just now. Throughout this vibrant discussion, they gaze at each other tenderly.

"I totally agree," says Olga. "And believe me, I'm devastated. Days like this simply shouldn't exist. Every year when May Day comes around, we say the same thing. Who invented this day anyway? Working helps us meet the challenge of Sundays, but who can cope with International Workers Day?"

He puts on his hat and looks in the mirror. He takes out an old red flag from the wardrobe opposite.

"I'm ready," he says.

"Right, let's go. What a nuisance, eh? What a drag having to go to the Champs-Élysées for a demonstration. Why can't we just go to the workshop like we do every day? The thought just fills me with anxiety. Whose idea was this holiday anyway?"

"Probably the same person who invented Sundays."

"It was better when we were in Spain, because then attending a demonstration was a really risky business. It demanded a bit of effort, some hard work. Plus, of course—why fool ourselves—we were in Spain."

I see them leave. It seems to me that Benito shoots me a furtive— possibly sympathetic—glance. Trucks pass. They close the apartment door, and I hear them go down the stairs. Soon afterward, their footsteps are drowned out by the infernal racket made by the taps. I hear the street door close, and it begins to rain. I would say it was pouring. It seems to me that I, too, am an idle soul, especially now that they have gone. A red flag begins to fade. They say the imagination is a place where it's always raining.

MEUDON, 1974

INVENTED MEMORIES

I

I remember that on my trip to the Azores, I visited Peter's Bar in Horta, a café frequented by whalers near the yachting club: a mixture of inn, meeting place, information center and post office. Peter's has ended up being the destination for all those precarious, fortunate messages that would, otherwise, have no address. On the wooden bulletin board at Peter's, people stick notes, telegrams, and letters that wait there for someone to come and claim them. On this bulletin board, I found a mysterious series of notes and messages and voices that seemed to be closely related, coming as they did from Antonio Tabucchi's world of small, unimportant misunderstandings: these voices seemed to pay homage to him as they traveled along together in an imaginary caravan of invented memories, voices brought there by something—it's impossible to say what, but which I have no hesitation in summoning up again here.

II

I am at the head of this expedition about which we have all dreamed at some point, and, among my memories is hearing the Italian writer Antonio Tabucchi say that, in a way, literature is like a message in a bottle (or like those messages pinned on the bulletin board in Peter's Bar), because literature needs a recipient too; and so, just as we know that someone, some unknown person, will read our shipwrecked sailor's message, we also know that someone will read our literary writings: someone who is not so much the intended recipient as an accomplice, insofar as he or she is the one who will give meaning to our writing. That is what allows every message to be added to, to acquire new meaning, to grow in resonance. And that is precisely what is so strange and fascinating about literature, the fact that it is not a static organism, but something that mutates with every reading, something that is constantly changing.

III

I must add something to the message written by myself, the leader of this caravan. What matters is that everything always leaves something behind, some trace. When my name was Carlos Drummond de Andrade, I wrote this: "Sometimes a button, sometimes a mouse." What matters is that everything always leaves something behind, and however small the flame, someone might be able to take it up and use it to find something else.

IV

Fire. I'd like to burn this sad bulletin board. It would be the revenge of someone who recalls having spent his entire life searching in vain, like Borges in that poem about the tiger, the other tiger. I've spent my life looking behind words for that other tiger—the one in the jungle, not the one in the poem. And because of this, my life has been ruined.... Fire, I say.

V

I can remember a lot of men swearing on their lives, and yet no one knows what life really is.

VI

I remember always thinking that life itself doesn't actually exist, because if no one tells it as a story or turns it into a narrative, life is merely something that happens, nothing more. To understand life, you have to tell it, even if only to yourself. This doesn't mean that a story can make life comprehensible, because there are always gaps in any narrative, whatever sutures or remedies you might try to apply. That is why a narrative only restores life in fragmentary form.

VII

My name is Sergio Pitol, and whenever I read this fellow Tabucchi, who everyone talks about so much here, I think of certain metaphysical Italian landscapes in which everything is very clear, exact, true, and, at the same time, completely unreal.

VIII

I was Tabucchi's shadow. Once I was drawn to the idea of becoming a gaze outside of myself. Like Pessoa. To make myself a ghost, a way of seeing, a detached gaze. Like Tabucchi, who was Pessoa's shadow. Now, when I recall those days, I remember what José Bergamín used to say about himself: "I am ooonly a shadoooow."

IX

Since nothing very memorable had happened in my life, I used to be a man with scarcely any biography. Until I decided to invent one for myself. I took refuge in the universe of various writers and, using other people's memories—which were, I realized, related to their books or imaginations—I forged a memory of my own and a new identity. I treated other people's memories as mine, and that is why I can boast now of having had a life. After all, isn't that what everyone does? My life is a biography just like everyone else's, built on invented memories.

X

I don't want any dates or inscriptions on my gravestone, please, just my name, but not Ettore; instead, put the name with which I sign this letter, which is none other than Giosefine.

XI

Like the whales from the world of Porto Pim, I communicate over immense distances, leaving desperate messages like the one from this person Giosefine, like all the messages pinned on this bulletin board. I spend much time observing men who are always in such a hurry. Sometimes they sing, but only to themselves, and their song is not a call but a heart-rending lament. When night falls on these small islands, and the men grow tired, they silently slip away and are clearly very sad.

XII

If I remember that I am Pessoa, then all I want to say is that I'm torn between the loyalty I owe to the tobacconist's shop opposite—a real thing in the outside world—and the feeling that everything is a dream, a real thing in the inner world.

XIII

I remember the hours I spent reading in bed, night after night, a history of solitudes in which everything was both despair and, paradoxically, a game. I think it's similar to what happens to the messages on this bulletin board when night falls on them and on us, and we all feel very strange and laugh awkwardly, as if *we* were playing a game.

XIV

I remember the words of the young woman hoping to disturb the perfect peace of the city in Donald Barthelme's story, "A City of Churches": "I'll dream the life you are most afraid of."

XV

I remember that it was by sheer chance, in a Paris street, when I was very young, dreaming of fearful future lives and other disquiets, that I bought a little book entitled *Bureau de tabac*. That same night, I read it on the train traveling back home to Italy. It made such a strong impression on me that I felt an immediate desire to learn Portuguese.

XVI

I used to travel by train a lot and it wasn't always as peaceful as it is now, traveling in this friendly caravan of fleeting smiles and the thrill of being among the disparate. I remember traveling through lands of fever and adventure. Then, I remember traveling to India, which is the ideal place to lose oneself. I set off in search of a disappeared friend, a shadow of the shadows of the hermetic past. Bombay, Goa, Madras saw me pass through in search of the hidden, nocturnal side of things. But for me, the Orient continues to be an unknown. I was there, but I understood nothing. A barbarian in Asia, a stranger in my own country and, worse still, filled with the suspicion that the universe is a prison from which one is never ever released and never will be.

XVII

I have escaped from a book by Álvaro Mutis, but I continue to repeat some of the things I was asked about there: Who summoned all these characters? Where do they come from and where are they being sent by the anonymous destiny that keeps parading them past us? Will their invented memories vanish one day into the kindly void that will one day accommodate us all?

XVIII

I'm an escapee from the lunatic asylum. Yes, I've escaped, even though I was having a good time writing novels on the asylum walls. In my shameless flight, I am now accompanying this expedition. I scream like a wounded seagull. I am a seagull. I am the seagull that spied on the spy Spino, on the very edge of the horizon of an unforgettable book. They say I'm mad. And that's because, while

I say the book is unforgettable, I have forgotten everything about it apart from a single sentence, which is a single question: "What is your imagination inventing in the guise of memory?" I can only remember that one sentence from the book by that writer from Pisa after whom this caravan is named, this caravan over which I am patiently, protectively keeping watch as I fly. And even though I scream and scream and am a seagull, I am not mad.

XIX

I remember that Valéry came to see me one afternoon at home, after lunch, to ask if I wanted to go for a walk. While I was getting ready, he picked up a sheet of paper and wrote:

Story
Once upon a time, there was a writer ... who wrote.

–Valéry

XX

I, too, devote myself to dreaming the life people will be most afraid of. I, too, am only a shadow. People call me Xavier Janata Pinto. I've finished my day's work; I am leaving Europe. The sea air will scorch my lungs, lost climates will tan my skin. I will swim, cut the grass, hunt, and, above all, smoke; I will drink alcohol as strong as molten metal. I will return with iron limbs, dark skin and a furious glint in my eye; and, because of this mask, people will think I come from a powerful race. I will have gold, I will be idle and brutal. Women take care of these fierce crippled men returning from warmer climes ...

XXI

I remember being a bartender in Lisbon who invented a cocktail called a Janelas Verdes Dream, but I would say that I was also the character who, by dint of inventing a past for himself, as if performing a sleight of hand in which he practiced different styles, ended up becoming a writer. He was, if I remember rightly, a marginal character, who was trying to say that he existed, and he said this through writing, reconstructing and even inventing an identity he never had, but which became true once written down; because this character didn't ask to take the floor, he simply spoke, doing so by writing and inventing his own story.

XXII

I take the floor in order to say that I remember Emil Zatopek, and that I also remember Georges Perec, who wrote a book entitled *Je me souviens*, in which none of the memories were invented.

XXIII

I am approaching Death and I approach very slowly. I am the last passenger on this caravan, and the Black Angel who awaits us all is waiting at the end of this journey ending here. I am a ghost beneath the night sky of an Atlantic coast, opposite an old house that used to be called São José da Guia, and which no longer exists. As a ghost, I receive many stories, but transmit very few, I confess, because I spend most of my time listening and trying to decipher all those often somewhat obscure and disconnected communications interfering with the normal process of reading these messages on the wooden bulletin board.

XXIV

I am truly the last passenger, tragic and strange. Today is September 11, 1891, and we are standing outside the convent of hope, Ponta Delgada on San Miguel Island, the Azores. I am going to end my life, and my memories will be taken up by the kindly void that will one day accommodate us all. Among the children of this accursed century, I, too, sat down at the cruel table, where, beneath all the laughter, there moans the sadness of an impotent longing for the infinite. I am going to say goodbye to everyone here, facing this sea, from this bench beneath the cool wall of the convent, where there is a blue anchor painted on the last, sad, whitewashed wall of my life.

XXV

I remember now that this has happened to me before. All the guests were beginning to leave. And those who remained did nothing but speak in ever quieter voices, especially as the light began to fade. No one turned on the lamps. I, who was Tabucchi's shadow, am now only the shadow of myself, although, when I tell stories, I can be anyone's shadow. I am your shadow. As well as the shadow of the person who said: "The succession of shadows and the dead that is me."

XXVI

I am among the last to leave, bumping into the furniture. I was a friend of Roberto Arlt. I remember one morning, we, his colleagues, found him sitting in the newspaper office, his shoes off, his feet on the table, holes in his socks, and he was weeping. Before him stood a vase containing a faded rose. When we asked what was wrong, he said: "Can't you see this flower? Can't you see that it's dying?"

XXVII

I am number XXVII. I am a man from the 1920s: I continue to wait for excitement, strong drinks, lively conversation, happiness, brilliant writing, the free exchange of ideas, revolution. I used to write short pieces, and in each collection there would be one, two, or perhaps three that I preferred to the others, and even though those preferences varied by the day and by the minute, a day and a moment came when, on a whim, I set them down in a personal anthology of remembered inventions that I titled *Invented Memories*.

THE VAMPIRE IN LOVE

This man called José Ferrato with a somewhat unprepossessing physique, whom we can see waking up in his apartment in Plaza de San Lorenzo, has just been dreaming about a donkey that resembled a very cautious greyhound. He observed that donkey closely throughout the dream, because he was aware what a rare phenomenon it was. However, on waking, all he can recall of the creature are its unpleasantly long, slender, symmetrical, human feet.

That donkey who always longed to be a greyhound is me, the man says to himself, and, for a few seconds, we see him lying in bed, motionless and distraught and deeply depressed. Then he remembers that when he went to bed last night, he had promised himself that, this morning, he would go to the cathedral to see the boy with the unsurpassable, Murilloesque face, the marvelous, unattainable boy who wants nothing whatever to do with him.

I will go and see him, José Ferrato thinks, his head resting on his pillow, and it will be the last time, for I have pestered him long enough. I will trouble Beauty no more. This is what José Ferrato says to himself as he lies in bed, remembering his excitement the previous afternoon in the cathedral, when he again spotted the boy among the other boys standing before the high altar, all dressed in blue and silver and wearing plumed hats, and dancing slowly and on tiptoe to the sound of castanets and a strange liturgy halfway between a *seguidilla* and a minuet: the *baile de los seises*, an ancient tradition in the cathedral of Seville.

Last night, he fell asleep thinking about Beauty, and a donkey ruled his dreams, and now, on waking, we have seen how this donkey—which is none other than himself, or so at least he believes—this donkey is trying not to forget that in two hours, the boy will reappear in the cathedral, this time in the guise of an altar boy in a side chapel where Sunday mass will be held.

Into his mind comes the memory of another liturgy, as strange as the *baile de los seises*, but belonging to the private world of his family. He recalls another processional dance, this time from his childhood, the eccentric game that his giant of a father had invented. He can see his father so clearly now, so very tall in his black boots, processing majestically and slowly through the house, tapping lightly with his heels to mark the different sections of his route, as if each section were important to him, as if none deserved to be dismissed and all were worthy of being drawn to the boy's attention, tapped out, suggested, signaled. Thus his giant of a father continued his crazy progress, dancing slowly from the dining room in their house in Carmona to another forbidden room, thus his father made his mad progress, and the boy would follow, respectfully, adoringly, the two of them forming a strange, slow procession whose familiar itinerary his father never changed, always going from the dining room, down the long, gloomy corridor to a room that was kept in permanent darkness and which no one could enter because it belonged to his grandfather; and so when his father reached the threshold of that secret room, he would spin around and make his way back down the gloomy corridor to where the procession or dance had begun, always respectfully followed by the boy who—knowing that he would be forgiven everything because he was ugly and hunch-backed—occasionally dared to break the light tapping rhythm of that processional dance and linger for a few long seconds hidden in the darkness of the forbidden room; and then his father, greatly surprised to find his offspring following neither the rules of the game nor his footsteps, would angrily interrupt the dance lesson and turn back and peer into the forbidden shadows in which his son had taken fleeting, fugitive refuge.

José Ferrato abandons his childhood memories now and remains for a long time pondering what he had heard people talk about yesterday, that strange business of the Russians sending up a second Sputnik into space with only a dog called Laika as passenger. Those Russians really are bizarre, he thinks. This is exactly what he said yesterday when he first heard the news and was plunged into a state of utter perplexity. A dog journeying through space, he says several times. What will God think when he sees a dog flying toward the Kingdom of Heaven? Only a Russian would consider it normal to send a dog up to see the stars. Besides, José Ferrato continues to reflect, why didn't they consult the rest of humankind? They never ask us what we think about some decision they're making. Obviously, we're not Russians, but the same thing happens here in Spain, and they never consult us, they don't care if we have a particular interest in whatever it is, or if anything's what they call "a matter of national interest." Of course, History goes one way and we, poor anonymous citizens, go another, and no one listens to or consults with us. At least we have the consolation of knowing that they didn't treat God with complete irreverence and send a greyhound or a donkey up to heaven, because that would have been even worse …

While he's shaving, he thinks again about the boy with the unsurpassable, Murilloesque face, whom he will soon be able to glimpse again in a side chapel of the cathedral. It will be the last time he will enjoy this vision, of that he is quite sure. As he contemplates the boy, he will try to experience, one last time, the matchless feeling that, at that precise moment, his eyes are the most fortunate on earth.

We see him, well-dressed and well-shaven, go down to have breakfast, as he does every morning, at the Sardinero, the bar next to the Basílica del Gran Poder, the church whose Christ has always listened to him so attentively, although whether he was able to understand him is another matter, because it still is a sin for a man to fall in love with a boy.

We see him go into the bar and, although he is of medium height, José Ferrato seems small, mainly because of his hump. He has very stubby, white hands, a soft voice, and rather effeminate gestures; he takes almost excessive care—perhaps because he is a barber—of his lank hair and moustache, and uses an extravagantly perfumed handkerchief. When he smiles, he reveals two sharp vampire's teeth. He has clearly not been blessed with good looks, but he has always tried to make up for his monstrous appearance with his infallibly good manners and his infinite kindness and patience—he's a real saint—in putting up with the locals, who, affectionately, but also cruelly, insist on calling him Nosferatu.

As soon as he enters the Sardinero, the waiters—of whom there are many, because there have always been hordes of them in this bar—make the usual jokes at his expense: José Ferrato, Nosferatu! Today, though, he doesn't even bother to respond, which is unusual for him, because, according to his philosophy—elementary, but perfectly reasonable for a single man of his status—it is always best to be on good terms with your fellow man, because we men are bound together by threads, and it would be a bad business if the threads binding us slackened and sent one of us plunging a little further than the others into the void. For Nosferatu, it would be more horrible still if one of those threads broke entirely and someone fell. That is why we should remain bound to each other, he tells himself several times a day, the first being when he has breakfast at the Sardinero and, armed with infinite patience and saintliness, has to listen to the nonsensical remarks and other innocently mocking comments given by that veritable cloud or horde of waiters: one for every two square yards of that small bar.

This morning, however—and this is most unusual—he does not respond to their jokes. This is because he has the impression that his whole small world is beginning to drift definitively away and it seems to him that the moment has come to say goodbye to it all. He enters the Sardinero with surprising haste. He orders a hot chocolate, and the customer beside him orders exactly the same. Nosferatu gives him a scornful, censorious look, indicating how much he dislikes having someone order the same drink as him. However, the two end up talking to each other and commenting on how well the soccer player Campanal has been playing lately, until a mistake—a mere slip of the tongue on Nosferatu's part—leads them into a completely different, more meaningful conversation. They find themselves discussing old age. Nosferatu says that he has always found it hard to accept his ugliness and his hump back, but the worst thing of all is that, lately, he is constantly, painfully aware that he is growing old.

"Oh, I really like getting old," says the other man. "I hate the golden curls of childhood, the spots and pimples of adolescence, all that nonsense about being in one's prime. Old age, on the other hand, brings calm and equilibrium. Friendship, love, and work take their proper places. Getting old is an excellent thing."

Nosferatu is so troubled by these words that he decides to leave the bar at once. Raising his left hand, he waves a silent farewell to the waiters. Farewell forever, he thinks. And he leaves. He knows perfectly well where he's going and what he's going to do, he knows exactly what his intentions are on this November morning. He's walking very fast, thinking to himself that if he keeps up this pace, he'll take off. It's clear that all he wants is to see the boy's perfect beauty one last time and then, yes, take off, fly, free forever, through the cold, silent air of that Seville morning, along with the angels, because there are (they say) no hunchbacks in the infinite.

As he quickens his pace, he thinks how little he cares now about his fellow man, those waiters at the Sardinero, for example. They don't matter one jot, just as he doesn't give a fig for the collective fate of humanity, and yet he cares enormously about his own personal fate, around which, this morning, his tortured thoughts keep circling and circling.

He has turned the corner now and is just leaving the Plaza de San Lorenzo, when a waiter grabs his arm and tells him that he forgot to pass on a message from his mother, saying that he should call her urgently.

His mother is the least alarmist of people; she's normally a very calm person. She would never worry her son for no reason, and so it really must be very urgent, assuming that anything ever is. Nosferatu goes back to the bar and phones his mother at her home in

Carmona, the village she has barely left in recent years. His mother's voice sounds rather distant, her tone surprisingly shrill, the message bewildering: Uncle Adolfo has died at the age of ninety-five.

"So?" says Nosferatu, most put out that such a trivial incident should have interrupted his walk to the cathedral.

Uncle Adolfo is almost a stranger. He has heard nothing of him for years and years and wasn't even aware that he was still alive. In fact, he only met his uncle Adolfo once, when he was taken to visit him in Madrid—almost half a century ago—a visit to what his mother believed to be a house of ill repute, the house of an outrageous sinner and a confirmed bachelor.

What he remembers most about that visit—he was quite small—was all the talk about his uncle's influential job as director of the Spanish railways. He also remembers a silk dressing gown—which revealed to him the existence of something called luxury—and the evil look on his uncle's face when he asked him if he wanted to hear a great truth. When Nosferatu said yes he would, his uncle merely told him that God was dead.

This malign, gratuitous action meant that the uncle never again saw his nephew. This nephew is now fifty years old and has never felt particularly affected by his uncle's words. He is very devout and has all the saintliness of the hunchbacked buffoon, who is almost pleased when he finds himself the butt of other people's jokes. The nephew believes in God, although he does regret God making him so ugly and so hunchbacked, and when he attends mass, he always feels very annoyed, because the son of that same God won't really suffer the little children to come anywhere near him. He believes in God and is a good man and a real saint, if we understand by this everything that goes with that, namely, that he is also drawn to sin and fascinated by profound Evil (which is radically opposed to Good), the perfect evil that is perfect beauty.

Nosferatu had been heading toward that beauty when his mother called him back.

"So?" he asks, rather tetchily. "Do you mean my uncle in Madrid?"

"Yes, Uncle Adolfo. He's died."

"That's very interesting, but I always assumed he'd died years ago. What is so urgent about that?"

"Nosferatu, bugaboo!" a regular customer who has just arrived calls out to him, intending this as an affectionate, everyday greeting.

Nosferatu picks up a bowl of Russian salad from the counter and hurls it at the head of the surprised customer, just missing his target.

"Are you still there, son?" can be heard coming down the telephone line.

"Let me at him!" yells the regular, restrained by a legion of waiters.

"Uncle Adolfo," says the voice, "has left you his entire fortune."

"Have you gone raving mad, you old queen!" screams the customer, beside himself with rage.

"Isn't that amazing, son? Two hundred or three hundred million, we don't know exactly how much, but a real fortune. Can you hear me?" His mother sounds very excited. "Say something, son."

There is no reaction from Nosferatu.

"I can understand why you're at a loss for words," his mother says. "Uncle Adolfo left a note explaining why he made you his sole heir. He was obviously a bit loopy at the end, but we won't say that too loudly in case the lawyers declare the inheritance null and void. Shall I read the note out to you?"

Nosferatu still says nothing, as if he had suddenly been frozen into silence by an arctic blast, but in fact for him it's as if nothing had changed and everything was the same when he first came into the bar that morning; he still feels as if his small world is beginning to move away from him, that the time has come for him to say goodbye to everything, to everyone who has, up until now, accompanied his wretched existence as a barber fascinated by perfect evil.

"All right, I'll read it out to you," says the voice on the line. "This is what it says, son, now listen carefully: 'I really took to you the one time I met you all those years ago. This money is a bulwark against all your unhappiness, because I know you have been very unhappy. I have my sources and I am making you my heir, because I feel proud to know that you, too, have remained free of any matrimonial ties. I want you to set up a brotherhood of bachelors in my honor and to use my money to the detriment of those ever-proliferating large families receiving all those government hand-outs."

"What?" is the only response Nosferatu can manage.

"Are you still there, son? I think your uncle was suffering from senile dementia, but, like I said, best not mention that in case the lawyers declare the inheritance null and void. Are you still there? Say something."

Nosferatu doesn't reply, he seems to be in shock.

"Apparently," his mother goes on, "this is his revenge on his other nieces and nephews, whom he hates.... You may wonder why he hates them, and I have no idea, but what matters is that you are his sole beneficiary. Please, say something."

Nosferatu is completely bowled over by the news, unable to respond. He leans his hump against the wall and, very slowly, slides down until he is sitting on the floor, laughing like a madman and with a calendar bearing a photo of the Giralda tower perched on his head like a hat. He sits there laughing for quite a while and when he recovers, there is no one at the other end of the line. The others tell him not to bother calling his mother back because she has already left her house in Carmona and is on her way to the bar to administer first aid.

He spends a few seconds seriously pondering his fate before starting to laugh again, feebly at first, then desperately, wildly.

"What did your mother say?" the other men in the bar ask.

Nosferatu doesn't answer, he merely pulls a face.

"Are you thirsty?" they ask and, in an attempt to gain his confidence, offer him an aperitif, which he drinks, slowly, calmly, silently.

"You're certainly in a very strange mood today," says the regular customer, who seems to be the one most startled by Nosferatu's reactions.

"What did your mother say to upset you so much?" they ask again.

"You're like a swarm of flies," he says suddenly, "pesky creatures, always sticking your nose in where it isn't wanted."

"You really are in a most peculiar mood," insists the regular.

Nosferatu pays and, without another word, leaves the bar. Two of

the waiters run after him and remind him that his mother is traveling from Carmona to see him.

"Are you coming back? What shall we say to her if she arrives?"

"I'm not coming back," says Nosferatu. "Beloved flies, give my
mother a big kiss from me and tell her it wasn't her fault I was born
with a hump."

Leaving the astonished waiters behind, he hurries off. He's thinking about the boy with the unsurpassable, Murilloesque face, about
the perfect evil that so afflicts his soul, about the perfect beauty
which, for days now, has gripped, overwhelmed and seduced him,
reminding him constantly that he is ugly and hunchbacked, and,
above all, that he is growing old. And while he is thinking this, he
looks up at the sky above the rooftops, which is no longer clear blue
but white, overlaid by an opaque patina similar to that in his soul,
which is trying, unsuccessfully, to erase the image of the forbidden
boy and of perfect evil, but he can still see that same perfect beauty
even in the smudge of light that is the sun, glowing like the very
dullest of love's pangs. Yes, perfect evil awaits him in the Cathedral.
Beauty is sinful, he thinks. And Nosferatu's saintliness has never before been more obvious. His concern about sin would vanish if he
knew that saintliness derives from the sacred, which is another word
for the forbidden. However, he knows nothing of this. Nosferatu suddenly slows down and begins to take pleasure in what he sees along
the way. He's heading toward the river now, almost dancing, mark-
ing each step with a slight tap of the heel, just as his father used to do,
as if pointing out anything of interest along the way.

Near the river, still keeping up that light, musical tapping, he goes
into the butcher's shop owned by a friend of his, a woman who has
always been very kind to him. Nosferatu goes in, intending to say
goodbye, because he wants to say goodbye to many things today.
Somewhat perversely, he hopes to say goodbye to his friend, because he has always found her exaggerated kindness unbearable.
He is tired of being pitied. That's all over, he thinks.

"Business is very bad," she says when she sees him standing there,
staring at her, not saying a word.

Saint Nosferatu—I'm going to call him that because, like all those in love, he is both vampire and martyr—maintains a rigorous silence.

The sun sidesteps the obstacle of the clouds and reappears in triumph. For a moment, it looks as if Nosferatu is about to speak, but he doesn't.

"Yes, business is very bad," she says again, feeling slightly uneasy now, "because everyone walks past on the other side of the street. As you see, I'm on the sunny side, but it seems people around here prefer the shade."

Nosferatu's face remains a complete blank. He is a very good man, who has grown tired of being good. Rather than having an unattractive face, he would like to have a brutal, false face, to smile only rarely and always insincerely, and thus win an obscene victory over his whole person. Nosferatu is silently bidding farewell to the butcher. To do this, he smiles shyly and reveals his two sharp vampire teeth.

"Have you nothing to say? Is something wrong?" she asks.

Nosferatu rests his elbows on the counter and stares even more fixedly at his friend. At that moment, a group walks past the sunny door of the shop. This, for him, disproves her statement that no one walks on the sunny side of the street. As if she had been found out, she changes the subject and says the first thing that comes to mind, something that is guaranteed to neither please nor amuse Nosferatu. She says:

"Do you know, for a moment there, I thought you wouldn't be able to reach the counter with your elbows. How silly of me."

Nosferatu now hates the butcher and thinks that he was quite right to come in and bid farewell forever to such a monster.

"Why don't you say something, Nosferatu? You're behaving very strangely."

Then he makes as if to open his mouth and say goodbye, but instead says nothing, and leaves, looking pleased not to have uttered a word in that pathetic butcher's shop.

He continues on toward the river, still keeping up that slow, light tapping, and when he is already some distance away, he turns for a moment, not in order to see his friend, but to confirm what he thought he had noticed when he was talking to her: her shop window is as tiny as the windows on the opposite side of the road.

It's a real disadvantage having a small shop window like that—he thinks—that's the real reason why business is so bad, but she, poor thing—and the word "poor" reminds him that he has suddenly become rich, one of those men whom others call "fortunate"—she blames it on people preferring to walk in the shade, which is pure self-deception.

When he woke up this morning, he, too, had succumbed to self-deception. He remembers that, shortly after thinking about the Sputnik, he had sat in bed reading one of those adventure stories he had liked so much as a child, but, when it failed to drive from his mind thoughts of the boy with the Murilloesque face, he had stopped reading to see what the weather was doing. A clear sky with a few clouds. He had gone back to bed after looking intently out of the window. He went back to bed and again tried to read, and it was then, without noticing and while he was still reading, that he changed the angle of the hand holding the book, which led him to think—erroneously—that a large cloud must have covered the sun, and everything suddenly seemed darker, even though the light in his room hadn't changed at all.

The same thing is happening to my butcher friend, he thinks. And it occurs to Nosferatu now that this is what often happens: we look for distant causes when the real one is to be found much closer to home, in ourselves.

Nosferatu keeps up the rhythm of his ceremonial dance, and when he passes the cinema next to the Torre del Oro, he is surprised to see what sounds like a vampire movie called *Rhapsody of Blood*, which has been declared to be "of national interest"; but he soon realizes that he was wrong to think that the movie dealt with the hellish, humiliating world of vampires like him, poor devils who, on a cold Sunday morning in winter in Seville, have suddenly become fortunate men. The movie is about something quite different: it's an apologia for the Hungarian uprising against the Communists. And he thinks: I did find it rather strange that a movie about sad Nosferatus should be declared to be of national interest.

His thoughts turn to Hungarians and he realizes that he doesn't know a single one. On the other hand, he does know a few vampires, because he is one himself. And he thinks: We look for distant people who are often to be found much closer to home; in movies, we look for the vampires that exist inside us.

This conclusion seems to him rather clever, although he doesn't quite understand it. Not that it matters, he thinks, as he sees the sun disappear once more behind the clouds. His footsteps slow right down, adopt the rhythm of his father's dance, a dance of initiation into life and also—for him—into the forbidden. He passes an acquaintance, one of his customers at the barber shop, who smiles with pleasure to see him dancing in that strange way along the edge of the pavement. With his slow, tapping gait, Nosferatu cuts such a jaunty, eccentric figure that the acquaintance assumes he must be celebrating something and says how glad he is to see him finally looking so contented and in such a festive mood.

"Have you won the lottery?" he asks.

For a few seconds, Nosferatu continues his tapping dance, then says:

"No, I'm simply moving more slowly, much more slowly."

And he resumes his dance, continuing to focus on each stretch of the road that leads him along the river to the cathedral. He meets another friend, a fellow member of the Rifle Club. Since they saw each other just a few days ago, he doesn't have much to say to him and so—rather hastily and still tap-tapping, on the spot this time—he ends up telling him about his recent confusion over the rhapsodic and bloody title of the movie being shown at the local cinema. The friend listens to him gravely, and, although at first, one would assume that he was concerned by Nosferatu's permanently tapping feet, it soon becomes clear that it is the movie about Hungarians that he finds so troubling.

"The other day," he tells Nosferatu, "I asked to be taken to the movies. I hadn't been to see a movie for years and I'd forgotten what cinemas were like, the darkened room and all that. Anyway, what I saw was that movie about the Hungarians and, to be honest, I couldn't follow the plot at all. Besides, the Hungarians were all Spaniards: one was even called Parra, yes, every single one of them was Spanish. I didn't understand a thing and fell asleep on the shoulder of the woman who had bought me the ticket."

Nosferatu can't contain his anger, first, because he feels that his friend is lying when he says that he'd forgotten what cinemas were like, and, second, his friend is boasting about being invited to the movies by a woman, which is something that might happen in Paris, but definitely not in Seville. He feels so indignant that he immediately says goodbye to his friend and continues his dance, meanwhile thinking what a ridiculous thing the cinema is with its absurd rhapsodies being declared to be of national interest—and without even being consulted about it. He feels so indignant that he decides to bid farewell to the cinema too, to bid farewell forever to the darkened rooms in which so many traps are laid for our imagination, traps that go uncriticized. Am I perhaps saying goodbye to traps of all kinds? he wonders, and then he even says goodbye to the Guadalquivir river despite its calm, luminous waters, he says goodbye to the flowering acacia trees and the marvelous clayey slopes of the river bank. He is saying goodbye to beauty, which is, after all, the very first thing to lay a trap for us. He says goodbye to the magnolias, to the unforgettable pages of those adventure stories, to the limpid blue sky of Seville. And in passing—although this is something he has been doing since he was a child—he also says goodbye to women, whom he now can't forgive for never having invited him to the cinema. He even says goodbye to the pedestrian walking past him now.

"Goodbye, my good sir," he says to me.

He, of course, is unaware that I know everything about him, which is why I'm writing this.

"Are you kidding?" I ask.

"No, I'm just moving more slowly."

He is indeed walking more slowly, almost wearily, meticulously saying goodbye to every stretch of the road, and at last we see him reach the cathedral. In the semi-darkness, apart from the rays of light sometimes snaking in through the glass panes, the great harmonious nave welcomes him and soothes his soul. He stops his slow dance and goes over to where he can see the perfectly beautiful boy, who, dressed now as an altar boy, is assisting at mass. And just as happened yesterday, Nosferatu again feels overwhelmed as he contemplates what will never be his; he is left defeated and ecstatic before the beauty of perfect evil, pierced by the pain of knowing he can never have the Murilloesque face that condemns him to endure in silence the bitter, intoxicating emotion filling his eyes with tears. He spends the entire mass looking at the boy and remembering him as he was yesterday, dressed in his blue and silver uniform and his plumed hat, in perfect harmony with perfect evil and the Christian liturgy. He is troubled by the memory of the moment when, caught up in his innocent dance and oblivious to the fact that he was being watched, the boy, on tiptoe, lightly clicked his castanets before the obscene, repellent eyes of those pederast monsignors.

Mass ends, and Nosferatu hides near the sacristy, where he knows the boy and the priest will pass. He takes refuge in a dark corner and feels as if he had regained the strange darkness of the forbidden room of his childhood. He takes a 7.65 automatic out of his pocket, removes the magazine, examines it, then puts it back. When the boy and the priest walk past, he emerges from the shadows and follows them, his feet again tap-tapping lightly to attract the attention of the boy, who, when he feels someone tugging hard at his surplice, turns and, with a look of horror, sees the intruder.

"Blessed are the eyes that see what I see," Nosferatu whispers.

"Sir, sir, you've been told before to stop bothering me," the boy warns him.

"But I just wanted to see you one last time," says Nosferatu. He succumbs to a burst of wild, desperate laughter, and hoping that his farewell will be the culminating point of the day, he fires the gun, only to discover that he has left the bullets at home.

I have no luck even when it comes to killing myself, thinks Nosferatu, completely exhausted now and kneeling before the fierce gaze of the priest, who reproaches him for committing so many sins in one day. And there he stays, defeated by the things of this world and of the Church, defeated by the greatest of all misfortunes, when, looking up, he senses a faint ray of light flagellating him from on high and sending him the dullest, most perfect pang of pain at the sight of so much beauty.

MODESTY

For years I've worked as an occasional spy on the number 24 bus that takes you up Calle Mayor de Gracia in Barcelona. At home, I have a whole archive of gestures, phrases, and conversations heard on that route, and I even think I could write a novel as infinite as the one Joe Gould wanted to write about New York, because I have stolen and recorded all kinds of odd phrases, strange conversations, and weird situations.

Recently, a modest delinquent seems to have fallen in love with this same bus route. He is called—because some passengers know him well—the No. 24 thief. As soon as he gets on the bus, the passengers who know him warn the unwary by shouting: "Look out, look out, the No. 24 thief has just got on!"

This is always a touching scene and even has about it a certain grandeur, a touch of the popular epic, and, obvious differences aside, it reminds me of a movie I saw as a boy in which people from the slums come together to corner and capture a child-murderer. The No. 24 thief has been arrested about five hundred times already, but when he's released, he always returns to the bus, where he has become quite famous. He doesn't seem interested in any other route or any other bus. He must simply enjoy—as I do—being a regular, or perhaps he simply loves doing the same thing over and over. He's not unlike me in a way: we are both of us thieves. Of course, he steals wallets and purses, while I only snatch phrases, faces, gestures…

In my archive, I have all kinds of phrases that I've picked up on the bus that, for years now, has taken me from home to work and back again. Obviously some phrases make better hunting trophies than others. One of them I heard from a woman sitting behind me near the back of the bus: "I can remember English and French, but I've completely forgotten my Swahili." This struck me as a very sophisticated phrase for the No. 24. When I turned around, I saw that the speaker was one of two nuns. They had probably lived in Africa, which would explain everything, but I still think it was a rather sophisticated phrase.

On another equally memorable occasion, two young men were getting off the bus, when one of them suddenly said to the other in a very angry voice, loud enough for the whole bus to hear: "This is the last time I'm telling you: my mother is my mother, and your mother is your mother. Is that clear? Do you understand?" This was obviously a major bone of contention between them. I felt like following them and finding out what it was all about.

I particularly remember, among the many other phrases heard and noted down: "I gave her some magnolias and she's never forgiven me." And this: "The secret of happiness lies in martyrdom." And this: "If you earn a lot of money before you're forty, you're lost."

I note all these down, along with their corresponding dates. I have a huge dossier so big it's almost toppling over, a vast archive on the world of the No. 24 bus.

One day, I heard a woman telling her husband that the moon isn't what we think it is: "It isn't a natural satellite of the earth, but an immense, hollow minor planet, designed by a very technically advanced civilization and put into orbit around the Earth many centuries ago." I carefully noted this down, as well as the reply made by her very stupid-looking husband (I noted that down, too, I mean, the fact that he had the face of an imbecile): "The moon is the moon and that's that."

I really liked the imbecile's response, and I sometimes say it myself:

"The moon is the moon and that's that."

No one knows why I say it, no one knows it's something I overheard on the bus. The life of the No. 24 is part of my most private archive. Up until today, I've always been under the impression that everything that happened on the No. 24 route directly concerned me.

The archive—like my life—has become large and complex, which is understandable, because in both areas—the bus and life—there have always been many things worthy of note, so many gestures, people, phrases ... And yet, a week ago, I was too deep in thought to spy on anyone. Lately for some reason, I've been taking a break from spying. I forget that I'm the bus's word-thief. Last Monday was one of those days, but then something unexpected happened. I was standing up on the packed and sweltering bus, leaning distractedly on one of the middle rails, when a woman behind me, talking on her cell phone, said:

"I'm getting off the bus now, at Fontana station. I'm thirty years old, although I don't think I look it, but I'm nothing out of the ordinary really. I'm wearing a gray overcoat. Anyway, we'll find each other. See you soon."

She had her back to me, and so I couldn't see her face, or only if I were to take a couple of steps (which was quite impossible) and stand right in front of her, or crane my neck in an exaggerated fashion, and with so many people around, that would have seemed most unnatural. Her words "I'm nothing out of the ordinary really" touched my heart. It was a phrase I'd heard a thousand times, but now it took on a different intensity. It worried me. Can anyone really be so unprepossessing? What could have happened in the life of that woman for her to value herself so little and to have no compunction about saying so? Did she just want to appear modest? Or did modesty come naturally to her? I found it troubling that someone should resign themselves to such grayness. Seen from behind, she was rather short and entirely dressed in gray; indeed, even her dark hair seemed to be turning gray, and she was carrying a bag from Zara, which would have been a more useful identifying mark than "I'm nothing out of the ordinary really".

I thought about following her when she got off at Fontana station, just to see who she was meeting and to plunge into the beginning of a real-life novel. But I was already late getting home. Plus, I had never followed anyone in the street before and I couldn't see myself starting now. Your space is the bus, I thought. And that helped quash my desire to follow her.

I thought of the book I was reading about Gérard de Nerval and remembered a particularly touching quote: "I have never seen my mother. Any pictures of her were lost or stolen. I only know that she resembled an engraving from the period, an engraving titled *Modesty*, in the style of Prud'hon or Fragonard."

Did that woman in gray resemble Nerval's mother? But how could I possibly know what Nerval's mother was like if even he didn't know? I could, at any rate, try to see what the woman with the cell phone looked like. I was full of curiosity to know if she really was nothing out of the ordinary. I waited patiently so as to catch a glimpse of her face. When the bus stopped at Fontana station, the woman turned and began pushing her way toward the exit door. I saw her then from up close: she had a very beautiful face with green, almond-shaped eyes, a face marked by sadness and modesty and, I would say, by despair. Again I was seized by the temptation to get off the bus and follow her and find out who she had arranged to meet.

She got off the bus at Fontana and I stayed on, fearing that in Calle Mayor de Gracia, her beauty would change, depending on the looks on the faces of other people. I realized then that I felt jealous of her. She was a captivatingly modest woman in gray. I stayed on the bus watching foolishly as she became lost in the crowd walking up Calle Mayor de Gracia. I still had time, as the bus pulled away, to see her passing all kinds of people and possibly offering each of them her best image.

That night, I dreamed I was coming home on the No. 24 and that another bus, immediately ahead of mine—they were almost nose to tail—was traveling so fast that it ended up crashing into Fontana metro station. Instinctively, to celebrate the fact that I had been saved because I was on the bus behind, I looked to see if the woman silently accompanying me was also safe and well. And she was, she was the woman in gray whom I'd seen a few hours before, *Modesty* personified, still carrying her Zara bag. And her eyes seemed even sadder and more irresistible and more almond-shaped than they had the first time I saw her.

I chose not to give too much importance to the dream (although I knew it *was* important) and went off to work. For more than twenty years now, I've worked at the Fundación Rougemont in Barcelona, where I hold an important position. I've been lucky in life, I can't complain. I'm very comfortably off and can feel proud of my wife and my three children. I spend every weekend with my family in Sant Hilari Sacalm, where we have a second home. I always do the driving—I never let anyone else take the wheel—and that's because it helps me let off steam and, besides, I like to drive fast. Sometimes, my car seems to me to be a symbol of everything I've achieved.

I'm very vain, although almost no one would know, because I keep a tight rein on my vanity. That's probably why I like to drive so fast when I leave Barcelona. It may be that I drive so fast simply because, even if it takes the form of speeding down the highway, I need a private, unostentatious way of showing my pride for what I've achieved in life. I can't do that on the bus, which, fortunately, is like a very salutary course in humility. Otherwise, I might turn into the vainest person in the world.

I suppress these feelings—a lot. When I get into the elevator with some of our neighbors, for example, I would love to tell them of my great feats and let them know how well everything is going for me. In a few weeks' time, I'm off to Paris to receive an award for my achievements at work, but I say nothing about this. And yet I would love to be able to tell them, to shout it out right now to all of the building's other inhabitants, who seem to think I'm rather a pathetic individual, because, of course, they see me humbly, modestly getting off the bus. "It's really convenient," I explain, "because it drops me right at the door," but they clearly assume I take the bus because I'm short on money and can only afford to spend it on gas on the weekends.

Perhaps my dream about the bus crashing was linked to my

213

frustration with myself for not having followed the woman in gray, who, all unknowing, had punished me with her sadness and modesty. Later on, in the office, I couldn't get her out of my head. In the afternoon, coming back from work on the bus, something very unexpected happened. At the Fontana stop, there was an old man in a wheelchair waiting to get on, and the driver immediately began the slow process of lowering the ramp. However, the ramp got stuck, perhaps because it wasn't used very much. In fact, I'd never before seen anyone disabled get on the No. 24. After five minutes of indecision, we were told that we all had to get off because the bus had broken down. It wasn't clear whether this was due to the failure of the ramp or was just an odd coincidence, but we all duly got off and waited for the next bus to arrive. There were, I felt, certain parallels with last night's dream: not only was there a first and a second bus, it was also the one in front that had broken down, *and* it had all happened outside Fontana metro station.

Whatever the truth of the matter, the breakdown of the bus vividly brought back to me the memory of the woman with the sad, almond-shaped eyes whom I'd seen the previous afternoon. I looked for her, but she wasn't there. I even imagined her spending the entire day wandering around outside the station. I couldn't help it. This woman in gray's description of herself as nothing out of the ordinary had really intrigued me. It was odd. I'd heard the expression thousands of times and had never given it much thought, because it had always seemed perfectly normal, insignificant, and yet now it really troubled me; my whole life seemed suddenly to turn on those words.

I looked for her among the crowd, but there was no sign of her. I did the same on Wednesday and Thursday, especially when the bus passed the Fontana stop. On Friday, I went out to lunch with some work colleagues at a restaurant near the Ramblas. There were loads of people gathered around the so-called "living statues". The one representing Che Guevara was particularly popular, but the others—the soccer player Eto'o, Don Quixote, and Evita Perón—were also attracting quite a crowd. Only one of them had no audience at all and was incredibly discreet, for she was barely perceptible, as if she didn't exist. In fact, I almost bumped into her, only noticing her when she was right there before me. She represented a beggar woman—from nineteenth-century London I would say—but there was something odd about her that meant she went entirely unnoticed by the tourists and the passersby. She was wearing a ragged gray outfit that reached down to the ground, where she had placed a metal bowl, also gray, in which people could leave coins. With some surprise, I thought: it's *Modesty*.

The following day, I used the rain as an excuse not to go away for the weekend. And on Sunday morning—that is, yesterday, when the sun came out again, I took the family to see a Fragonard exhibit in a museum located in the hills above Barcelona. I thought I might come across some clue as to where to find that engraving of *Modesty* mentioned by Nerval, assuming it existed of course. And I thought, too, that it was also a way of feeling, in some way, closer to the woman in gray.

"When do they give you your award?" my oldest son asked, taking me by surprise.

He's seventeen now and still believes in me and, just then, I couldn't help but feel proud of that—yes, why not admit it?—proud of that award I was going to receive. Then, almost immediately, I felt ashamed of my vain response and, to make up for it, I intensified my search for some clue as to that engraving, thinking instead about people who didn't have a high opinion of themselves, people who are modest.

Most unexpectedly, the museum shop had a book about Prud'hon, which I immediately bought. It contained no images of the engraving I was looking for, but I saw that *Modesty* did exist and was indeed attributed to Prud'hon (thus removing the possibility that it was by any of Fragonard's followers). Armed with this information, I would be able to track it down on the internet. That evening, at home, with the help of my older daughter, I found the engraving on Google. Modesty, the figure that Nerval believed resembled his mother, was a beautiful woman. I think I fell in love with that engraving, because now I carry in my wallet the printout my daughter made.

"You know, not going to Sant Hilari this weekend was a really good idea," my youngest daughter said yesterday, when dusk was coming on and we were all happily watching a good movie on TV.

Today, Monday, going to work on the bus, I heard a woman saying to someone on her cell phone:

"No, that's not it, but you're getting warmer, you're very close. I love you. You're the best."

I thought at first she was talking to me. I turned around and was so disappointed: not because those words weren't intended for me, but because the woman was nothing like the woman I was looking for and whose image I was carrying around in my wallet. This woman was clearly talking to her boyfriend, saying:

"A bulbul is a Persian nightingale. I thought you knew that."

This was a very strange comment, but I didn't feel like noting it down. Sad to say, I think I'm beginning to lose interest in my hunt for phrases, in the world in general, in almost everything. From one day to the next, I've begun to run out of steam. It's as if the ancestral hunter in me were beginning to lose his curiosity, along with the necessary attention, agility, and patience. As if my only interest now lay in meeting that woman again and being able to tell her—I don't know—to tell her my most modest truths: that I'm getting older, that I'm no longer such a good hunter of phrases, that I don't much care about awards anymore, or the world, only about her.

NIÑO

I

If my son survives the operation, we'll have a family celebration party for his sixtieth birthday. He's getting on, my son Francisco, whom we all know as Niño. Then again, I can't say I'd be exactly thrilled if he did survive.

To be honest, Niño has always been unbearable.

"Why did you *beget* me?" he asked when he was only seven years old. Even at that young age, he had an extraordinarily wide vocabulary, which even included the verb "to beget."

He exempted his mother from all blame, because—quite gratuitously really—he has always forgiven her everything.

"Mama is innocent," he would say, using the same highly developed, but whimsical vocabulary he still uses today. Did he know what he was saying when he said his mother was innocent? Innocent of what? It really got on my nerves.

"Innocent of what?" I would ask, exasperated.

He would say nothing, but gaze at me indulgently, and I preferred to think that my eldest really didn't know what he was saying.

My other children—two girls and three boys—turned out to be perfectly normal, and if you'll forgive my waxing sentimental, they're an absolute joy. A historian, a teacher, two architects, and a designer. They're all perfect, but Niño has always been the exception.

"I don't want to finish my degree," he said when he was not yet twenty and, at my instigation, reluctantly studying to be an architect.

He didn't want to continue, he didn't want to be an architect like me (which, while a bit of a setback for the family practice, was nonetheless reasonable enough), but more than that, he didn't want to be in any way like me, not that anyone had asked him to be.

So one day, he left Barcelona and the School of Architecture and hitchhiked his way to Paris, where the May Revolution was in full swing. He arrived there on his twentieth birthday. When he returned, I had a pleasant surprise. I had ceased to be the only person who was to blame for everything. The battalion of guilty parties had swelled its ranks, and those who were to blame for everything and anything that happened to him were: his father, capitalist architecture, the three local barbers, all my friends, the coal merchant and the local policeman (both retired), the workers in a nearby patisserie, the newspaper vendor, and even the young women he passed in the street and who walked too briskly for him to get a good look.

He didn't resume his architectural studies—he let two of his brothers follow that path—and instead devoted himself to the rather odd business of needling me at all hours of the day or night; at the time, his most frequently asked question was: why had I begotten him? A complete nightmare. One day, when I could bear it no longer, we sat down to talk in my office. I remember it was raining heavily outside, and that it stopped raining at the precise moment our brief encounter ended. He wanted to discuss Godard's movies, and I wanted to talk about my supposed guilt for having brought him into the world. We ended up discussing the latter.

"I just want you to explain why, a few years ago, during that family holiday we spent in Málaga at Easter, you gathered us all together in the hotel lounge to explain that you were having a crisis of faith. Do you remember? I was fourteen, and the others were even younger..."

I remembered it perfectly. I had spoken to my children when I was in the middle of a nervous breakdown brought on by doubts about the resurrection of the flesh and my religious faith in general.

"All I want to know," Niño went on, "is why you gathered all your children together to tell us that you felt it was your fatherly duty to tell us that one day we would have to die, that we were born to die, that there is no life after this one. Do you think that was a good thing to do?"

I hadn't behaved well, it was true, but I wasn't going to admit as much to my son.

"You even told little Javier he was going to die," Niño went on, "and he was only five. Were you really trying to say that you wanted to see all your children dead and buried? Isn't it true that you never really wanted children in the first place?"

"What nonsense," I said, stopping him in his tracks. "Perhaps I was just having my revenge on you, because you'd been asking me why I begot you ever since you were little. And you haven't changed one bit. You were and still are a real pest, Niño."

"What were you thinking of when you gave me life, knowing that you were also giving me death? You should explain that. You owe me an explanation."

I slowly looked up and, seeing that it had stopped raining, opened the window, pretending to be too occupied in doing that to answer him. I caught the exquisite smell of damp earth, at once so ancestral and so new. I told him to leave, that I wanted to go for a walk alone. Once out in the street, I thought about what Niño had said and about how he always managed to wind me up, and how, that day, he had been even more successful than usual.

Today, I went to see him in his apartment and shared with him and his beautiful Martinique wife some excellent Pakistani tea (bought, they told me, in some huge store in London), and when she went out for a moment to buy some bottles of mineral water from the Pakistani supermarket downstairs (everything is Pakistani today, I thought), Niño took advantage of her absence to tell me that at first, he hadn't given much thought to the operation awaiting him, "as long, of course, as I wasn't obliged to"; but now, he said, "the operation hangs over me all the time, it's getting closer and closer."

I felt rather sorry for him and tried to change the subject and talk instead about mountaineering, a sport that continues to fascinate me, although I no longer practice it. In fact, for a long time, mountaineering was our favorite hobby, Niño's and mine. I instilled all my children with a love of sport, but not all responded with the same enthusiasm and eagerness as Niño. He wasn't interested now though, and interrupted me to insist on his anxiety about that imminent operation.

"It will all be over soon, you'll see," I said.

A silence fell, during which I felt tempted to tell him that I'd started writing these notes about him—but, in the end, I preferred him not to know that, on the eve of his operation (I didn't want to make him even more worried than he already was), I had started writing about some of the good and bad aspects of our relationship, and about some more memorable episodes in his life as occasional researcher into what might exist after death, and some of the more picturesque milestones in his biography as a supposedly indefatigable investigator into the more shadowy areas of human knowledge.

I've decided to recall certain moments from his life, and, in passing, certain moments from my own. I think I'm doing this because of a doubtless debatable and superstitious belief that, by talking about Niño, I am, in a way, praying for him, perhaps lighting candles that will bring him luck during his operation. I may wish he were dead, but he's still my son …

I wonder if he's ever heard about how the movie director Werner Herzog once walked from Munich to Paris to save his friend Lotte Eisner. "When I arrive, she will have left hospital," he said. And so it turned out. Eight years later, Eisner, who, by then, could barely walk or see, asked him to free her from "the spell," and two weeks later, she died.

As a father, I need to do something for my son—some would say I've done quite enough. I think that recovering these moments from the past will help me dispel the image of myself as having simply stood by and done nothing, an image I could not bear.

"I'm aware that, basically, I'm just waiting," he said suddenly, breaking the silence.

And he went on to explain that he now belonged to the vast horde of people filling the health system, waiting, for example, to have tests done. Indeed, he's been seen many times by various health workers, and he has frequently been part of the amorphous mass. He has been subject to long lines for a simple pin prick—a blood test—"what the doctors and ordinary people now call 'a barrage of tests.'" He says he feels part of that army of patients.

"Basically," he concluded, "I am someone who is waiting, and, even though I am objectively sitting at home, I'm really milling around with that endless amorphous mass of people, slowly disappearing into the dark."

I thought his words were ridiculously overdramatic, but I'm used to that.

"I am living a nonexistent life," he added.

Fortunately, at this point, his wife Claudine came back. I have always thought her really beautiful, the lean, limber prototype of the Caribbean woman. She has a wonderfully feline bone structure, and it's a pleasure just to watch her move. She returned bearing bottles of mineral water and asked if I wanted more Pakistani tea or another cake.

Niño didn't give me time to answer and began telling me that he hadn't, at first, realized he was in the anteroom.

"What anteroom?" I asked, prepared to hear some nonsense or other.

He told me that, a few days before, when he had just come back from the hospital after yet more tests and was sitting at home listening to "the melancholy music of Debussy," he noticed that everything around him was the same as always— Claudine, for example, was singing in the kitchen, as she did on other mornings—yes, everything was the same, but suddenly it seemed to him that the light was different, it was much more real, far brighter than anything he had known before. At first, he wondered if he had unwittingly taken some powerful drug. However, he soon came to see that his whole world had been subtly changing around him. He only realized this when he noticed that there was something unnatural about the light. He was still in his house, Claudine was singing in the kitchen, and everything seemed almost normal, but he was in that anteroom, or intermediate zone between life and the other world. Fortunately, Claudine was with him in that region of the spirits. "And now you are too," he added, with an apparently warm and friendly expression.

I remember looking around at that point to see if everything really was more real than it had been, to find out if I, too, was in the anteroom, and it struck me that the only thing that had changed was my son. In the best-case scenario, I was someone who would one day enter that anteroom, that intermediate zone with which Niño was already so familiar.

"There are no nihilists in the anteroom, so don't try to be one," he said very bluntly. "And there are no sceptics either. We believe in the dignity of mankind, in the value of science, in the relative truth of art. We are not devoid of beliefs so we don't feel entirely desolate and alone. Here, desolation is seen as the fruit of a terrible narrow-mindedness. Desolation is seen as mere stupidity. Ah, and there's no praying in the anteroom."

I wondered why he should mention praying. Perhaps he had read my thoughts and knew that, since yesterday, I've been appeasing my bad conscience for wishing him dead and that to do so, I've been trying to bring him luck by praying or—which comes to the same thing—writing these notes that seek to keep him alive; notes that I will continue to write over the next few days, however often Niño may say that he has left life behind, caught in that intermediate zone between the truth of fiction and sumptuous truth itself.

At any rate, with his capacity for seduction, he has achieved what one might call the miracle of making me feel as if I, too, were in the intermediate zone, in that same anteroom or waiting room. But then he has always been able to pull the wool over my eyes. The wall at the far end of his living room even began to take on the color of the abyss.

"It's late," I said.

"For everything," was his automatic response.

He said this as we both used to do in happier times, when our motto was, "It's too late for everything," the motto we consoled ourselves with whenever we found ourselves floundering in our philosophical debates about the beyond, our painful investigations into the existence of other worlds: our pursuit of facts—often to be found in the most remote of places—that would provide us with information about the human condition, about our terrible solitude in the face of the vastness of the universe, the origins of life ...

Yes, in happier times.... Except that now we found ourselves in an unexpected anteroom. We had perhaps, for the first time in our lives, even made some progress after all those years of investigation. It was as if, suddenly, we'd both arrived at exactly the same moment in time, the right moment, neither too early nor too late. As if we'd finally caught up and been able to *see something*. I needed desperately to believe him, even though I didn't believe him at all.

I thought about this and, with the aid of a little cynicism, told myself that, just then, it really didn't matter if I believed him or not; what mattered was that the anteroom—that temporary intermediate zone—seemed a logical destination for both of us and almost a proper reward for our long journey as tireless researchers into the nature of the other world.

I said goodbye and set off down the corridor toward the front door. In the kitchen, Claudine was singing an unusually jolly piece by Debussy.

"I'll be back tomorrow," I shouted back when I reached the front door.

"And what about that other business?" Niño fired at me from his armchair in the anteroom.

I stood frozen to the spot, not understanding what he meant at first.

"What business?" I asked.

There was a brief silence.

"The help you promised!" he yelled.

Ah, he was reminding me that he needed money. He was broke again, and needed my help. It seemed to me that I knew by heart what he was going to say. The illness, the cost of the operation, our wretched human condition, the way ruin always awaits us after a brief burst of good fortune, life as catastrophe …

I wasn't surprised, but it seemed decidedly the wrong moment to say that he wanted money from me, and I was bothered, too, by the way he had said it. I was annoyed and disappointed. I decided to play him at his own game and not tell him that any sympathy I'd felt for him had just been demolished, along with any tolerance I had for his abyss-colored anteroom and his limitless capacity for pretense. It was a shame. I had made a real effort to reconcile his time with mine, for us to arrive together at the right moment, but he had ruined all this by the inelegant way in which he had reminded me that I should continue to provide him with financial help.

I realized that it had been naive of me to pray for him to survive the operation. At that point, I decided that I wished him dead. It's his own fault, he's managed to make me feel utterly fed up with helping him. He's a poor, sad good-for-nothing, a drain on his father, a fake explorer of the enigma of the world, the most superficial creature on the planet.

I considered saying that for someone supposedly sitting in the anteroom to the next world, he seemed surprisingly concerned with material things, but I didn't. I preferred to let him bask in the belief that he had managed to hypnotize me as he used to do, in this case with his shadowy anteroom and its walls the color of the abyss.

"I'll bring you the money tomorrow," I said.

And I left, slamming the door, leaving behind me an anteroom so cold that going out into the street was like hurling myself into the unexpected warmth of the abyss.

II

I would like to see Niño's final fantastical journey to that abyss-colored waiting area, or anteroom, as the logical consequence of our own eccentric trajectory over all those years, years in which we both investigated and discussed, like men possessed, the inexhaustible subject of life after death, with me always the modest research assistant trailing behind my son, as if this were my way of paying for my guilt for having brought him into the world.

Yes, apart from a few brief interruptions, I've always been Niño's attentive assistant, ever since that now-distant day in 1972 when, on his return from a turbulent time doing military service in Cartagena, he spoke with strange emotion about the no less strange volcano Licancabur, located on the border between Chile and Bolivia. "The lake at the top," he told me, "is the highest in the world, and, according to the local population, it contains the souls of all the world's dead."

According to the people of the Atacama desert, the lake was the place where all living beings go when they die. "It must be very full," I commented ironically while calmly lighting a cigarette. At the time, I was used to taking Niño's views in my stride. A long silence followed, during which it seemed to me that my son looked at me with real anger. He appeared even more on edge than usual, and I had no idea what would happen when he spoke again. Finally, he told me that he wanted to go to Licancabur and climb it, to see if those legends had any basis in fact. "And I'll need your help," he concluded, "I would be grateful if you could be both my financier and my helper." I smiled. "You mean you want me to help you financially," I said. "No, they're two quite different things. You can be a helper all your life if you want. Being a helper is a very specific job, whereas being a financier is ethereal and temporary. No, I want you to be both my financier *and* my helper, neither more nor less, exactly as I said," he explained, and he looked very pleased with himself.

Once again, he had succeeded in surprising me. And then he surprised me again when he said he was thinking of preparing an exhibition of photographs "of our discoveries." Then he went on to give me more details. For example: in Kunza (once the local language), Licancabur meant *village of the heavens*. Some had Christianized the name to *village of heaven* or quite simply *heaven*. Then, he started giving me further details and drawing me deeper into that investigation of otherworldly souls who could possibly all be found on top of that Chilean volcano.

"We'll find out the truth about the beyond," he said.

"Be careful," I warned. "Those who seek the truth deserve the punishment of finding it."

The unbearably hot days of August were approaching. August is always a terrible month to be in Barcelona. I decided that I wouldn't mind doing a little mountaineering, which was by far my favorite pastime. However, having agreed to go on this trip with my eldest to the cold heights of Licancabur, I made it a condition that we travel via Argentina and, before climbing the twenty-thousand-foot volcano, spend a few days in La Cumbrecita, a charming little village in the province of Córdoba at the foot of Mount Champaquí, and which was full of all kinds of Tyrolean architecture. The village has Swiss-German connections, an architecture that has always attracted me. I still harbored desperate hopes that the architecture might also attract Niño, who was growing up before my eyes like an ever more alarming urchin, becoming increasingly lost in life as he invented his own character. And so my agreement to finance our research on the Chilean side of Licancabur was conditional on our spending a brief holiday in La Cumbrecita. Niño had no alternative but to accept. We spent a pleasant few days in that Argentinian village, but I've never known anyone less interested in things architectural; he was interested in everything else, even the most trivial aspects of La Cumbrecita, but he didn't show the slightest flicker of interest in the timber framework of any of those Tyrolean edifices.

Finally, we traveled on to the Chilean volcano. One memorable day in early August 1972—along with various helpers dressed rather like Himalayan sherpas, a style that had become fashionable in the world of climbing—we set off on foot toward the volcano. We began on Chilean route 241, which then (I don't know how it is today) started in San Pedro de Atacama. We headed, first, for the foot of the other volcano, Juriques, where, hours later, we set up camp. The following day, we walked several miles to a narrow pass, a pleasant route over low ridges and past ravines, where we saw impressive rock formations sculpted by the wind. Niño greedily photographed them. When we reached the pass, we began to climb Juriques, keeping more or less at the same altitude, and finally found another suitable campsite: a beautiful place beside a shallow gulley beginning at the crater of Juriques. The site was fairly sheltered from the wind and liberally photographed by our would-be photographer.

The following day, we continued around Juriques, trying not to lose height, until we reached another narrow pass, between Juriques and Licancabur. And there we began what could properly be considered our ascent to the highest lake in the world. We climbed up a path flanked by huge boulders and lumps of lava, making good progress until we were brought to a halt by a great wall of rock (I actually sketched it in a notebook, which, alas, I have since lost). After scaling the gigantic wall more easily than expected, we had to scramble over rubble and scree as we began to make our way toward the Bolivian side of the volcano until we reached the abrupt edge of a cliff. There, we could see that the way ahead was over firmer ground and would lead us straight to the base of what was a false summit. From there, the climbing was fairly straightforward, past rocks and over firm ground that was not too steep. Thus we reached the small pass between the false and the real summit; from there we trudged up until, only a hundred yards away—it was unbelievably cold—we saw the crater with the lake inside it, the highest lake in the world. When we got to the real summit, all we saw was a humble, completely frozen lake.

God and the angels and all the dead and all the devils that have ever existed or will exist in the world might be hidden beneath the waters of that lake. My common sense was telling me, though, that, just as I'd always thought, there was nothing out of the ordinary beneath the icy surface. Niño appeared to reject this and began photographing that *village of the heavens*, even though there were no living dead, no lost souls (apart from ours), and not an actual dead person either. There was no village, and although the heavens seemed very close, the lake clearly didn't contain heaven or anything resembling it. What we saw was pretty much what I expected, but Niño continued impassively taking photographs, until he began going on and on (as if trying to come up with an excuse for our obvious failure) about "paths leading nowhere, but which, nonetheless, must be walked, in case one day someone should find something, quite what no one knows."

To keep from weeping, I decided instead to laugh fondly at his ingenuousness. "But our path *has* led us somewhere," I said, "to this wretched frozen, entirely unmysterious lake! There's absolutely nothing to make us think that we're about to encounter a world in which all the dead of the universe have taken up residence or sought refuge."

Needless to say, he caught the complaining note in my voice and also the fact that I was laughing at him (I was laughing at myself, too, but he didn't pick up on that); and then, shooting me a glance that was icier than the lake itself, he decided to join the sherpas, even eating with them and recounting—if I heard correctly—mad, spine-chilling tales from beyond the grave. Then he came back, as if regretting having left me alone (perhaps afraid of what I might be thinking about him there on my own) and I saw at once that he was in a better, more conciliatory mood, as I found out when he said: "It's too late for everything," which was our motto and the thing that perhaps bound us most closely together. We shook hands. And I thought that I forgave him. I looked around me; the snow, isolated from the rest of the landscape, was winking and blinking in its usual brilliant, enigmatic way and, in its solitary perfection, it seemed to glow as never before. The light it gave off was blinding, a sensation that lasted for a long time, until, inevitably and perhaps inopportunely, I began to think nostalgically of the days when my private world was one long party, or, rather, I remembered that London bar where, while leaning on its gleaming counter, I had once drunk the best gin cocktail of my life.

"There's nothing here," declared Niño.

"You're right, there's nothing here," I answered with British phlegm, imagining myself leaning on the counter of that bar, where there were lots of things, all of them attractive.

My eldest must have sensed what I was thinking because he shot me another suspicious glance, as if he could see that imaginary gin cocktail and found this deeply strange. He remained silent for some time, until I saw him bow his head and move slowly off into a fringe of yellow sunlight, and suddenly, as if he felt trapped by that fringe of light, I saw him stumble forward, as if about to step into the abyss and thus take the first-ever photograph of the beyond.

III

It must have been as we were coming down from Licancabur that my firstborn began to see himself as a reputable—or perhaps I should say apparent—expert in all things strange. I remember that when we reached the first pass on our way down, he came over to me to say that he was suddenly filled with a feeling of stupefaction, which he described thus: "I have a feeling of utter strangeness, not because we failed to find any souls from beyond the grave, but because I felt that icy lake at the summit literally in my forehead, the way a wall feels the tip of a nail about to be hammered into it, that is, I *didn't* feel it."

Obviously, the really strange thing was what he had just said and there was no need to go looking for anything strange in a lake at the top of a Chilean volcano or anywhere else apart from inside himself. *He* definitely was strange. In the days, months, and years that followed, he continued to cultivate that tendency, to which he always applied the same rigid rule: everything familiar and everyday was strange and everything unusual was perfectly normal. To give one example among thousands: seeing me and his mother lining up to go into a cinema seemed to him very strange indeed.... And so on.

Of course, no one has ever been able to deny his astonishing ability to see strangeness where ordinary folk do not. Indeed, his expedition to Licancabur turned into an exhibition of disconcerting photographs, where his investigation into the frozen lake and the *village of the heavens* appeared in an irritatingly tangential form. He seemed to have done this on purpose to annoy me, because in the exhibition there were hardly any photos of the volcano or the frozen lake, nor was there any suggestion that the objective of the expedition had been to probe the mysteries of the world and of the beyond. All that talk for nothing. This strange exhibition was only on for four days in an obscure venue in an obscure part of town and met with not the slightest success—apart from visits by family members, because every one of our relatives dutifully trooped through. The photos set out to show something very different from our adventure. What Niño presented to the public was, rather, a series of images of clouds glimpsed in the skies of Chile and Bolivia, a kind of general catalog of oddities, beginning with the photographer himself, who was the oddest of all.

As a photographer, he had got off to a bad start, and despite that first frustrated artistic sortie, I continued to finance my son's expenses. Unlike his brothers and sisters, who had quickly learned how to earn their own living, my tricksy firstborn settled into a stubbornly picaresque way of life, believing (sometimes quite rightly) that he could win my admiration by becoming a tireless investigator of the beyond, an activity that brought in no money and required, instead, my generous financial support.

I helped him in many of his investigations. Around 1984, for example, I financed his trip to the Amazon jungle of Colombia and Peru, where he went to follow in the footsteps of William S. Burroughs, who had gone there to experiment with yagé or ayahuasca, a plant with mythical hallucinogenic and telepathic properties that allows one, as Niño put it, "to connect with the spectral presences of our dead and to begin seeing or feeling what seems to be the Great Being, something that approaches us like a big wet vagina or a big black divine hole through which we peer, in a very real way, into a mystery wrapped in colored snakes".

Niño went to Mocoa, the capital of the Colombian region of Putumayo, a ghastly town recently devastated by floods and where he found only rusty machinery scattered everywhere and swampy waters right in the town's center: the same "unlighted streets you sink up to your knees in" that Burroughs had described. According to what Niño told me on his return, he was, nonetheless, able to organize an unforgettable expedition into the jungle that led him to a shaman, who held a ceremony exclusively for him, and which involved drinking a concoction made from an exotic blend including ayahuasca, and this, he wrote in a letter: "helped me, right from the start, to hear the ghost approaching inside my mind, but also to connect with the spectral presences that are transformed on contact with the single mysterious Thing that is our fate and which sooner or later will kill us ..."

The whole experience, it seems, was a terrifying one. To cap it all, the ayahuasca played tricks on him, told him appalling Spanish jokes, and, when a few hours had passed after drinking the brew, showed him his dead children. "But you have no children," I said at once. And Niño explained that these were potential children, children that could have existed at some point, there was nothing odd about that. The more you saturated yourself with ayahuasca, the deeper in you went: you visited the moon, you saw your dead children, saw God, saw the tree spirits.

In other words, Niño felt he was standing before the very Nose of God. He had a sense that he could confront the Big Question right then and there. Of course, to confront that Question, you would have to die, but dying would lead to a complete understanding of everything and thus free you from the big problem, which was none other than that Great Being we all carry within us.

Niño hadn't made contact with the beyond while on top of the Licancabur volcano or anywhere else, but in the jungle of Putumayo he'd had the most important experience of his life—it was just such a shame I couldn't have shared it with him, he said—he had peered into the Great and complicated Void.

He returned from there with a box full of abuarasca, which is not the same as ayahuasca, but a substitute that I could try whenever I wanted, because he had learned how to make a potion. More than that, he had learned the songs the shaman intoned—softly and re-petitively at first, then with a very slight change of rhythm—while he prepared the extraordinary, inspired mixture.

After much hesitation, I agreed that Niño would be my shaman and we would drink that repellent, viscous brew. We waited for a trip to Ibiza to try and connect with our dead and with the Eye of God. The result of that long, elaborate ceremony was zero, an absolute cosmic void, we didn't even see the Nose of God. The abuarasca concoction hadn't the slightest effect on either of us. It may, at most, have affected my dreams, because, that night—we were staying in a house built on what had once been a goat track—I had a sense that the pleasures of this life were not *mine*, but belonged to someone living inside me, who looked like a goat and was clearly afraid of progressing to a higher life form.

IV

Despite my issuing several ultimatums, Niño turned fifty-one having never done a day's work in his life—no, I'm being too hasty, that isn't quite true, he never did anything apart from being a photographer, whose ever more bewildering exhibitions were always total failures. For example, out of that expedition in search of experiences with ayahuasca came a collection of insipid photographs that were displayed in a savings bank in Granollers, a town just outside Barcelona: an absurd sequence of blown-up images of microbes found on the surface of ayahuasca leaves. He had all the latest camera equipment, but all he produced was a disastrous and embarrassingly microbial art.

What I found rather disappointing and increasingly annoying was that his ethereal photographic exhibitions never illuminated the questions with which, in private, he was so preoccupied and about which he was always ranting on to me: life after death, the essence of the human condition, our terrible solitude in the universe, the visions provoked by certain dangerous drugs, the first step beyond the abyss, the experience of the void … And so, as the song says, the days slipped by. And I despaired, still paying his expenses and the cost of various expeditions required for his peculiar research (which never found expression in his talentless exhibitions);

I always picked up the bill for his squanderings while he prepared for each of those exhibitions, which were always linked—at least when they were only in the planning stage—to the search for "a truth hidden from humanity since the dawn of time", but which, when he showed them to the public, bore no relation to his investigations into the beyond or into hidden truths; they consisted of very dull images with only the most tenuous connection to those initial questions.

Not that I actually believed my eldest would ever find any hidden truths about the other world, but you never know. On the other hand, I didn't want to leave him in the lurch, without a euro, and so I always ended up defraying the costs of his research, even accompanying him in long conversations on the subject of life after death or about one of his adventures that, afterward—I could see it coming, but I always fell for it anyway—never appeared in his photographs.

Fool that I am, I was always behind him, financing his many quests to discover the secret of the universe through the photographic image. Until that day in April 1999 when I decided not to give him any more money. Niño had turned fifty-one, and it was high time he faced up to reality, as all his siblings had. I could continue being his helper, even his sparring partner in conversations about the great mystery of the world, but I no longer wanted to go on helping him financially. I told him so over the phone and, that same day, he stormed into my office. I had, he said, turned off the financial tap just when he was about to join a troupe headed by Maurice Forest-Meyer (whom I had never heard of), "a famous and utterly amazing tightrope walker," a celebrated and extraordinarily gifted acrobat, whom he had just met and with whom he had discovered the simple charms—far superior to those of mountaineering—of walking the tightrope.

"I have finally found someone who truly does confront the void, not like me. I've spent my time merely flirting with the abyss, daring only to skirt around the edge," he said very gravely.

According to him, his friends in the troupe really did approach the mystery of the void. For some days, he'd been having classes

233

in tightrope walking and was hoping to delve still deeper into the subject of the abyss, when he finally dared to give his first public performance. He wasn't afraid of falling, because tightrope walking was an art of life not death. His intention was to channel all the positive energy from that experience— a year spent touring Europe with the troupe—into photographing the void from the tightrope. It would be the first-ever exhibition of photographs made of the void and nothing else. He would finally be able to capture absolute nothingness in his photographs. The moment had come to lay bare his old preoccupations about life after the abyss that follows death. Tightrope walking was the perfect activity because it required no explanation, it was based on the excitement of observing and photographing the void …

Niño paused as if he had lost the thread of his argument, but then I realized that he simply had the hiccups. That was the decisive moment, although it could have been any other moment or any other day. It was doubtless something that had to happen sooner or later, I couldn't remain so lacking in insight and so innocent forever. It could have happened on another day, but it happened at that precise moment, when he started hiccupping. It was horrible, one of those things you know you'll never forget. I suddenly understood what my wife had long suspected and that I had resisted accepting.

Suddenly, at that precise moment, I saw clearly that Niño had always been a complete fraud. It had almost all been pure theater, and almost all of it shockingly immoral: his speeches about the abyss and his inexhaustible ability to find everything strange had simply been a way to get money out of me. As outrageous as that, as simple as that! He probably didn't care a fig about the art of photography! And as for how much genuine interest he felt in "the strange," it was minimal, sub-zero, frozen beneath a layer of ice, possibly the same layer of ice he saw that day at the summit of Licancabur.

Not realizing that, thanks to a tiny but significant contradiction on his part, I had discovered, with horror, that the famous Maurice Forest-Meyer did actually exist, but that their supposed friendship was pure invention, all it occurred to him to do was to recover from his hiccups and start talking to me again, returning once more to those "paths that lead nowhere, but which, nonetheless, must be walked, in case one day someone should find something, quite what no one knows." Then he took to philosophizing about "the not necessarily eternal enigma of the human being," not necessarily eternal because he'd sensed that the time was approaching when some would know how to cross the threshold and take a step into the beyond ...

That was far enough. I found listening to him now utterly infuriating. And I decided to turn off the money tap. I explained that, just as I had told him over the phone, from that day on, there would be no financial help of any kind. I was, after all, nearly eighty and felt I should take better care of my personal fortune.

Everything indicated that my words had fallen on deaf ears. Niño didn't appear to understand why I should react like that. He had come to take it for granted that he could always dupe me. And the expression of profound bewilderment—at that instant, he seemed to have become a consummate professional in feigned astonishment—was a poem in itself. He asked me if I knew what we are, where we come from and where we are going. I will never forget that supremely comic moment. I smiled with the same British phlegm as I had many years before, when we reached the top of Licancabur. I explained that there was nothing to be done, that it was monstrous at his age for me to still be giving him so much money. I said that I'd had enough of him playing at being the eternal child, hovering absurdly on the threshold of the adult world (an utterly childish pose), gazing at everything in amazement and never daring to take a step into this world he found so astonishing.

I asked if he had noticed that none of his brothers and sisters were hovering on any kind of threshold. They didn't spend all day wondering what lies beyond. Instead of taking photographs of clouds, it was time, I said, for him to penetrate those clouds, not just stand there in the mist.

"You're trying to make me cry," he said.

Over the following months, and since it would cost me nothing,

I agreed to pose for an exhibition of portraits of "the Catalan bour-geoisie" that he was planning. The success of that exhibition—with me as the sole subject—was astonishing. Who would have thought it? He sold every one of the photographs and at very good prices too. Obviously, some were bought by my many friends and employ-ees and, of course, my reputation as an architect helped boost sales. Some visitors sent by my enemies doubtless bought a few too, in order to take them home and have a good laugh. The fact is, though, that all the photos were sold, and, for the first time in his life, Niño stopped being economically dependent on me—temporarily. For a while, he even became quite a wealthy, well-known artist, and all thanks to the unexpected success of his photographic collection *The Faces of One Architect*. He remained famous for about a year, but his fame proved short-lived, and his money even more so.

V

Now Niño is ruined, in all senses. You can tell the moment you walk into his apartment. Today, as promised, I went to see him again. He didn't know that I wished him dead. He told me that his fear of the operating room was eating away at him, and yet, I could see, too, that he was convinced he had recovered his talent for deceiving me. He thinks I swallowed every word of the story he told me yesterday about being in the anteroom of the next world. And since he hasn't a euro to his name—he spent it all, no, squandered it, and his re-cent metaphysical exhibition of hugely enlarged photos of butterfly wings and, more especially, his latest exhibition on "metaphotogra-phy," have met with no public acclaim whatsoever—he seems to be waiting for me to give him money as I always used to do. Or perhaps he's waiting for something more than that: for me to not only hand over money, but also to give him a new idea that will allow him to put on another exhibition about me, one that will restore to him his brief, dazzling moment of critical acclaim.

He told me this morning that he has started visiting a special ward at the hospital where he is being injected intravenously as part of a five-day treatment to destroy the strange microbe or bacteria with which he has been infected (he wishes he could photograph it and enlarge the photos, but doesn't know how). So far, ordinary oral antibiotics have failed to be effective.

He told me it's a strange place, that it is—needless to say!—the very epitome of strangeness. At first sight, because of the style of the chairs, it resembled a ladies' hairdressing salon. There weren't many infected patients, only a select minority. And, as everyone knows, any select minority contains a majority of imbeciles. There were loads of them in that ward for the infected, which is also an annex of the anteroom in which he currently spends his days. This morning, he was sitting opposite a man who was Spanish through and through, and yet claimed to have lived in Manchuria ...

At this point, I stopped listening to my son, who now hopes for nothing more in this world than my money, not that this stopped him from going on at length about the infected ward and then, in his blind logorrhea, telling me, for example, that he's no longer interested in adventures per se, but in what surrounds the "shadow line" in his anteroom—that line which "once crossed, delineates an unknown space in which everything has to be learned anew, where nothing is clear, because there are only shadows and more shadows ..."

He rambled on like this for a long time, as if he really had died or really was in the anteroom to the void, which, depending on how you look at it, comes to the same thing. But I also saw him behaving as if he were never going to die and, quite unconsciously (which is why his attitude was so absurd), as if he were, if you'll forgive the odious comparison, Socrates on the evening after he had drunk the hemlock, when he simply carried on as usual, chatting to his friends who had come to visit him in prison and glancing several times out of the window to see if it was going to rain.... The truth is, though, that Socrates is the very last person my own dear swindler resembles.

To start with, he lacks nobility of mind, as well as any of Socrates's many other qualities. My commercially-minded firstborn, that trader in fake anxieties, that expert in nonexistent strangenesses, that photographer of butterfly wings, has more than enough quackery, and more than enough immorality to earn his living from our very human dread of unanswerable questions. He knows all there is to know about the theatrical moment.

For example, when I arrived at his apartment, I heard the words, "In this realm, time becomes space," sung by the Knights of the Grail in Wagner's opera, when Parsifal solemnly enters the room in which the Grail is hidden. I assume that Niño wanted to pretend that in his anteroom to the next world, time had become space or eternity. He clearly wanted to immerse me in the re-creation of a timeless myth; for he knows—and I was the one who taught him—that the search for the Holy Grail is relevant to every age. He would have been horrified if he had known that yesterday I once again judged everything he does to be quite simply immoral and that, even though I'm over eighty now, I remain more lucid and alert, and even though I have deliberately led him to believe the contrary, I haven't been taken in by the pathos of his anteroom, where my eyes are gladdened only by the lovely, gentle, undulating, and sometimes aggressive or haughty steps, so very Caribbean, of the beautiful Claudine.

As a fake explorer of the abyss, Niño doesn't realize that there is always a high price to pay for trading in feigned angst and for inflicting fake emotions on one's loved ones.

Today, I could only take twenty minutes of sitting in his anteroom. Seeing him childishly playing the fool, I couldn't help but think that being nice to someone almost always encourages that person to reduce you to slavery. I should have realized all this a long time ago and then I wouldn't have ended up wishing Niño dead.

That was it. Unable to stand it any longer, I left, slamming the door behind me, leaving my son with his fantasies about the ward for the infected or the annex to his anteroom to hell, or his wild imaginings about Manchuria, because, although he doesn't know it, he's already in hell. I'll go see him tomorrow too, but he'll never get another cent out of me. He doesn't know this, of course. How could he? He finds *everything* so strange that it seems to me impossible he'll ever find anything genuinely so.

Niño has only the vaguest idea of what constitutes strange, and that very vagueness constitutes for him a definition of it. I loathe him. He's nothing but a self-proclaimed expert in strangeness. He will die, as we all will. And if he doesn't like it, he can lump it. He should not, therefore, complain so much. Didn't I give him plenty of notice of this fact on that Easter day in Málaga, when I told him he'd been born to die? Given the way he has behaved for the last two days, you would think he had done all this just to be freed from my spell, to get me to stop praying for him. If so, he has certainly succeeded. Niño will die like everyone else. In his case—as is only right—he will die without my prayers. He can be sure of that. Enough of his flippant mind games.

After all, it's always the same for everyone. And Niño is no exception, however much he would like to be. We're propelled into life, shown its rules, and the moment we drop our guard, we find ourselves in the anteroom, facing death. Yes, it's always the same, but if you happen to be my eldest, you die twice over. That second time, he became dead to me. He won't reach sixty. You're dead to me for being a superficial bastard, a "metaphotographer," for having only toyed with the essential human questions, and for swindling your father, for being a fake explorer of the abyss, for reflecting on the world with such ineptitude and for failing to take seriously how utterly alone we are in the universe.

The devil I've always carried inside me has now emerged into the outside world. Yes, he will die twice. For the simple reason that his father gave him life in order for him to die. You see, Niño, you were right when, on that day in Málaga, you suspected me of imagining all my children dead. You saw them as surely as I now see you, although now I'm contemplating you from slightly higher up, I'm observing you in silence from the highest point on the Nose of God, just days before they wheel you into the operating room. And I see that there's no hope for you, none at all. With these words, Niño, I am writing your death certificate. You will travel from the anteroom to the room itself far more quickly than you expected. And once conclusively dead, Niño, you will wonder, seriously for the first time, why you are so absent, so hidden away in the darkest crevices of my universe.

I'M NOT GOING TO READ
ANY MORE E-MAILS

Erik Satie never used to open the letters he received, but he always answered them. He would check the sender's name and address and write a reply. After he died, his friends found all those unopened letters and some felt quite upset, but there was no need to be. The letters were published alongside Satie's replies, and the results were fascinating. Ricardo Piglia wrote: "This is an amazing correspondence in which everyone is talking about different things, which is, of course, the essence of dialogue."

This summer, I set off on the yacht *Zacapa*, a Frers Dorado 36, named after the rum of the same name because of the color of the wood. Two expert sailors—one is a publicist and owner of the yacht and the other is a fellow writer and friend—allowed me to come on board in Marseilles, the city where I have spent the last few months in a whirlwind of activity, writing my latest novel and generally getting up to no good.

I should say that at no point did they force me to share in the work while we were on the high seas, although when they saw that I didn't lift a finger to help, but merely eavesdropped on their conversations, there were times it seemed when they both felt a great desire to throw me overboard.

In the end, they left me in a small hotel in the Bay of Nora, on the south coast of Sardinia, next to the ruins of the Phoenician town of Pula. I've been here now for five days, dividing my time between the beach, the swimming pool and obsessive visits to the ruins, which are the most interesting thing in the area.

The wi-fi in the hotel is so unreliable that it has nearly driven me mad. In revenge, but also as a kind of farewell game and a nod to Satie, I am going to pay homage today to the true essence of any dialogue by responding to the e-mails that arrived during my holiday and which I haven't read and now have no intention of reading.

To e-mail no. 1 (a dear friend), I said that we writers are not really such utter bastards, the proof being that some big literary names owe their success partly to our reluctance to appear envious.

To e-mail no. 2 (an interviewer I suspect), I replied that when asked how much of her work is autobiographical, the novelist Elisabeth Robinson always answers: "Seventeen percent. Next question, please."

To e-mail no. 3, I recommended ignoring anyone who tries to impose a particular kind of writing style on everyone else, because only a fool would deny that there are as many forms of literature as there are forms of life.

To e-mail no. 4 (the trainer for Bayern Munich), I wrote to say that conceited critics only improve when they have a bit of a suntan.

To e-mail no. 5, I confided that, while in Marseilles, I repeatedly dreamt that I kept finding live bullets in the street.

To e-mail no. 6 (a publisher in crisis, who has only ever defended commercial rather than intellectual interests), I suggested that, in adversity, it is often best, finally, to take a bold path.

To e-mail no. 7, I said that I wished I had taken refuge for a whole year in Paris or in New York and escaped from all the idiots in my own country, but it's too late for that now.

To e-mail no. 8 (a correspondent who is, by nature, envious), I reported that, any moment now, I was going to spread some butter on a piece of toast.

To e-mail no. 9, I wrote that truth has the same structure as fiction.

To e-mail no. 10, I explained that I wouldn't mind visiting Abu Dhabi, as long as I could come back the same day.

To e-mail no. 11, I said that among my favorite authors are David Markson and Flann O'Brien, as well as Markson and O'Brien's favorite authors, and all the favorite authors of their favorite authors.

To e-mail no. 12, I replied as if I were sending a postcard: On holiday in Sardinia. Ruins and a full moon. Amazing food. I have refused to make any friends. Love.

To e-mail no. 13, I said that I had grown tired now of waiting, beginning, succeeding, fastening and unfastening, persevering and persisting.

To e-mail no. 14 (a young writer), I said that I never read anything for fear of reading something good.

To e-mail no. 15, I explained that I have now been able to confirm as true that when you look into the abyss, the abyss looks back at you.

To e-mail no. 16, I wrote that the biggest argument in my life took place in Soria and lasted two days and ended up with us coming to blows. I was arguing about how to pronounce Robert Mitchum's name.

To e-mail no. 17, I confirmed that Norma Jean Baker committed suicide.

To e-mail no. 18, I said that everything stays the same but changes, because the eternal inevitably repeats itself in the new, which quickly becomes old.

When I was about to turn off my computer, e-mail no. 19 arrived from Marseilles, in extremis, and I replied, saying that I had no intention of paying my debt and that I'm very sorry, but I'm in a hurry, because I'm just about to go and visit the ruins of Pula where—and I'm sure you'll forgive me—I have everything all set up to commit suicide tonight.

Perhaps that person will send me another e-mail. No matter. Let's be quite clear, this is a serious and definitive decision: I'm not going to read any more e-mails.

VOK'S SUCCESSORS

Sooner or later, something always happens. Something I can make a story out of. I'm a quiet fellow. If nothing happens, I simply wait. But that day in Barcelona, in my new part of town, it seemed to me that too many things were happening. Most serious of all: someone was following me.

I saw the man emerge from Bernat's bookshop in Calle Buenos Aires soon after I had left, and I immediately started walking more quickly. I really don't like that kind of thing. Fifteen minutes earlier in Pipper's, I had already suspected that he was spying on me from his table. It became clear that this young man wanted something from me. I set off at a brisk pace and took refuge in Bar Warum, where I ordered a good whisky. Soon afterward, he came into the bar too and, when he saw me, he immediately looked away. It was odd, because he didn't seem like a policeman or a hit man, more like a shy intellectual. Of course, I would much prefer it if he weren't a policeman. A gay guy for example. It would be much easier to shake him off.

Two minutes later, I saw him coming over to me. Even though I hadn't committed any crime, I could already see me being sentenced to at least fifteen years in prison.

"Excuse me, are you Vilém Vok?" he asked.

I gave a sigh of relief. It was as if all my previous misdemeanors had been forgiven.

"Yes, I'm Vok."

"My name's Eguren. At your service."

He held out his hand. He had a pleasant, friendly face. The face of an affectionate reader. The only thing I could have done without was that awful "At your service."

"I wasn't quite sure if it was you," he said, smiling. "You know, since you supplanted the real Vok ..."

"Supplanted! You took my words too literally. I only said that, after Vok's physical breakdown four years ago, I feel like his heir, a kind of literary executor, looking after his work."

"Yes, I know."

"I look after it and, now and then, I add to it, bringing to Vok's work a serenity it previously lacked ..."

"Because of the drinking, yes, I know, I know. Listen, I just wanted to say that I wrote a letter last week and I wasn't sure if it arrived."

"You wrote it to Vok or to me?" I asked ironically.

"To you. I just thought that it must be very tiring having to spend all your time completing Vok's work, and it seemed to me that I could perhaps relieve you. I mean I could do the writing instead of you. I'd charge almost nothing. And that way I would be freeing you slightly from the Vokian legacy."

That is what he said and then went on to explain that he enjoyed writing, but didn't want to put his own name to anything. Supplanting Vok's supplanter would allow him to be creative in private, and in complete freedom.

"Besides," he said, "you're basically an actor, a great impostor, not a writer. You're a terrific public speaker. Unlike Vok, who was useless at it, you're positively histrionic."

"Yes, well, speaking in public is a completely different skill from writing. The two things are entirely unrelated. Each one requires a different technique, and I have a special technique for speaking to people."

"Well, if I wrote the books, you could concentrate on your daily bit of theater, on your excellent characterisation of Vok. I went to your last lecture, and it was brilliant. I particularly liked the bit when you said that you're trying to stop people seeing you as some sort of weirdo and getting them to focus attention on what you write, which is what really matters after all.... I loved that. But I thought: if I were to take care of the writing, that would leave you far more time to perfect your impersonation."

I found his proposal very attractive, since it would free me from a job I felt chained to. Yes, chained to. Because as everyone knows, you have to keep a writer in the public eye. That was why I was laboring away at writing Vok's new novels, his serene works, the books from his quiet phase. But, as I said, it was hard going. I used to enjoy writing, but lately, I've found it a bit of a chore, especially now that, to cap it all, I've been having to work even harder to outdo Vok at his brilliant, alcohol-fuelled best ...

"I can write you a novel in six months," said Eguren. "What do you think? I have an intimate knowledge of your style as the sober continuer of Vok's work. Well, perhaps 'sober' isn't the word, because I see, my friend, that you are no teetotaller. That *is* a surprise."

I bought him a drink. And after a matter of seconds, once he had downed it in two resounding gulps, he began to tell me—using the most scandalously rhetorical oratory—that he was glad to see that my spirit had found such serene and blissful repose, as in the heavens of my birth, and that he was also very pleased to see that I was surrounded by a divine harmony (whether audible or not).

I said: "I assume you're aware that you must achieve the same state of serenity in order to write under the name of Vok, because we definitely don't want a third Vok to appear who is clearly under the influence."

"So you'll let me be your replacement?" he said with sudden and very genuine excitement.

"Yes, drop by my house tomorrow and we'll draw up an agreement."

He embraced me warmly and, soon afterward, he left. I saw him shoot out of the bar like a bullet.

An hour later, I found him in another local dive. He didn't notice me, and I was able to get close enough to hear what he was saying to another young man of about his age. To my amazement, he was coming to a financial arrangement by which his friend would write Vok's books, a task for which—he said—he himself had neither the time nor the talent.

"Yes, I'll do a really good job," his friend was saying. "I've read and studied the serene Vok very closely and he holds no secrets for me. It's all a question of calming the passions and knowing how to live and die in a state of elegant resignation."

When I had recovered from my initial surprise, I decided that it would be best to give way to that fourth Vok, who seemed harder working than the third.

It remained to be seen, though, how it would affect me in the long run having these young people so ruthlessly sharing out my inheritance, my life's work.